TIE
DIE

Also By Max Tomlinson

The Colleen Hayes Series:
Vanishing in the Haight
Bad Scene

The Sendero Series:
Sendero
Who Sings to the Dead

The Agency Series:
The Cain File
The Darknet File

Standalone:
Lethal Dispatch

TIE
DIE

A COLLEEN HAYES MYSTERY

MAX TOMLINSON

OCEANVIEW PUBLISHING
SARASOTA, FLORIDA

ISBN 978-1-60809-440-0

Published in the United States of America by Oceanview Publishing

Sarasota, Florida

www.oceanviewpub.com

10 9 8 7 6 5 4 3 2

PRINTED IN THE UNITED STATES OF AMERICA

This one's for Evan Marshall,
agent extraordinaire, a man who never stops, and one
who knows how to come up with a great book title!

ACKNOWLEDGMENTS

I would like to thank my writing group, whose steadfast critiquing helped whip *Tie Die* into shape. They are (in no particular order): Barbara McHugh, Dot Edwards, Heather King, and Eric Seder. Thank you for many years of enduring early drafts!

Special thanks to Stan Kaufman for helping with various details, and Carl Gonser for answering legal questions.

And, as always, thanks to my wife, Kate, the ultimate beta reader, and my dog, Floyd, whose extremely slow walks allow me to ruminate on stickier story questions.

TIE
DIE

PROLOGUE

THE HAMMERSMITH ODEON

LONDON 1966

"Ladies and gentlemen, the group you've been waiting for—number one on *Top of the Pops*—on their way to America—will you put your hands together for—*The Lost Chords*!"

Eighteen-year-old Stevie Cook stood backstage behind the safety curtain, smoking a Player's No. 6, listening to the Odeon burst into a massive, collective roar. He shut his eyes and relished the noise. Screaming: the girls were bloody *screaming* out there. The Chords had sold out the Hammersmith Odeon. A year ago, they couldn't fill the front row of Andover Church End Youth Club on a Saturday night.

Onstage he heard Tich starting it up, bass drums like sledgehammers, snares and tom-toms making Stevie's feet move. Cymbals crashed as Nev's raucous guitar cut in. Thousands of pairs of hands clapping now. The audience knew the tune, yelled it at football matches. He might have written it, but now it was theirs.

Frenzy. You've got me in a Frenzy.

Stevie sucked tobacco smoke while he listened to Nev slashing out the intro on his white Vox Teardrop, an African rhythm tempered on wet English cobblestones. Then the bass guitar came thundering in, like a locomotive out of the station.

He'd stay behind the curtain just one second longer, savor it *just* a bit longer.

"Right, Stevie. You've had your fun. And put that bloody cigarette out."

Steve opened his eyes, saw Ian Ellis, their manager, a ferret of a man, mustache trimmed too tight, a boarding school bully in a Savile Row suit.

"When I'm good and ready, Ian." He gave the man who'd been robbing them blind a hard stare as he took a luxurious drag of smoke. And blew it directly into Ian's face.

"You might have a crowd of *yobs* out there tonight," Ian spat, his face turning red as he fanned smoke away. "But you won't have them long. Yesterday's papers are what you'll soon be. I've seen it all before." Ian gave Steve's arm a light double pat, military, cold, patronizing. Beyond the curtain the band vamped out the song's intro, over and over, waiting for Stevie to come out. The crowd was chanting the opening lines.

Steve looked at his arm where Ian had touched him, then he looked back at him, the look saying: touch me like that again and I might bloody well touch you back. Ian didn't have his thugs to protect him now.

"I've got one question, Ian," Steve said. "Where's our money?"

Ian Ellis gave a smirk. "You might want to read your contract, boy. You get paid when I say. Not a moment sooner."

"You're a bloody thief and that's about the size of it."

"Best watch your step, lad. And end on the new song—American girls won't wet their knickers like some West Country trollop over a tune you wrote in the back of the van." Ian gave Steve another shoulder pat.

Steve flared, jerking his fist back, holding it a few short moments to let Ian know what it was about to become before it actually did, then let it fly. He thought he heard a crunch of cartilage above the music and managed to get Ian again with his left fist on the way down to the floor, twisting it on a smudge of opened nose.

"Pay us, Ian," Steve said, wiping his hands. "Final warning."

Ian sprawled on the rough wooden boards.

"You're finished!" Ian shouted, clutching his face. A streak of red ran through his fingers. Steve dropped and stomped his smoldering fag next to Ian's head, then fluffed his dark mod haircut back with his bricklayer's fingers. Straightened his skinny tie.

Sauntered out from behind the curtain.

The house exploded, a blast of applause.

Up to the mic in a jog, the roar deafening his ears.

"Are you ready?" Stevie yelled, eyes screwed up.

Shouting back: *Ready!*

"No, I said, 'Are you *ready?*'" Steve bounced up with the mic stand and spun, turning midair, landing to face Nev, who was planted firmly onstage, beanpole legs splayed wide in his stovepipes, chopping out power chords. Grinning at Steve from under a mop of fine blond hair.

Steve whirled toward Dave, on bass, in his white shoes and big-striped suit, working away. Dave nodded back with a shy smile, thumping along.

To Tich, on drums, the sweat already making his face shine, thick neck bulging out of a purple Ben Sherman collar. Beating every drum he owned.

Play every gig as if it was your last. Steve gyrated back to the audience, whipping a leg around the way he'd seen Wilson Pickett do at The Marquee, adding his own bit of British flair. The crowd, rising out of the seats, bellowed with approval.

He leaned into the microphone.

"*Alright*, then."

*   *   *

A throbbing head and full bladder woke Steve from a drink-induced coma the next morning. The clicking in the corner of his hotel room was like a metronome from hell, tapping on his skull.

He didn't know where he was at first. Then he remembered: Dorchester Arms, Mayfair. But how he'd gotten into his hotel room after the show last night, he hadn't a clue.

He peeled back the sheet that had been covering his head, squinted through the stabbing of his optic nerves, saw his clothes strewn across the floor. The *tick-tick-ticking* of the record player scratching the final groove of an LP in the corner of the room was drilling a hole in his cranium. The tonearm bobbed as the black vinyl turned. Cold gray morning light seeped in around the edges of the curtains.

Steve threw the sheet off and climbed out of the king-size bed in his socks and tie-dye underpants. Standing now, he swayed like a boat on a stormy sea as blood rushed up the back of his spine and slammed the base of his skull like a hammer. He grabbed the back of his neck with one hand; his hand felt bruised. He examined his knuckles. Swollen. A fight?

He recalled something about Sir Ian.

He stumbled over to the record player on the floor. LPs and 45s out of their sleeves, scattered around. He pulled the tonearm off the end of *Rubber Soul.* He didn't remember listening to that.

There was a lot he didn't know.

Back to bed. He turned, the room spinning a split-second behind.

And flinched when he saw that the bed he'd passed out in wasn't his alone.

A slim girl lay facedown, a satin sheet just covering her curved, bare derrière. The gray pall leaking in around the curtains highlighted the delicate bumps of her spine. Pale skin like cream. Her short blond hair reminded him of Twiggy, and she was an English rose, to be sure, but one that was probably smashed with drink the way he had been.

He didn't remember that either. Christ.

Staggering into the bathroom, he shut the door behind him, took a long strangling piss, bracing one hand against the red and gold wallpaper above the loo so he wouldn't fall in and be flushed away. Examined Mr. Johnson while he drained: he didn't appear to have seen any action last night.

God, his head hurt. He could normally handle his drink better than that.

Back out into the room, he picked up the phone, dialed zero.

"Reception," a woman's crisp voice said. "Good morning, Mr. Cook. And how may I help you?"

"You can start by telling me what time it is, love."

"Five thirty in the morning, sir."

"Right," he said, glancing around for his cigarettes. He found a near-empty pack of Player's on the floor next to a pair of white lace knickers. He pulled a fag out with his lips, found some hotel matches in a glass ashtray.

Then he remembered he had a guest.

"Tea or coffee, pet?" he said to the girl facedown in his bed.

No response.

"A pot of tea," he said into the phone. "Two cups. Milk and sugar. And a bottle of brown ale to chase it down with." Christ but his head was screaming.

"The bar's closed, I'm afraid, Mr. Cook."

He got a cigarette going, sucked in acrid smoke, bringing some minor relief to his ravaged system. "Just the tea, then, please."

"Straightaway, Mr. Cook."

He hung up. Looked at the curvature of the flared hips exposed above the shiny sheet. In the half-light she looked like a painting. One he wished he'd known better.

He called the front desk again while he waited for room service and was put through to Nev's room. On the fifth ring, the phone was answered, dropped, picked up again.

"Who the fucking hell *is* this?" Nev croaked.

"Wakey, wakey, Nev."

"Fuck me dead, Steve. Do you have any idea what the bloody time is?"

"Around five thirty, I'm told." Steve blew smoke across the room.

"My point exactly. Call me when the bar opens."

"Just curious, Nev. What the hell happened last night?"

"You don't remember?"

"Wouldn't be asking if I did."

"You don't recall guzzling scotch in your dressing room after the show? You know, mate, it's not considered classy to drink right out of the bottle."

"I do *not* remember."

"Thank Sir Ian for that. Apparently the two of you got into it before the gig. You were a tad upset."

He remembered something about that now. Punching him in the nose.

"Well, at least the evening wasn't a total write-off," Steve said.

"That would explain Sir Ian's purple, enlarged beak." Nev laughed. "We all hit the booze pretty hard, mate. But you outdid yourself. But, for the record, it was a great show."

Steve lowered his voice. "Any chance you might know the name of the bird I came back to my room with, Nev?"

Nev laughed again. "There were a couple at the bar waiting to meet you."

"She probably got past the guard. Waited at my hotel room door."

"Lucky git."

"Funny thing is, Nev, I'm not feeling all that lucky at the moment."

"Well, my heart bleeds. I can't think straight, mate. I'm back to my beddy byes. Ta-rah." Nev hung up.

Steve ran his fingers through his hair, his head numb and buzzing. The ding of an elevator outside was followed by a gentle knock at his door.

Cigarette in the corner of his mouth, he pulled on hasty trousers, let Room Service in, the woman in the white frilly apron blushing when she saw Steve's unclothed guest flat out on the bed. The maid put the silver tray with the pot of tea and cups down on the table and, having no cash, Steve tipped her a pound on the room service receipt. Sir Ian could pay for that, tight arse.

He poured a cup of tea, stirred in three sugars and milk, drank it down in a single burning gulp, gasped, poured another cup. His belly radiated heat.

Took the cup over to her side of the bed. Set it down on the stand.

"Rise and shine, love."

No movement.

"Not to be too personal about it," he said, "but would you mind telling me your name?"

Still no movement. That wasn't right. He pulled in a breath.

He reached down, gently touched her bare shoulder. "Come on, pet . . ."

Her skin was cool.

Still.

Dead.

He recoiled back, heart pounding between his ears as a million thoughts screamed through his aching head.

* * *

The Daily Mirror, April 16th, 1966:

ROCKER RUNS!

Reports have confirmed that pop star Steve Cook, lead singer of Britain's chart-topping Lost Chords, has fled the United Kingdom whilst under investigation over the death of an underage girl found nude in his Mayfair hotel room bed.

The *Mirror* has learned that Cook, eighteen, traveled to France by ferry under an assumed identity, and has since boarded a flight to Rio de Janeiro. Cook has been the center of an investigation over an unidentified sixteen-year-old girl found dead of a drug overdose in Cook's hotel room in Mayfair's Dorchester Arms the night after a sold-out concert at the Hammersmith Odeon. Cook was taken into custody and had been helping the police with their inquiries and was released on bail earlier this week.

Cook maintains his innocence.

"It certainly doesn't help matters that he's left the country illegally," Scotland Yard said. Brazil does not recognize extradition treaties with Great Britain.

Delco Records sacked Cook when the investigation began.

"We are appalled by the criminal behavior of one of our recording artists," said Sir Ian Ellis, manager of The Lost Chords. "Cook should come back and face the music—so to speak."

The Lost Chords shot to fame earlier this year after "Underground Girl," a song penned by Cook, hit number one on the British pop charts. Their current hit, "Frenzy," has been sitting at number one for three weeks and, ironically, the bad

news about Steve Cook seems to be fueling its continued success. The Lost Chords hail from Andover where the former
childhood friends until recently played youth clubs and small
venues while Cook worked as a bricklayer's apprentice.

"My mate is completely innocent," said Lost Chords' guitarist Nev Ashdown. "Steve and I spoke right after the incident.
Steve told me he found the girl in his hotel room and thought
she was asleep. Fans will do anything to get near a star sometimes. Tragic, but it happens. The poor girl died of drugs they
say. Steve never did drugs. Drink, yeah, but drugs—never. I
would know; we've been friends since we were kids. Steve hates
drugs. My heart goes out to the poor girl's mum and dad. But
if Steve said he didn't give her drugs, and he didn't touch her,
then he didn't do it."

CHAPTER ONE

"It sure beats sleeping on a cot in a condemned warehouse," Alex said, admiring Colleen's new flat. In one hand she held a bottle of champagne in a paper bag. Behind her, beyond the sunroom facing the rooftop deck, the city was fast disappearing in fog.

"You can say that again," Colleen said. Her last residence had been an abandoned paint factory she guarded for a client.

Alex was a former client, a petite blond decked out in one of her runway-worthy outfits, today a dark blue linen pantsuit with a long, draped jacket and outrageous bell-bottoms that hid her stacked platform heels. Her aristocratic features seemed heightened by the fact that she'd just inherited a fortune.

The silver tips of the Bay Bridge's spans were vanishing. Behind them, up the hill toward Potrero, the whir of traffic on an elevated section of 101 provided white noise.

Colleen set a bag of groceries down on the kitchen counter, already occupied with boxes and tools and other artifacts of the recent move-in. She shifted a can of paint on the floor out of the way with the tip of a white Pony Topstar and pulled open the door to an empty refrigerator where she began putting groceries away.

"It's about time you had something nice," Alex said.

Colleen felt like an Amazon next to Alex, although that was overstatement. But she was taller, darker, moodier, with brown eyes and chestnut hair that she'd let reach her shoulders, with a feathered look that was in fashion. She was more muscular, thanks to her decade in prison inhabiting the weight room. And she had to earn a living, presently as owner and operator and sole employee of Hayes Confidential, investigator license pending. She also wore clothes that came off the rack, acid-washed denim flares today, along with her beloved beat-up tan leather jacket over a white V-neck T-shirt. A pair of silver magpie earrings that once belonged to her daughter dangled from her ears. Pale pink lipstick softened her lips.

"Want the fifty-cent tour?" she asked as she slid a stack of TV dinners into the freezer compartment. "I actually have furniture."

Bottle in hand, Alex came in close, the scent of her hair filling Colleen's nostrils. She touched the tip of Colleen's nose softly with a fingertip. "You bet."

Colleen led Alex through a long living room with polished hardwood floors, where a new chrome and black leather sofa sat under a bank of tall, white-framed wooden windows. The smell of fresh paint prevailed. At one end of the flat was a corner room that served as Colleen's office. French doors led to a large bedroom with a bay window. "Technically, you can see the Ferry Building from here," Colleen said. "If the sun comes out."

"Seriously, Coll?" Alex said, nodding at the king-size waterbed, where a ton of liquid bulged inside rainbow-striped sheets. Next to the bed, on the floor, a lava lamp, off for the moment. "When is the porno shoot?"

"I could use the money," Colleen said. "But no, this one's virgin—unless they were abusing it in the showroom."

"How old-fashioned you are." Alex peeled back the wrinkled brown paper bag around the bottle, worked off the wire net around the cork, positioned herself with the base of the bottle on one thigh in a little squat, eased the cork out with both thumbs, generating a *pop,* followed by the cork bouncing off the ceiling. Froth dripped on the hardwood floor.

"I'll get some glasses," Colleen said.

"Don't bother." Head back, Alex drank, a hefty slug for a woman her size. She held the bottle out. "To your new home, Coll."

"*Merci.*" Colleen took the bagged champagne, brushed her hair back, drank. Cool, effervescent, and delightful. There was a definite difference between the champagne Alex bought and the stuff you found in the corner store.

"The new Colleen," Alex said, taking the bottle back. "You've come a long way, baby. But I'm curious—why no curtains?"

"Light," Colleen said. A decade within four gray prison walls still lingered. Colleen wanted them gone. "Besides, from this side of the hill, no one can see a thing."

"You said you had another bedroom?" Alex asked.

Colleen nodded, serious now. "Pamela's," she said.

"Ah," Alex said gently.

She led Alex next door to a tidy bedroom, where a single bed was made up for her teenage daughter, if—*when*—she got Pam back. There was a photo of Pam on the nightstand, taken over five years ago, when she had just turned thirteen. Her soft red hair hung in her freckled face, and her shy smile was one of the last Colleen remembered. Pam hadn't hit the Goth stage yet. She wasn't using yet. She was still coming to visit Colleen in prison. If there was any regret Colleen felt over killing her ex, it wasn't the nine years and four months spent inside Denver Women's Correctional Facility; it was losing *that* Pam. The innocent Pam.

Alex's voice softened. "Any news?"

Colleen shook her head. "She's still up at Moon Ranch in Point Arenas."

"And you still can't see her?"

"They've taken out a restraining order. If I get within five hundred yards, I'll violate parole." The orange-robed sect that Pam had fallen in with had not only taken her red locks, leaving her with a botched crew cut, they'd turned Pam against her. Not that there was that much further to go. Colleen had come out to California last year, when she got out of prison, to bring Pamela back home.

Alex reached over, gave Colleen's hand a squeeze. "You'll get her back, Coll."

"Yes." Colleen squeezed back, took the bottle, drank. "That is what I tell myself. Every day."

"Then you will."

In the living room, the phone rang, pulling Colleen out of her thoughts.

She handed Alex the bottle, went to answer the white Princess phone on the low glass coffee table.

"Is this Hayes Confidential?" a man said in a working-class British accent. He didn't sound young, or old, but he had a distinctive, authoritative voice. But he sounded tired. More than tired. Exhausted.

"It is," Colleen said. "How can I help you?"

"My name is Steve Cook." The name sounded familiar, as did the voice, although she couldn't quite place it. "I need to talk to the private investigator, yeah?"

"You are," she said. "Colleen Hayes."

There was a pause while static crackled across the wire. Colleen turned to the window by the sofa, watching the lights down the hill start to burn fuzzy through the fog as evening approached. She knew exactly what he was thinking: a *female* private investigator.

But his desperation must have gotten the better of him because he didn't hang up or beg off the call.

"It's my daughter," he said finally, in a tone that underscored a deliberate attempt to sound calm. "She's eleven years old. And she's gone missing."

CHAPTER TWO

Steve Cook lived in the heart of the Mission, in a dilapidated Victorian apartment building with flaking blue paint and faded white trim. He had told Colleen to park in the driveway, which she did, nosing her red Torino up to a garage door built before there were cars. She was partially blocking the sidewalk but that was the way it was done in the Mission, where little parking was to be had.

She got out, locked up the car, the wet evening mist cooling her face. She still wore her jeans, white T-shirt, and brown bomber jacket, but had run a brush through her hair. Steve's phone message had been brief but anxious and the sense of urgency was unmistakable.

Trotting up the wooden stairs to the porch to three doors, she found Steve's first-floor flat on the left. A tarp served as a curtain over the bay window. The pounding of a hammer came from within. Upstairs, Cheap Trick blasted on a stereo.

"You must be Colleen."

He was of medium height, around thirty, well built, no extra weight. He wore work clothes. A hammer dangled from his right hand. A burnt-down cigarette stuck out of the corner of his mouth. He had short dark hair that needed combing, square features, and a nose that might have been broken at one time. He needed a shave about three days ago, which is when he had probably last slept, judging by the rings around his dark, drowsy eyes that still bore a hint of smolder despite the fact that he looked like fifty miles of bad road. The way he carried himself said he was weathering a missing daughter better than the average male would have.

Because he was not the average male.

Colleen realized, with a start, why the voice on the phone had sounded so familiar, along with the name. She was immediately taken back to the year before her disastrous marriage ended with the death of her husband, when a certain English rock 'n' roll band spent the summer of '66 on her turntable in West Denver. She had willingly escaped into an album that spoke to her in her bleaker moments, with its brooding, moody, soulful singer who stood before her now.

At that time, he had been a teenager, dressed in the height of Carnaby Street fashion, with a fluffy mod haircut, ruffled shirt, and a jacket made of a Union Jack. He had sold millions of records. Even now, he still had that way of standing to one side, and he had a lot of what most men didn't. He had plenty to spare.

She did her best to contain her surprise.

"Yeah," he said with a wry look that said he read what she was thinking, "I used to be *that* bloke—for all of fifteen minutes. But that was a million years ago. Thanks for coming, yeah?"

She collected herself, handed him a business card. "It sounded important."

He took the card, hammer in his free hand. Working on the house while his daughter was missing. There were worse ways to cope.

She followed him into an old flat, resembling a construction zone. The front room was a skeleton of aged redwood studs and joists, lit by a single bare bulb that cast broken shadows up to the floor above. A few sheets of new wallboard had been hung. Another sheet sat on two sawhorses in the middle of the room, with the rectangle of a light switch cut out. A ladder leaned up against a wall, a box of tools was out, and a radio murmured with oldies on the bare subfloor. The only other furniture in the former living room was a sofa covered with a sheet of plastic and a folded-up cot in the corner, which had a small backpack and a sleeping bag next to it. Colleen wondered who the cot was for. His daughter?

Steve went over to the radio, turned it off, set his hammer on top. He took the cigarette out of his mouth, held it between thumb and forefinger.

"Sorry about the mess. Trying to get this place ready to sell."

He was stalling. Upstairs, "Surrender" throbbed.

"Your eleven-year-old daughter is missing," Colleen said.

He nodded, stubbed out his cigarette in a tuna can on a section of blocking between two studs. He picked up a can of Foster's lager from another block and took a long pull.

"Have you done this kind of work before?" he asked.

Colleen took a calming breath. *This* again. "You knew I was a woman when you called me."

"Sorry, love. But it's not the norm, is it? Women private detectives, I mean."

She had left a bottle of Dom Perignon for this.

"If you want to look elsewhere," she said, "go ahead. Call back if you feel like moving forward." She turned to go.

He put his free hand up to stop her. "Sorry, love. I can see you're the real deal. I just had to make sure. We are talking about my daughter, yeah."

She stopped, nodded. "Who gave you my home number?"

"Al Lennox."

Al Lennox. A shady bail bondsman Colleen had used to connect her with someone who could get her an illegal peek at some case evidence in police storage once.

"If you know Al," she said, "then you must be in trouble."

There was a pause while Steve gulped beer, his Adam's apple bouncing. Under pressure. He wiped his mouth with the back of his hand.

"I don't want the police involved," he said.

"If the police don't need to be involved, that's fine. But if you've committed a crime, I can't work for you."

"Everything we talk about is just between you and me, right?"

"Hayes *Confidential*," she said.

"Do you carry a gun?"

"Not if I can help it. What *is* the situation with your daughter?"

The skin tightened around his eyes. "Mel's been taken," he said with a small gasp.

A bolt of alarm shot up Colleen's back. "Your daughter's been *kidnapped*?"

Steve gave a single nod.

"Why didn't you tell me this when you called?" Colleen said.

"I had to be sure. And I can't have you going to the police."

She understood, for the most part. "How long has she been gone?"

"Two days now."

"Two *days*?"

"I didn't get the call until last night. I wasn't sure if she'd run off again. She's done that before."

"The call last night being from someone who claimed they took her?"

He confirmed with a nod.

"Did they let you talk to your daughter?"

Shook his head *no*.

Problem. "And you haven't notified the police?"

"Only when she first went missing. Two days ago. Not since."

"I'm not generally a big fan of the cops," she said, "but they really need to be brought in."

"No." He drained his beer, set the empty can on the sheetrock on the sawhorses. "They said *no cops*."

"The kidnappers?"

"Right. So, if you want the police in on this, I don't need you."

"Got it." She'd circle back on that. Right now, time was critical. "Tell me about your daughter. Do you have a recent photo?"

Steve had one pinned to a stud. He plucked it, handed it over. "Mel. Melanie."

Colleen studied the Polaroid of a prepubescent girl on a horse in full riding gear. Her helmet hid most of what looked like a mousy bob. She was a young version of her father, with a firm face, but she had a mean streak. You could see it in her eyes. The lack of a smile when sitting on a horse, something most girls her age dreamt of.

"Where's her mother?" Colleen asked.

"We're divorced. Lynda lives in town. She knows the situation with Mel." He dug a pack of Lucky Strikes out of his shirt pocket, shook one out, stuck it between his lips. "She's not going to like you working for me, by the way."

"It's not confirmed I'm working for you yet." Colleen placed the photo on the wallboard, took another look at the cot. Things made more sense now. "Your daughter was staying with you when she disappeared?"

He lit up his smoke, nodded in acknowledgment as he shook out a match. "Lynda had to go out of town for work. She's a record producer for NewMedia and they don't always get much notice when things come up. Mel had to stay with me. Lynda wasn't happy about that either, but she had nowhere else to put her. I'm not allowed custody. But Lynda's au pair had just quit. Mel can be a handful."

A difficult kid. Two parents who didn't get along, one holding her position over the other. Steve didn't look like he could afford horses and riding lessons. He wasn't the parent with custody. So he probably wasn't the parent who won many arguments.

She asked about possible friends and family Melanie might be with. They were few and Steve had already checked. No luck.

"How did Melanie disappear?"

"I was playing a gig. Nearby. I wasn't supposed to take Mel to any more gigs. I promised Lynda. But Deena'd already booked it—it's her band, yeah?—and was set to lose her residency if I didn't show. So, against Lynda's wishes, I took Mel. I had our roadie keeping an eye on her while we performed, but the venue was packed, and things got out of hand. Mel went to the restroom, disappeared. I called the cops, and they went through the motions, but, like I said, Mel has run off before, so it was wait and see. And then last night, I got the phone call."

"Was the caller male? Female?"

Steve smoked. He was looking brittle, his neck tight. He was hanging on; she could see that now that she knew him a little better. "The voice on the other end of the phone was distorted, electronic, like something out of a film. Couldn't tell if it was a man or woman."

"What did he or she say? As close as you can remember."

"'Don't talk. Listen,' it said. 'I'm going to say this once. Do exactly as I say. No police. Otherwise she dies.'"

An involuntary shiver ran down Colleen's back. It was quickly replaced by anger at the monster—or monsters—who would take an eleven-year-old girl. And what she must be going through. Colleen just prayed that Melanie was still alive.

CHAPTER THREE

"How much do the kidnappers want?" Colleen asked Steve.

"Twenty K," he said, taking a hit on his cigarette so hard it crumpled. "Nothing larger than a twenty, used bills. They'll let me know when and where to drop it off. That's where I need your help. Dropping it off."

Twenty thousand was a fair amount of money for a guy who didn't look like he had any. It was twice what most people made in a year.

"You've already got the cash?" she asked, surprised.

"I do, yeah."

"And your plan is to just pay them off?"

"What other choice do I have?"

"Pay them off with no conditions and you won't have any choices left except to keep paying them."

"But they say they're going to kill her."

"We say you're prepared to pay them once you have *absolute* proof that your daughter is unharmed and it's certain you're getting her back. This is the time you have leverage. Meanwhile, we try to find out who they are."

He shook his head. "God, that sounds risky."

"Everything about this is risky, Steve. But giving kidnappers money without any guarantee is riskier. Did they say when they would call you back?"

Steve took a drag, blew smoke across the empty torn-down room. "They said just to raise the money and wait." He nodded at a black phone on the floor by the bay window. "So here I am, waiting."

Colleen thought about SFPD putting a trace on the line. But those things took days and didn't always work. And Steve was adamant he didn't want the police involved.

"They want you on edge," she said.

"They've got that part working."

"They might not even phone," she said. "They might get a message to you some other way."

Steve flicked ash into the tuna can on the wall block. "Christ."

Colleen eyed the cot again, the backpack. It had a red ribbon tied to a zipper. "That's Melanie's bag?"

"Yah," he said with a crack in his voice.

"I need to go through it."

"Help yourself."

She found little to go on in the backpack. A sweatshirt. A folded copy of *Teen Beat* magazine, with Leif Garrett shirtless on the cover. Half a bag of jelly beans. A crumpled dollar bill. Some loose change rattled around in the bottom, along with a torn bus transfer.

But no change of clothes. No hairbrush. No toothbrush. No clean underwear. Not much of an overnight bag for a girl who was going to spend time at her father's.

"Does Melanie pack her own bag when she stays with you, Steve?"

"Mel doesn't do anything for herself. The au pair would take care of it. But she'd just quit. So it would have been up to Lynda."

"I need to see the club where Melanie disappeared," Colleen said. "I want to talk to the people who were with her besides you. The person who was looking after her right before she vanished. And your ex."

"Lynda's not going to like talking to you."

"Steve, if I'm involved, your ex is going to have to put up with me. How soon can you call the people in your band, and your ex, get them to meet me at the bar where Melanie disappeared? Right now would be ideal. Melanie's already been gone two days. You stay here, wait for the kidnappers to call—if they do call."

"I can't come with you?"

She shook her head. She didn't need him around when she was interviewing people who knew him anyway. "You wait for the call."

Steve frowned. "I reckon I just need help paying them off. Not the rest of it."

"I have to get a better handle on this first. And before you pay anyone, we need to speak to Melanie, confirm that she's okay. I know it's not easy, but we have to establish we're not just going to do whatever they say without getting something in return. The next step you make is the most important." Melanie Cook might not even be alive, but she wasn't going to say that.

"We're talking about my daughter."

"Steve, if you just want to pay them off, no questions asked, then you don't need me. Save my fee because you'll need it when they make another demand. Which they will."

He looked at her, uncertain. "I'll need to talk to Lynda about this."

Colleen checked her watch. "Call me when you two make up your mind. If you can't get hold of me at home, I've got an answering service I check regularly. It's on the card. Like I say, you should call the police. But if you refuse to do that, and if we do go ahead, then you and your ex have to let me drive. And that means I talk to the people who last saw Melanie." And make sure what he was telling her was what it was purported to be. "And one last thing . . . if we do go ahead and I find out I'm being kept in the dark on something, or being played in any way, I'm out." She raised her eyebrows, left him there, headed out, down the steps. On the second floor, Cheap Trick were singing about a California man.

She fished out her keys, walked around the back of the car.

The door to Steve's flat opened and he came out on the porch. He had a fresh cigarette going.

"Okay," he said. "You're the boss."

Colleen felt a shudder of relief. But she knew things were going to get rockier.

CHAPTER FOUR

Colleen motored over to The Pitt, the Mission bar where Melanie Cook had disappeared. The lights of the stores and bars and little Mexican restaurants twinkled in the low, wet fog. People were out, all ages and shapes and sizes, most of them Hispanic, some double-parked in lowriders, others hanging out on street corners, others just walking. Anyone with money lived elsewhere, but a genuine vibe prevailed in the neighborhood.

Steve told Colleen the band he sang with—*the band with no name*—would be available to talk to her as they were playing tonight. He wasn't singing with them for obvious reasons, which irked the owner of The Pitt apparently. Steve left a message with Lynda, his ex, to hopefully meet Colleen there, too, but hadn't been able to speak to her directly. And Lynda wasn't the most cooperative person, he said.

On Mission Street, Colleen could hear The Pitt throbbing with rock 'n' roll before she saw the place. A '50s-style neon sign flickered with a red "P" as she passed by. A sullen-looking bouncer with a Fu Manchu mustache, sunglasses on at night, stood out front.

She parked up the street and headed down. A raunchy version of "Johnny B. Goode" was in progress, '70s style, which meant distortion, pounding bass, and crashing drums. The doorman didn't actually smile but he did pull open one of the double doors for Colleen, so she figured she wasn't too old. A screaming guitar assailed her ears. The rough floorboards gave off a stale beer odor.

The Pitt was bigger inside than it seemed from out front, with a long, lovely old bar on the left and a small stage at the far end, where a trio was shifting into high gear as they broke for a guitar solo. A small clump of denim- and leather-clad clients stood in front, heads bobbing. The band was pretty decent, even without Steve, their singer. In the dim light from the beer sign, a tall guy with chiseled looks and a sculpted blond ducktail thumped a bass while a character who looked like an extra from *Night of the Living Dead* staggered around, ripping out an eloquent guitar solo that belied his less-than-sober appearance. Hunched over an old Fender Stratocaster, he was ill or beholden to some narcotic. At the drums sat a striking young woman in a tight black tank top and a punk cat-style hairdo, black, replete with little peroxide tufts that resembled ears. She had dark mascara to carry it off and tight muscled arms that offset her slim, feminine torso. The guys in the crowd were watching her while the girls watched the bass player.

Behind the bar, a big man with wild long gray hair and a beard to match eyed Colleen. His beer gut stretched out a Stones lapping tongue T-shirt. Colleen went up, shouted for a beer. He gave her what was probably meant to be a winsome smile as he pushed a foamy glass her way.

"On the house," his lips mouthed, his words obliterated by the music.

She shouted her thanks as she took a token sip. She didn't do any serious drinking while working.

The *band with no name* returned from their solo, earning a shout of praise, and the bass player got behind the mic and sang the final chorus to "Johnny B. Goode." He looked a lot better than he sang, but then again, he was filling in for Steve. And he could play bass. The band slammed the song into a brick wall, ending it with a crash of drums and squeal of guitar. The guitarist managed to break a string as he beat his Strat into submission.

"We'll be back after a short break," the drummer said in a sharp New York accent as she slotted her sticks next to the snare. Colleen set her beer down on the bar and headed over. A big black man in glasses and a camouflage jacket had jumped up onstage and taken the guitar from the emaciated guitarist and began changing the string. The guitar player teetered off the stage and down the hallway to the back. The bass player with the hair took off as well.

Colleen caught the drummer stepping offstage before she could leave.

"You must be Deena."

She gave Colleen a guarded squint. "That's right."

Colleen introduced herself, handed Deena a business card. "Steve hired me to find Melanie."

Deena took the card, read it, handed it back. "And how is you talking to me going to find Melanie?"

"Maybe it won't. But it might. Buy you a drink?"

Deena shrugged. "Draft." Colleen went to the bar while Deena sat at a table, breaking out a pack of Marlboros. Colleen retrieved her beer and bought one for Deena. By the time Colleen sat down across from her, Deena's legs were stretched out under the table and she was leaning back, chair tipped, blowing a smoke ring at the ceiling.

Colleen sat down. "What can you tell me about the night Melanie disappeared?"

Deena set her cigarette in the notch of a Budweiser ashtray. She took a slug of beer, smacked her lips, gave Colleen a frown. "Steve didn't tell you?"

"He told me what *he* knew. I'd like to hear your side of it."

"How much are you charging him? While his kid's off somewhere?"

"This is how it works. I ask questions."

"Like a cop. The same questions over and over. Instead of looking for Melanie."

"This is how I start looking. Get as many details as I can first. Maybe there's something you know that doesn't seem important but is."

Deena drank beer, set her glass down, eyed Colleen with suspicion. "Or maybe you're just trying to milk it."

"If you don't want to talk to me, that's your call. But please don't waste my time. Because right now, that's Melanie's time as well."

Deena picked up her cigarette, took a puff, smashed it out in the ashtray. Stood up. "I'm going to call Steve."

Deena returned a couple of minutes later, looking ashen. She sat down, trembling. "Why didn't you tell me someone called Steve, demanding ransom? That Melanie's been kidnapped?"

"It wasn't my place. I need to keep my client's affairs as confidential as possible."

"Fuck." Deena ran her black-nailed fingers through her hair. "*Fuck.*"

"Agreed," Colleen said. "You didn't think Melanie was kidnapped?"

Deena gave a deep sigh. "I thought she was playing games again."

"Because she's done it before."

"Melanie might be a kid technically, but she can be a full-grown Grade-A bitch when she puts her mind to it. Especially when she doesn't get what she wants. I shouldn't say that with what's going on, but it's the truth."

Don't hold back, Colleen thought. "Why was Mel being a pain this time?"

"She needs her own horse." Deena took a drink of beer, shook her head. "Apparently, the ones at the stables aren't good enough anymore. Like Steve's got that kind of money. But she'd just bust his chops for something else if she *did* get a horse. That's what she does. Like mother, like daughter."

Colleen was getting a distinct impression of Steve's ex. "What do you remember about that night? When Melanie disappeared? Your band was playing here."

"One of Steve's first big gigs with us. People were lined up down the street. The place was jammed. Steve's still got a lot of fans. A *lot* of fans. He's overdue for a comeback. I've been telling him."

"He hasn't played for some time."

"Took me forever to convince him to test the waters again. And when he did, it was a flood. All my life I've been looking for a front man like Steve. Finally talked him back into it. And then *this* happens." Meaning Melanie.

"So what happened to Steve? The Lost Chords were huge."

"He's been out of circulation since the sixties."

"Why?"

Deena gave Colleen a look. "You don't know?"

"I was married with a kid when The Lost Chords fell out of the top forty. Too busy watching *Romper Room*." And going to prison for killing her ex.

"Then it's not my place to tell you," Deena said with a smirk. "I have to respect Steve's privacy."

Touché, Colleen thought. But there was something in Steve's past she didn't know about that might have a bearing. "So the place was packed when Melanie disappeared."

"Yeah. Boom was watching her, but she got away. More typical Melanie bullshit, I thought. Always had—*has*—to be the center of attention. Now it's the real deal." She shook her head again. "I can't believe it."

"*Boom?*"

Deena took a drink of her beer and nodded at the black guy on-stage who had finished stringing up the guitar and was now tuning it up. "Our roadie. He was keeping an eye on Mel while we played."

"Sounds like I need to talk to Boom. What about the other two? Your bass player and the guitarist? Would they know anything?"

Deena frowned. "Finn was onstage. We were in the middle of our set. He didn't even see Melanie. And Jamie never notices much to begin with."

"Jamie's the guitarist?"

Deena gave a knowing look. "He was especially *not noticing much* two nights ago." She put her beer down, stared off. "Poor fucking Steve."

"Deena!" a deep voice shouted from the bar.

Colleen turned in her chair to see the wild man with the gut holding up his watch, pointing to it.

"In a minute, Vernon," Deena barked.

"I'm not paying you to drink."

"Lighten up!"

Colleen turned back. "Vernon's all heart."

"How am I supposed to go up there and play another set now? With Mel being held somewhere? But Vernon knows we're no big shakes without Steve. I better get back up there before he fires us."

"One last thing," Colleen said. "Steve called Lynda, left word for her to meet me here." She gave her a questioning look.

"Good luck with that."

"Lynda doesn't tend to do anything anybody asks her to?"

Deena stood up. "Especially if Steve is doing the asking. She's not gonna like someone like *you* sticking your nose into her business either. Double if it has to do with Melanie."

It didn't sound like Lynda was going to show up.

"Give me that card again," Deena said. "If anything else comes to me, I'll call."

Colleen gave her the business card. "You've got a great band."

"With Steve, we're a *great* band. Without him, we're a *good* band." She shook her head one more time. "Poor Steve."

Not *poor Melanie*. Poor *Steve*.

"Deena!" Vernon shouted from behind the bar.

"Jesus, Vernon!" Deena snapped, heading off to the stage.

The *band with no name* launched into more gutsy rock 'n' roll. A few more people had wandered in and it was almost enough to fill half the dance floor in front of the stage. Colleen caught the roadie's attention as he stood with his back to the bar, arms crossed over his big chest, watching the band.

"Got a minute?" she shouted over the music.

CHAPTER FIVE

"This is where Melanie was last seen," Boom said to Colleen. "Two nights ago."

They were standing in the alley behind The Pitt, Colleen and Boom, the roadie with the *band with no name*. He was a big, imposing black guy in his mid-twenties with a leveled haircut and dark-framed glasses and a well-worn camouflage military jacket.

A kid in a hoodie and high tops was leaning up against a dumpster that reeked of garbage, his head back, mouth open, about to lose balance. In the shadows, a couple of longhairs were making some sort of trade. Two youngsters in a lovers' clinch held up a brick wall, barely lit by the streetlight that drifted down the alley.

"Melanie had gone to the restroom when you lost her?" Colleen asked.

Boom's eyes blinked behind the lenses of his glasses. "The place was packed, crazy, people everywhere. A fight had just broken out. I told Melanie we were going across the street for pizza to wait until the show was over. She said she had to go to the bathroom first. I said it could wait until we got to the pizza place, but she said it couldn't. 'Not after five gallons of Coke,' she said." Boom shook his head sadly. "I went to tell Steve we were leaving but he was onstage in the middle of a number. When I got back to the restroom, no

Melanie. I waited a minute. A woman came out, and I asked her if she had seen anyone like her. She said yes, she had just left. Someone else said they had seen Melanie come out here." Meaning the alley. "I freaked, came out. It was packed out here, too. So busy no one really saw her, except one guy. Who was loaded. But he said he thought he saw her."

"Did he see anyone with her?"

"He said 'no.'" Boom grimaced, shook his head. "But, like I say, he was out of his head."

Maybe that's why Steve had thought Melanie might have taken off on her own.

"What's your honest opinion of Melanie Cook, Boom?"

Boom took a deep breath, looked away.

"Confidentially," Colleen said.

"In a word," Boom said, "*difficult.* In two words: *extremely* difficult."

Colleen gave Boom a business card. "If you think of anything else, please call."

Boom took the card, slipped it in the pocket of his jacket. "Two tours of Nam and *this* is where I fuck up. I never should have let her out of my sight. I should have just dragged her out of there, kicking and screaming."

"I'm not sure it would have made a difference," Colleen said.

"Why do you say that?"

"It seems she was intent on getting away from you."

Back in the bar *the band with no name* pounded out more tunes. Lynda never showed. Colleen had Lynda's number and she called it from a pay phone down the street where she wouldn't have to shout over the band. No answer. She had Lynda's address but wouldn't be going over there tonight. Lynda wouldn't exactly welcome her with open arms, she'd been told, and Colleen had done enough nosing around for one night. She wanted to check in with Steve anyway. She didn't have all the info, but she could tell he was telling the truth about the kidnapping. What he knew of it.

But something wasn't right.

CHAPTER SIX

It was close to midnight when Colleen got back to Steve's. It took time to find a parking space on 20th and she didn't want her car in the driveway where it might draw attention.

Steve answered the door, cigarette in the corner of his mouth, eyes tight with stress and exhaustion. Once they got inside, Colleen spoke first. "Any phone calls?"

"Just Deena, after she met you," he said. "But you probably know about that one."

"She needed to get her comfort level up about me."

"And?" he said.

"I met Deena. Boom. And sweet Vernon. Lynda was a no-show."

"Typical."

They looked at each other in the light of the single bulb.

"Where did you get the ransom money, Steve?" she asked. "The twenty K?"

"Borrowed it."

"From who?"

"That's none of your business."

"Everything about this is my business," she said. "Every little detail."

"I have the money. There's your little detail."

"You have money you owe. To who?"

"You already asked me that."

"You didn't answer."

"Some guys Al Lennox put me in touch with."

That was the kind of thing she was worried about. "If Al Lennox set you up with a loan shark, Steve, you've got more problems."

Steve stubbed his cigarette out in the tuna can. "I don't care about the money."

"You will if some leg breakers come around to collect."

"I'll cross that bridge when I get to it."

"If you can walk."

"I do like your positive mental attitude, love."

Having the once-famous Steve Cook call her "love" meant absolutely nothing, but it still made her heart beat a little faster.

"So what's the verdict?" he said. "You good to help me get Mel back? Or do you still need to talk to Lynda?"

She didn't have a complete handle on the situation yet. But Steve was depending on her. Her own daughter had run off and she knew what kind of toll that took on a person. Steve apparently had the ex from hell. She'd have to run with what she had and keep her eyes open. "We are going to get your daughter back, Steve."

One way or another, she thought.

He gave a sigh and the muscles in his face eased a millimeter or two and that made her feel better. "Thanks, Colleen. Thanks a lot, yeah?"

Steve Cook. Calling her by her first name. For a moment she felt like a teenager in her thirties. Just a little starstruck.

"So what happens now?" Steve asked.

She went over to the sofa, pulled the plastic sheet off, sat on blue velour. "We wait. With any luck they'll call. You get some sleep. If the phone rings, I'll wake you."

"You think I'm going to bloody sleep? Knowing some bastard's got my daughter?"

"It was worth a try."

"Beer?"

"No."

"Something stronger?"

"Not for me."

He went back into the kitchen, and she heard the sucking pop of a refrigerator. He came back, drinking an oil can of Foster's. He sat down on the unfinished subfloor, his back up against a stud.

"When is the first payment due?" she asked.

"Not until next week."

"I'm guessing you don't have any assets to pay anyone back twenty K, beyond this building, and that's iffy, too."

"You, madam, are bloody clairvoyant."

"You're my client. One who is in a jam. Now you're in two. See where I might be concerned?"

"I had a limited education, but I can count to two. Just help me get Mel back. I'll worry about the rest."

"You really should get some sleep," she said. "You're no good if you're exhausted."

"I'll sleep when we get Mel back."

Colleen gave a sigh. "So tell me your story." It would change the subject, possibly get him to relax a little. She needed to learn more about his past, anyway. Why he stopped singing. Was there any connection to the situation he was in now?

Steve left to get a fresh beer, returned, sat back down against the stud, popped the beer, and told Colleen he worked construction here and there. The flat was a work in progress between jobs. He bought the building when he came to the U.S. over ten years ago, when they were still affordable, with what money he had left. He rented the upper two flats out but Señora Rojas on the top floor was eighty-seven, with no family, hadn't paid rent in over a year. He wasn't about to throw her out. The building was mortgaged to the hilt. He was a few inches away from losing it.

"What about Lynda?"

Steve laughed out loud. Lynda was a record producer and his former manager with NewMedia who had tried to revive his career. It was not a success, due, mostly, to his apparent inability to make a fresh start with a fast-moving industry that had left him behind. His tumultuous marriage had resulted in Melanie.

"But The Lost Chords . . ." Colleen said. "You were huge."

"We made *one* album." He held up a single finger.

"Plus a bunch of singles. And that one album was a smash. You knocked the The Beatles off the top of the charts. Even I had a copy."

"That was 1966," he said, drinking. "This is 1978."

"What happened?" she said. "You guys were on your way."

"Got ripped off is what happened," he said. "Stupid working-class lads who thought a fancy meal in a restaurant meant we were on top of the world. Signing papers we didn't understand. I never saw a penny beyond what I could eat, drink, or wear. And I wrote the bloody songs. 'Frenzy' sold over a million copies."

"I loved 'Shades of Summer.'" A hippy-dippy song about love being everywhere.

He actually smiled. "That was secretly one of my favorites, too."

"Really? It wasn't your usual fare."

"Wrote it for my mum."

"Get away."

"*Lovely Louise, she makes my summer sun shine,*" he sang softly, vaudeville style. "Louise Cook." He drank. "My mum."

"Kind of ruins your bad boy image."

"Delco—my old record company—hated it, but I was big enough at the time to call the shots, so they put it out. 'Shades of Summer.' Never got anywhere as a single. So they threw it on the album as filler. But my mum heard it on the radio. So there you are. Never got a penny for that, either."

What was the reason he quit performing?

"I'd just gotten married," she said. "Worst mistake I ever made. And that album of yours . . . and 'Shades of Summer' . . . let's just say I listened to that song a *lot*. The way you sang it. It was like you were singing it to me." She wasn't just digging for info now; she was opening up. "I wish I still had my copy."

He looked at her close from where he sat. "That makes my day, Colleen. Because, at the end of it, it's not about the money—especially since I never bloody got any. It's about connecting. Yeah, I know, it sounds like new-age bullshit, but I'm really chuffed you liked that silly song. So did my mum."

He said it in such a way that she felt special, and she realized that was what being a real artist was about—connecting.

"But, even so," she said. "After 1966, you just disappeared."

He drank, turned his head away. "Yep." He looked back, smile gone.

"So, what happened, Steve?"

He shook his head.

"Come on," she said. "I'm asking as a fan."

Steve drained the beer, crumpled the empty, tossed it into the plastic garbage can again from where he sat on the floor. "I don't need to lose any more fans. I'm down to about three." He got up, went to the back of the house.

She could tell that was the end of that conversation. For now.

He returned, carrying a record album. She recognized it.

He came up, handed it to her. "Long out of print. Enjoy."

Colleen took it, looked at the cover she had studied many times in her room in West Denver while her husband was at work. The Lost Chords in a grainy black-and-white photo, standing in front of a white van parked in front of some old brick building. There was Steve in front, modded out in a wild paisley shirt, 19th-century military uniform jacket with epaulettes. His thumbs were hooked into the belt loops of his hip-huggers. His eyes were glowing. The rest of the band weren't bad either. All in high sixties fashion.

"How much did you guys spend on clothes?" she asked.

"The band had open accounts all over Carnaby Street. Since we never got paid, we took our revenge in accumulating the latest gear. Ran our clothing allowance through the bloody roof! I spent five hundred quid one month at I Was Lord Kitchener's Valet alone. That's 1966 quid. Nev—our guitarist—had silk underwear tailor made. We were always trying to outdo each other." He actually laughed. It was good to see.

She smiled, studied the album cover again. "I can't take this, Steve."

"I've got a gold one on my bedroom wall. And Deena has a copy if I really need to hear myself sing 'Frenzy' for the millionth time."

"Handed to me by the man himself." She held the record up to the light. "How cool is that?"

"Not too much anymore, truth be told."

She set it down, carefully, to one side against the sofa. "Are you still in touch with anyone from the old days?" Maybe there was a link.

He shook his head, patted his shirt for cigarettes. None. "Sorry to say, no."

"No one who could have anything to do with the current situation?"

"That bridge was crossed long ago. Hang on. I need to get some smokes." He headed back to the rear of the house again.

Outside, Colleen heard quick feet coming up the front steps, on the porch now, followed by the sound of a key sliding into the front door lock. The door opened.

And there stood a blond woman, early thirties, a year or two shy of Colleen's age, dressed in smart jeans and a short black coat that matched the mascara under her hard blue eyes. A faux fur collar highlighted a face as striking as it was fierce-looking.

She gave Colleen a sneer.

"Who the fuck're you?"

So it was going to be like that. "Colleen Hayes," Colleen said, standing up.

"Where's Steve?"

Steve returned from the rear of the house with a pack of cigarettes. His smile faded.

"Lynda," he said.

She dumped her handbag on the floor with a clunk. "I can't believe you're trying to bang some tramp while your daughter is being held by maniacs."

"Stop." Steve grimaced. "This is Colleen Hayes. She's a private investigator. I've been trying to call you."

"What?" Lynda's face dropped—barely—before her sneer resumed its natural position. "An investigator? No, Steve. Why?"

"Because we need help."

"We *know* what to do. We don't need some rent-a-cop." She glowered at Colleen. "A female one at that. What is she gonna do? Attack them with her nail file?"

Colleen said, "You need all the help you can get right now."

"Shut the fuck up, bitch. I'm not talking to you."

Colleen let it slide, but saw more problems heading their way.

"That's enough, Lynda," Steve said. "Bloody stop it."

"You were supposed to call Daddy," Lynda said.

"Well, I changed my mind."

"Say *what*?" Lynda's face reddened. "Do you know how hard it was for me to talk him into helping us out?"

"I don't want your father's money."

Colleen wondered about a guy who would take a mob loan over his ex-father-in-law. But there was obviously plenty of bad blood between Steve and Lynda. She'd circle back on this when the screaming stopped.

Lynda shook her head angrily. "If Melanie dies because of you . . . you *motherfucker*, I'll see you go to prison. For the rest of your fucking life. Don't think I can't make it happen. Child endangerment just to start."

Steve worked a cigarette out of his pack, lit it up, put the pack in his shirt pocket. "Guess what, Lynda? I don't bleeding care. Once we get Mel back, you can do anything you like."

"And how are you going to get her back, hotshot? Get your drummer girlfriend to take up a collection for you?" Lynda flicked a nasty smile on Colleen. "Oh yeah, he's got one for every day of the week, in case you thought you were special."

Losing your temper with a woman like Lynda was counterproductive. Lynda would have fit in perfectly with the women Colleen spent almost a decade with behind bars. "None of this is helping get your daughter back," she said.

"And I thought I told you to shut your hole. You're not Melanie's mother. So fuck off."

"Lynda," Steve said. "I've *got* the money."

Now Lynda was well-and-truly taken off guard. Her perfect red lips dropped open for a moment, showing perfect white teeth. She looked at Steve and blinked.

"What?"

"It's covered."

"You got it?" Lynda said. "All of it?"

"Twenty K." Steve smoked.

"How?"

"Borrowed it."

Lynda let out a breath. "Borrowed it from who?"

"That's my business."

Her face softened. "Daddy had it all ready."

"Well, now you can tell him I don't want his money."

"Why not?"

Steve laughed. "Do you think I'm bloody stupid? You know why."

She shook her head violently. "Fuck!"

"That's all you have to say, Lynda? Here I was thinking a curt 'thank you' might be more in order."

"And all I can say is that if anything goes wrong, Steve, it'll be your damn funeral."

"You can thank me when we get Mel back."

Now that the fury had died down, Colleen spoke: "How you two handle the ransom money is your business. Mine is to make sure you get your daughter back. But giving twenty thousand dollars to total strangers without conditions is not the way to start. We don't hand it over unless we're certain we're getting Melanie back. That means proof before payment. That means we talk to her. That means we all have to agree to be tough and *stay* tough."

Lynda narrowed her eyes at Colleen. "And you're an expert."

"I've dealt with scum like these people before. I've got resources. And I'm not in the middle of an emotional shitstorm like you two are. I've got a daughter of my own who ran off. I know what it's like. I can be a lot more objective than you."

"Yeah," Lynda said, "you look like a load of help."

Colleen ignored her. "Twenty thousand is a lot of money, but it's not a fortune. So it's most likely their starting point. Ten to one the kidnappers are going to ask for more. It's important to negotiate *before* we start paying. This is our strongest time, before they've gotten anything."

Lynda shook her head, glared at Steve. "She's going to get my daughter fucking killed."

"She makes a point, Lynda," Steve said. "They could have asked for more, yeah?"

"*Yeah?*" Lynda mimicked Steve's accent. "You're such a fucking whiz with money. You damn loser. You don't know what the hell you're doing. I don't want her." She nodded at Colleen. "She's out."

"Lynda," Steve said. "I'm the one paying Colleen. *I'm* the one paying the ransom."

"Damn right, you're paying the ransom," Lynda said. "It was your fault Melanie was taken in the first place."

"Right. We've established that—several times. But since I'm footing the bill, I'm the one who decides. And Colleen is going to get us through this."

"No, she fucking isn't."

"Lynda, if you don't like it, feel free to leave."

"Fuck you and the horse you rode in on, Jack. I'll have you arrested for child endangerment right now."

Steve strolled over, put his hands on his hips. "Get out."

"Get the fuck away from me!" Lynda slapped his face. Hard. It echoed in the room without walls and ceiling.

Steve stood there, didn't move. "Lynda, you've got five seconds to leave before I throw you out. And that'll be the end of your involvement in getting Mel back."

"You can't do that, you sad sack. I'm her fucking mother!"

Steve still had his hands on his hips. "One . . ."

"Go ahead, tough guy. I fucking dare you. My lawyers will eat you alive."

"Two . . ."

"You pathetic loser. You could have had everything."

"Three . . ."

Lynda's face suddenly crumpled; she collapsed into tears. "I'm just so scared, Steve!" She buried her face in her hands and sobbed like a baby. "I just don't know what to do anymore!"

Steve immediately took his hands off his hips, stood back, mouth open. He came back up to Lynda, put one hand gently on her shoulder. "I know, Lynda. Me, too. But we're going to get Mel back. I *promise*."

"Don't make me go, Steve! She's my daughter. Please let me stay. *Please!*"

"Of course, Lynda. Of course."

Colleen watched, wondering how these two were going to hold up as things got bumpier. But she also wondered about Lynda. And her father. She was going to have to look him up as soon as she got the chance.

"We'll wait and see if they call tonight," Colleen said. "When they do, Steve, you'll do the talking—but I'll tell you what to say."

Steve looked at Colleen, his hand still on Lynda's shoulder. "We're counting on you, Colleen."

"Good," she said. "Then we have a plan."

Lynda sniffled, wiped her eyes, stared at Colleen with a glare carved from ice.

CHAPTER SEVEN

Steve's phone rang just after 2:00 a.m., the bell splitting the late-night silence. Colleen had been sitting on the sofa, resting her eyes. Steve sat on the floor in the shadows by the opposite wall, against a stud, his head hung low, catching a little rest. But he snapped to at the first ring. Lynda was sleeping in Steve's bed down the hall.

Colleen stood up, took a deep breath, went over to the window, bent down, picked the receiver up on the second ring. Steve came up and stood next to her, as arranged, his head cocked to listen into the call. Lynda came padding down the hall in her stocking feet, rubbing her eyes. She gathered on Colleen's other side. She was an inch or so shorter. She smelled of expensive perfume. Steve smelled of cigarettes.

They waited.

An electronic noise, like air being pushed through a fan, preceded a metallic, robotic voice.

"I do hope you have the money," it said. There was no way to make out sex, or accent, or any human characteristics of the voice.

Colleen made eye contact with Steve, gave him a single nod. She held the phone between the two of them, the mouthpiece aimed his way.

"Yes," Steve said.

"Tomorrow. Nine a.m. Transbay Terminal. The pay phone by the snack bar. Wait for the call. Bring the cash. Don't be late."

Colleen gave Steve another nod to continue as planned.

"I need to talk to Mel," he said.

"All in good time. Just bring the money. Anyone comes with you, is seen with you, or is even suspected of being with you, you'll see little Mellie's head. In a bag." There was a mechanical staccato laugh and then the phone was hung up. The buzzing of a dial tone droned.

Colleen hung up the phone.

"Christ," Steve said, wiping his hand across his forehead. Lynda was hyperventilating.

"They wouldn't even consider letting me talk to her," Steve said.

"It's too bad," Colleen said. "But not entirely unexpected."

"So now what?"

"We move forward," Colleen said. "Remember, I'm driving this."

"It's happening," Steve said, digging his cigarettes out of his shirt pocket. "It's actually happening."

"It's happening, alright." Colleen looked at her watch. "Stay calm. I'm going home, get cleaned up, take care of a few things. I'll be back in the morning, early."

"Don't think you're going with Steve to the drop," Lynda screeched at her. "You heard what they said. Anybody comes with Steve, they'll kill Melanie."

"I haven't decided exactly what we're doing yet," Colleen said. The less Lynda knew, the better.

"You'll get her killed!"

"The kidnappers aren't going to do anything rash—yet. They want the money. We still have time. To gain some kind of advantage."

Lynda turned to Steve. "You can't fucking let her go down there, Steve!"

Steve took a drag on a cigarette he had lit. "We agreed to let Colleen handle this, Lynda. She knows what she's doing—a lot better than we do."

Lynda shook her head, took a deep sigh, but finally nodded, too.

"You need to go home, Lynda," Colleen said. "I can't have you here."

"What?" Lynda spat. "No. Not only no, but *fuck* no!"

"I'm going to keep you up to date on everything."

Lynda let loose a string of expletives concerning Colleen's character.

Colleen turned to Steve. "If she's here when I get back, I'm out."

Steve looked at Lynda, then Colleen. "Got it."

"You damn bitch!" Lynda muttered.

"I understand what you're going through, Lynda," Colleen said, "but you need to get out of the way."

Colleen left the two of them there, went outside into the foggy street, walked down the block, got into the Torino, started up the big block V8 with a throaty rumble, turned on the windshield wipers to slap away the night dew, drove home. The dark streets through the Mission were clear and it took no time at all.

She called her answering service. There was a message from Alex. *Don't forget Thursday—Antonia's party—xxx, A.*

Colleen had forgotten about Antonia's surprise birthday party. Too preoccupied with Melanie Cook. She fired up Mr. Coffee, putting two scoops of dark roast in the basket for each cup of water.

After a very hot shower she dressed in loose black straight leg jeans and a burgundy turtleneck. She sat on the single chair in her bedroom and laced up her sneakers and sipped rich coffee with brown sugar.

She took her coffee into the living room still reeking of fresh paint. She sat on her new ebony leather sofa, pulled a Virginia Slim out of the pack on the glass coffee table. She lit the long white skinny cigarette, braced herself for making a phone call in the middle of the night to Moran. She prayed that he answered instead of his wife, who disliked Colleen at the best of times. Since Moran had retired, and quit drinking, Daphne was a pit bull when it came to intrusions.

The phone rang somewhere in Santa Cruz, down the coast. After six rings, Daphne's nasal voice bit across the wires.

"Yes? Who is it?"

Colleen apologized profusely for calling so late but told Daphne how important it was and how she needed to speak to her husband, very briefly.

"It's four in the morning!"

"I'm so sorry, Mrs. Moran, but a client's daughter is in serious trouble, and I really need your husband's advice."

"Just a minute!" The phone was smacked down on a hard surface, jarring Colleen's ear. But she was thankful Daphne didn't hang up.

Lieutenant Dennis Moran was a retired homicide detective Colleen knew from her first, traumatic year in California, when she had come out from Colorado looking for her daughter. After a rocky start, they became unlikely allies.

"I hope you're not calling about my garden, Hayes," Moran said in his low, soothing voice. It was a running joke between them. Moran hadn't adjusted to retirement and hated gardening, but Daphne had other ideas. Colleen pictured the quiet man of sixty-five, with his medium build and unassuming demeanor, pushing his heavy-framed glasses up his ample nose, a gesture he repeated many times a day. "I usually wait until sunrise before I start pulling weeds. Sometimes I wait much longer. Days, in fact."

"That's too bad," Colleen said. "I hear it builds character."

"How's the security business? I assume that's what this call is about?"

"Still waiting for my license to be approved," she said. Ex-cons didn't go to the front of the line for investigator licenses. "But that's not exactly stopping me. In fact, I've got a doozy."

"Shoot."

She told him everything she knew about Melanie Cook's abduction.

There was a pause while the wind howled through the gaps in the old windows behind her.

"My client is to take the money to a phone booth at Transbay Terminal at nine a.m.," she said.

"Less than five hours from now. What's your plan, Hayes?"

"I make the drop in my client's place, take the call, refuse to hand over the money until I get proof that Melanie is alive. Take it from there."

"You don't have much to work with but, under the circumstances, it's what I'd do."

Colleen breathed a sigh of relief. Moran had validated her plan, such as it was.

"You run the risk that the girl's already dead, Hayes. You know that, don't you?"

She swallowed. "I do."

"You also risk riling up the kidnappers. They kill the girl since it's not easy pickings."

"I know that, too."

"But they want the money. They don't have any yet. They'll play ball for a while. You can figure out how much ball once you make a demand to talk to the girl. You'll also set the tone for future interactions. Start on the offensive."

"That's what I thought. But I wasn't one hundred percent sure. My client is conflicted."

"Especially if his ex is what you say she is."

"She is. And more."

"Be prepared to get the runaround from the kidnappers. They might run you all over town."

"I've got my sneakers on."

"Don't take a gun. You'll probably get patted down at some point."

"That crossed my mind, too."

She took a puff of her Slim, hoping Moran was thinking what she was thinking. Listening to the message she was telepathically sending him across the phone wires.

Colleen took a breath. "I hate to ask . . ."

"Of course, I'll help," Moran said quietly.

A huge surge of relief came.

"I could really use it," she said with an exhalation of air. "This has all happened so fast. I don't want to ruin your marriage."

"The weeds will still be here when I get back. And the thought of some poor girl being held somewhere means I'm not going back to sleep."

"Daphne's going to hate me."

"*Going* to?"

She laughed. "I wish I had time to recruit more people. But there's only a few hours left. Thank God you're willing to help."

"Agreed, we're short on time. Where is your client?"

"I'd like to keep him out of it."

"Yes," Moran said. "He's too emotionally involved to be much help. And you don't want him to get hurt."

"I'll keep him nearby in the event we get to see his daughter."

"That'll work, Hayes."

"I think I'm going to call my friend—Alex. Just to park near the terminal and observe and report. Take photos. Call the police if needed. We can use another pair of eyes to keep watch outside the station."

"Sounds good. I'll be there by seven thirty."

"I owe you." Colleen let out another sigh of relief as she hung up the phone, smashed out her cigarette.

Then she called Alex's house—*mansion*—in Half Moon Bay. She wondered how long Alex would continue to live in the big rambling estate her father had left her. It wasn't very Alex. But living large was.

Harold, the butler, answered, sounding just a tad groggy.

"Copeland residence," he said in his British accent.

"I am really sorry to be calling so late, Harold. Or is it so *early*?"

"It's no trouble, Ms. Hayes."

"You're sweet to say so."

"I'll get Ms. Copeland."

A few moments later, Alex got on the phone.

"Checking up on me?" she said.

"You're the type who needs it."

"Good, because I'm in the middle of the biggest orgy you've ever seen. The floors are covered with plastic sheets and the Wesson Oil is flying. Some poor man pulled his back out. Everyone is exhausted. But if you hurry, you can catch the tail end."

"Ooh la la."

"How's the new client?"

"His daughter was kidnapped."

There was a pause.

"Jesus H, Coll," Alex said. "That's about as lousy as it gets."

"Tell me."

"You going to the police?"

"Kind of," she said. "I called Moran."

"Can I ask why you called me? Since you woke me up at four in the a.m."

"Because my client intends to pay the ransom. And I could really use your help, Alex."

CHAPTER EIGHT

"This is Moran," Colleen said. "He's a retired homicide cop. He's going to help us get your daughter back."

Lieutenant Daniel Moran shook hands with Steve Cook in Steve's construction zone living room, then pushed his thick glasses up his nose and stood back, feet slightly apart. Moran was a medium-size man in his sixties, with a dark mustache streaked with gray and a thick head of hair to match. Fine wrinkles etched his narrow face. But he looked good to Colleen. He'd been off the bottle for some time.

He shoved his hands in the pockets of a black jacket. Colleen saw the telltale heel of a pistol in a shoulder holster. He'd come prepared. Steve, for his part, was looking both weary and anxious, but coping, considering his daughter had been kidnapped. His heavy denim workpants and gray sweatshirt were powdered with white dust. Tools were scattered around the shell of a house. He'd been hammering wallboard when Colleen and Moran arrived. Couldn't sleep, he said, so he might as well get something done. He was smoking a cigarette in rapid puffs, a hard grimace on his face.

Lynda was nowhere in sight. That fact provided Colleen with some relief.

It was eight a.m. Friday morning. At nine Steve was to take a call from the kidnappers at a pay phone by the snack bar at the Transbay Terminal.

Colleen, however, would go in his place.

"What's the plan, Coll?" Steve asked, smoking.

Colleen handed Steve a paper grocery bag rolled up at the top. It contained ten bundles of cut-up newspaper banded with rubber bands to resemble the bulk of $20,000. "You take this, head down to Mission Street. Take a cab, or BART, or a bus. Get out at the Transbay Terminal. Quarter to nine, head to El Faro's restaurant, wait for one of us to contact you. I'll also have one more person nearby." She would have liked more people, but this was the best she could do with the time pressure. "I'll make my own way down to the Transbay Terminal with the cash, take the nine o'clock phone call by the snack bar inside the terminal. Moran will be nearby, keeping watch." If anyone could be sly, it was Moran. "After that, a lot depends on the call. With any luck, they'll let us talk to Melanie. We'll take it from there. If one of us can't make contact with you, I'll leave a message on my answering service. I've authorized the service to give you an update." Colleen eyed a gray gym bag sitting on the floor by the phone. "Is that the cash?"

"Yeah." Steve blew a blast of smoke as he looked inside the paper sack. "And this is the decoy cash, I take it?"

"In case someone follows you." Someone like Lynda, who Colleen didn't quite trust. "It'll look like you're on your way to make the drop."

"Are you sure about this, Coll? The kidnapper did say *I* was to make the call."

"You're too emotionally involved to deal with them. As a third party, I can be tougher, get away with more."

"Sure about that?"

"I know what you're thinking," she said. "I heard the threat they made. But the kidnappers didn't go through all this so they could walk away from the money. They'll play along, up to a point."

Moran spoke: "They're not going to like it, Steve, but they'll cooperate. For a while anyway."

"By 'cooperate' you mean not kill my daughter, right?" Steve said.

"We have to assume they're somewhat rational," Colleen said.

"Somewhat."

"And if they're not," she said, "it's another ball of wax. One we'll deal with, if it comes to that."

Steve took a long drag on his cigarette, exhaled twin plumes of smoke through his nostrils. He shut his eyes for a moment. "Something that's gone through my mind about a thousand times," he said, tapping ash into the air, "is that Melanie is . . . ah . . . Christ, I can't even bloody say it."

Colleen knew what was going through Steve's mind. She'd been in a similar spot once, with her own daughter. She went through a lesser nightmare now, every week or so, when she wondered how Pamela was holding up, living up at Moon Ranch with those religious lunatics.

"Melanie's alive, Steve," she said.

"You really believe that, Coll?"

Did she? She had to, for Steve's sake. "I do. But we need to take control of the situation. And this is how. You can't be in the middle of it. I can. We'll have you nearby, in the event that meeting with the kidnappers and getting Melanie moves ahead."

Steve looked at her, uncertain. "I hope you're right."

Moran interrupted. "The people who took your daughter will understand you have to have proof that Melanie's alive before you pay them, Steve. They're probably half expecting it. They're anxious, too. Listen to Colleen. She's got a handle on this."

"All I want is my daughter back, safe and sound," Steve said.

"And that's what we're going to make happen," Colleen said. "And then we're going to get those bastards."

Colleen was going to get them, or him, or her, regardless.

She checked her watch. "Time to go."

Steve reached down, picked up the gym bag, handed it to Colleen. Unzipping it, she peered inside. Ten bundles of rumpled twenties, various colors of rubber bands around them. Mob money, money Steve had borrowed. Another problem she'd worry about later. She zipped the bag back up. "It's important to stay calm."

"Easier said than done."

"You're handling it like a trooper."

Then they heard a car pull in the driveway with a squeal. Neither Colleen nor Moran had parked in front of the house, for anonymity's sake. They'd both arrived separately.

"Christ," Steve said, sucking on the last of his cigarette. "That's Lynda's car. I told her to stay away."

"If Lynda asks," Colleen said to Steve, "tell her *you're* going to take the phone call at Transbay Terminal. We don't need her flying off the handle. If she asks about Moran, tell her he's here to lend you the ransom money."

"Right," Steve said.

An engine shut off, a car door was flung open, and then slammed. And then the same angry heels that had stepped up the stairs last night repeated their journey to the front door. The key went into the lock and opened it.

There stood Lynda, wearing a gold Afghan coat. Her blond hair was swept over in a dramatic swoop and her face was armored with heavy makeup. Well put together considering her daughter had been kidnapped, Colleen thought. None of it managed to hide Lynda's fury, though.

"I can see that I'm going to need my key back," Steve said to her.

Lynda looked at Steve, Moran, Colleen. "What's going on?"

Steve went over, shut the front door. "Nothing."

"Don't you *nothing* me." She eyed the paper bag in Steve's hand. "You going to make the drop?"

Steve's eyes met briefly with Colleen's.

"I am," Steve said to Lynda.

Lynda squinted at Moran. "So who is this? Another dick scooping up a fee?"

"He's lending me the cash," Steve said, holding up the paper sack.

"Which you will pay back in seven days," Moran said to Steve, playing along. "Plus interest."

Lynda gave Moran a wary look and actually took a step back. Being connected to mob money scared most people, even her.

"Then what is *she* doing here?" Lynda shot Colleen a prison-yard stare.

"Helping me," Steve said.

"Doing nothing. What a fucking vulture."

Colleen ignored her.

"I'm paying her, Lynda," Steve said. "I'm paying the ransom. It's *my* decision, yeah? Now you best leave."

"Don't you tell me what to do, asshole."

"We don't have time for this," Colleen said. "Steve needs to be at the drop by nine."

Lynda spun on Colleen, jabbed a finger into her shoulder as she spoke. "Anything happens to my daughter, bitch, I'm holding *you* personally responsible."

Colleen grabbed Lynda's hand, moved it slowly to one side. "I know you're going through hell, but don't ever do that again. Now leave."

Lynda glared, turned, stormed out, leaving the front door open, her heels smacking the stairs. Tires squealed as she pulled out of the driveway and took off.

Moran, Colleen, and Steve reconvened.

"Let's do it," Colleen said.

Moran left.

Steve and Colleen stood across from each other, holding their respective bags.

"This is the longest bloody morning of my life," Steve said.

She squeezed his arm. "We're going to get Melanie back."

There was a pause.

"Good luck, Coll."

"I never plan on luck," she said, checking her watch. "You better get going."

Steve nodded, rubbed his face, left his apartment, carrying the bag of fake newspaper money.

Colleen left through the back of the house with the gym bag of cash, by the long narrow kitchen that had not been torn down. Through an overgrown yard and wooden garage to an alley behind the house she exited on Capp Street, checked both directions. She headed down to 21st. On 21st, a white Jaguar XJ6 drove up, stopped in the middle of the street, and Alex, wearing sunglasses, leaned over, gave Colleen a little wave. The electric window rolled down.

"My husband's out of town." She raised her eyebrows. "Interested?"

Alex's attempt to lighten the situation wasn't lost on Colleen. She smiled, shook her head, got in the car.

She saw that Alex was outfitted for speed: a white tennis skirt and running shoes, along with a black denim jacket with the collar turned up. Diamond studded earrings brought the outfit to another level. Alex's bare legs were firm and tanned.

"This is my first kidnapping," Alex said, setting the Jag into gear. "I didn't know if there might be running involved."

"Well, if there is, every eye will be on you in that outfit."

"Please don't hate me because I'm gorgeous, Coll," Alex said as she drove. "It's not like I can help it."

A smile found its way across Colleen's face. "I don't hate you."

"Likewise," Alex said, winking from behind a blue lens.

The car was silent inside for a while, apart from some cool jazz oozing out of multiple speakers. The ride was equally smooth as the luxury car softened the rough Mission streets.

"Try to park across the street from the terminal, Alex, and stay with the car. Just observe and report. Take photos. Nothing else. If the drop isn't a success, I'll find you, and we'll secure the cash." Colleen continued: "And if anything squirrely happens, I want you to simply take off."

Alex turned right at a stop sign with an old THE VIETNAM WAR bumper sticker under the word STOP, turned left at the next block, then took a right on Mission, into busy SF morning traffic. A beer truck trundled along in front of her.

Alex cleared her throat. "Do you think . . . this girl Melanie . . . is still . . . ?"

Alex's sister had been brutally murdered in the late sixties when Alex was a teenager. Colleen had tracked down the killer. Alex was no stranger to family tragedy.

"I have to think she's alive, Alex," Colleen said. "But, honestly—I don't know."

They drove in silence for a few minutes.

"You have your camera ready?" Colleen asked.

Alex nodded at the back seat. Colleen turned to see a Polaroid camera on the beige leather seat.

Alex studied the rearview mirror. "I hope you catch those fuckers, Coll."

"Ditto. But right now, I'll settle for Melanie."

Alex gave Colleen a knee squeeze as she drove. "Just don't go getting yourself hurt and expecting me to make a fuss over you."

"Yes," Colleen said, pressing her hand over Alex's. "I would hate that."

Twenty minutes later, they passed the Steinway Piano Gallery.

"Pull over here," Colleen said. "I'll walk the last couple of blocks. I don't want anyone seeing you."

Alex did.

Colleen got out of the car, grabbed the gym bag, leaned down, and looked inside. Despite Alex's sunglasses, her eyes were sharp.

"Thanks, Alex. It really means a lot."

"Please be careful, Coll."

"You, too." Colleen shut the door with a soft thump and patted the roof twice.

She zipped up her brown bomber jacket. Slung the bag over her shoulder, walked the last couple of blocks until she got to the station. Buses pulled up. Office workers were pouring out of the Transbay Terminal. The kidnappers had picked an opportune time of day for the drop. Rush hour. Crowds of people to hide amongst. She took a right, past the Wagon Wheel Café, and the Fun Terminal where the inane ringing of pinball machines and video games wafted out into the gray morning. She caught a glimpse of Alex's white Jag, parked on the far corner of Mission.

Inside the Transbay Terminal, hectic with commuters flooding into San Francisco, the low ceilings reverberated with noise. Colleen found the pay phone across from the snack bar. This was the place where Steve Cook was to take the call. A short man in a blue windbreaker, with a thatch of mousy hair sticking out from under a Giants cap, was on the phone, his back to Colleen. *Damn it.* She checked her watch. Eight fifty-five. Five minutes to go. She went over to the diner, sat on one of red leather stools, set the gray gym bag with the $20,000 in it down by her feet, ordered a cup of coffee she didn't want. No one was expecting her, as far as she knew. She lit up a Virginia Slim to create the illusion of relaxation and waited, scouring the bus station, looking for anyone suspicious in the morass of people. Voices, footsteps, and the clattering of handcarts echoed off the tiles and ceiling. Moran was out there, too, somewhere, watching.

Halfway through her cigarette, the short man in the windbreaker hung up the pay phone and left. She checked her watch. A couple of minutes before nine.

Colleen picked up the bag, went over to the phone, looked around. She saw Moran now, standing by a news kiosk not far from the snack bar, going through magazines on a rack. He looked over briefly. She returned an imperceptible nod.

She set the gym bag on top of the hanging phone books.

"I need to use the phone," a man's voice said.

She turned, cigarette in hand. Always a good impromptu weapon, if need be.

And saw a big swarthy guy, bordering on obese, with small eyes sunken in a pie-shaped face. He wore a grubby dark duffle coat, rumpled dungarees, and scuffed shoes. He needed a shave.

She couldn't give up the phone. The kidnappers were about to call.

And maybe he was one of them.

"I'm waiting for a call," Colleen said. "My daughter missed her bus from Portland."

"I need the phone."

"Well, you'll have to wait your turn."

He squinted at her. Trying to figure her out? Was he expecting Steve? "When is she calling?" he said. "Your daughter?"

"Nine," Colleen said, hooking her arm through the gym bag to secure it, "to let me know when she's going to arrive. I won't be long."

He eyed the gym bag furtively.

That did it. Something wasn't right.

"Thank you for your patience," she said curtly.

He huffed, lumbered over to the café, sat on a stool, drummed his fingers on the countertop, watched. She looked for a bulge in his coat, but it was a big coat, and he was a big dude.

She made brief eye contact with Moran, leafing through *Sports Illustrated*, who looked at her questioningly. His eyes shifted to Duffle Coat, then back. She couldn't really nod but she blinked. Moran got it, nodded back.

The phone rang.

This was it.

She took a drag on her cigarette, heartbeats rapping nicely, answered with a curt *hello*.

"Who's this?" a metallic voice said. The sound whooshed in and out, masked by electronics.

She had to put one finger over her free ear to block an announcement being made that reverberated through the station. The big guy in the duffle coat was still perched on the stool, his hands now jammed into the pockets of his coat. Moran, at the magazine rack, kept his eye on him over the top of his magazine.

"Not who you think it is," Colleen said.

"Where the hell is Steve?" the robot voice on the other end of the phone said.

"Steve couldn't make it." Colleen shifted the gym bag up on her shoulder.

"Why the fuck not?" Getting angry. Good. Maybe she could draw him out.

"Put Melanie on the phone," she said.

"Just shut the fuck up and listen to me. Leave the money by the phone. Someone will contact Steve when we have your little package ready."

Colleen turned, phone to her ear, eyed Duffle Coat by the snack bar. He was watching her, hands in his coat pockets, apprehensive. He caught her look. He was definitely here to pick up the cash. It made sense. He had expected Steve. Moran was still watching through the magazine rack.

"Let me speak to Melanie," Colleen said.

"When we're good and ready."

We. Colleen took a deep breath through her nose. "If you think I'm leaving a bag of money here, without Melanie, you are seriously mistaken."

"What do you fucking think this is, cunt? Do as you're told. Put the fucking money down. Then walk away."

She did her best to discern any kind of uniqueness out of the caller's robotic voice. No luck. She took a puff on her cigarette, looked around casually for anyone else suspicious. No one, so far. Duffle Coat stood up, hands still in his coat pockets. Pretending not to stare at her. But getting antsy. He could tell it wasn't going right.

Moran was watching.

"It's been great chatting with you," Colleen said. "Let's do it again soon. You know who to call. But we need to see Melanie alive before anything happens."

"You want to tell Steve you killed his daughter?" The caller swore, using a word she didn't know. Having spent a decade in prison, she thought she knew them all. But, then again, the voice was altered, and the line wasn't perfect, and the bus station was pandemonium. But it sounded something like "spite."

"Melanie first," she repeated, her heart hammering with the threat.

The caller hung up.

Damn!

Colleen looked over at the coffee shop.

Duffle Coat was standing, glaring at her. Moran was next to the magazine rack.

She stood where she was, bag in hand.

"Tell whoever it is you work for it's no go," she said. "Not until we see Melanie."

His small eyes popped open as he put two and two together. His hand came up inside his coat, pointing something at Colleen. Her heart did a hundred-meter dash.

Moran came around from the magazine rack, his hand inside his jacket. Ready to pull a gun.

"That'll be enough of that," he said to Duffle Coat.

Duffle Coat spun, mouth falling open when he saw Moran.

"Get away from me," Duffle Coat said, moving quickly for a big guy, putting distance between him and Moran. Colleen came at him, too, and he raised his hand inside his coat, pointed what had to be a gun into a crowd of commuters walking by. "One more step and someone gets it." His arm was shaking, but his hard frown said he was determined.

Moran's hand was under his arm, ready to draw.

"Just stay away from me!" Duffle Coat barked.

The three of them froze.

A standoff.

"What's going on?" a woman passerby shrieked. "What's he doing?"

A flurry of activity caused the crowd to heave around them. Voices picked up.

Duffle Coat backed away to the rear of the station, into the swarming crowd. Gone.

She couldn't risk it.

Colleen said to Moran, "We can't afford to get some innocent person killed. We're not going to get Melanie this time."

Moran nodded. "I'll follow him, Hayes. You get that bag to a safe place."

"Good luck," she said.

Moran turned, picked up the pace, pushed back toward the rear of the terminal.

Shit!

Colleen hoped she hadn't overplayed her hand. She hoped Melanie Cook was still alive. And stayed that way.

9:04 a.m. A lot could happen in four minutes.

She headed for the exit at the front of the terminal, bag in hand. She'd stow the cash in the trunk of Alex's car, get hold of Steve, bring him up to date. The crowd was tightly packed, pressing for the doors. More commuters had poured into the station.

Frustrated wasn't quite the word.

Colleen was just about to exit the front of the Transbay Terminal in a throng of people when someone came up behind her, quick, jabbed something hard in the small of her back.

Something a lot like a pistol. A bolt of panic shot up her spine.

"Stop right there," a thin voice whispered. "Don't turn around." He sounded young. Like a punk. "Drop the fucking bag."

CHAPTER NINE

"I said 'drop the bag,'" the guy behind Colleen said.

The gun pressed to her back, Colleen had frozen twenty paces from the main doors. Almost free. Commuters poured around them like a stream around a boulder. One or two started voicing their displeasure at being delayed.

"Get out of the damn way!" one said.

"Really!" said another.

So there were two of them, Colleen realized: this guy and Duffle Coat. He pressed up close against her. He needed a bath. "Drop it on the ground, already. Or I'll drop *you*."

"There's about a thousand witnesses," Colleen said, her heart thumping. She prayed Moran might show. But he'd gone after Duffle Coat.

"No one will hear a thing with all this noise," the man said. The gun stabbed her spine, making her jerk. He was probably hiding it inside a jacket. "Last chance."

She did her best to quell the fear of being shot and killed.

"Stay cool." She eased the gym bag off her shoulder, let it down, and before it even hit the tiles, he shoved her, hard, slamming her into a mob of people who immediately protested as she fell onto them, losing her balance.

She scrambled to get back up, but he'd already snatched the bag, taken off for the doors. He was the little guy who'd been on the phone when she first got to the terminal, wearing a Giants cap and a blue windbreaker.

"Watch out!" she yelled. "That guy just robbed me! He's got a gun."

Commotion rose. Shouts and people pushing.

Heart thundering, Colleen righted herself, broke into a sprint, shot outside, where she looked around frantically. A sea of heads in a small plaza in front of 1st and Mission.

Where the hell was he?

There!

She spotted the Giants cap, to her left, moving fast through the crowd to 1st Street, toward the Fun Terminal. She went after him, shouting.

"Stop him! Giants cap! He kidnapped a girl!"

One or two people flustered, spinning to look at her, and that didn't help. Most people paid no attention. Didn't want to get involved. Or she was coming off as a crazy lady. She pushed on, reached 1st, across from the arcade. The roar of a motorcycle filled her ears.

Then she spotted the Giants cap, blue windbreaker flapping, crossing 1st, running past the arcade, and the Wagon Wheel coffee shop. She heard the motorcycle roar off down 1st, in the opposite direction, fading away.

Dodging cars, she tore after the little guy, shouting for people to stop him. Horns blared as she zigzagged across the street. Once on the other side she saw the Giants cap turn left around a corner, south on Mission. She raced after him, drawing air in like a bellows, fueling her brain and body, laboring to keep her thoughts coherent.

At Mission she cut a hard left, leaving the Transbay Terminal behind her. Where was he? She kept going and spotted a Giants ball cap on the sidewalk. *Damn!* That would only make him that much harder to follow.

There. There he was, scurrying across Mission Street about half a block up in a barrage of car horns.

Colleen broke into a fresh run, looking for an opportunity to cross Mission. It was bumper to bumper with noisy, rush-hour traffic.

She sucked in air and shot out into the middle of the street, running down the double yellow line. Car horns screamed. But she was covering ground.

The little guy was on the other side of Mission now, getting close to 2nd Street, pumping his fists as he ran.

With a flash of alarm, she realized he no longer had the gym bag in his hand.

Shit!

Had he stashed it somewhere? Handed it off?

She kept going, knowing he was the only one who could answer that question. She hurtled across the middle of the intersection at 2nd amidst squealing tires. A blast of horns.

He'd crossed 2nd. She was ahead of him. She just had to cross over, get out of the street.

One more gulp of air and, heart thumping, she sprinted across two lanes of traffic to his side of the street, blocking his path.

She turned, faced him.

He saw her, his mouth dropping open. He reached inside his jacket, pulled a revolver from his waistband.

People yelled as he raised the gun. He fired. A wild shot. The crowd scattered amidst shouts and screams as the shot ricocheted off the buildings. Colleen flinched, dropping to the ground, her jeans ripping at one knee. It would hurt like sin when the adrenaline wore off. But that was later. She rose back up to see her little guy spin around, head back across Mission, trying any which way to lose her.

She kept on his tail. Darted back out into the street after him. She was gaining.

A white Muni bus groaned as it loped toward the Transbay Terminal.

She scurried after the little guy. Tires screeched. Horns blasted.

She caught up to him in the middle of Mission, grabbed at his thin, slippery jacket. He yelped, broke free, charged in front of a green Monte Carlo that slammed on its brakes just in time, bouncing. The horn screamed. A flurry of Spanish profanity came from within.

Colleen leapt across the green hood, sliding on her butt, landing on the asphalt on both feet on the passenger side, clutching at the blue windbreaker again. The little guy pulled away, but she had the jacket tight in one hand, and yanked it, making him reel around to face her.

The gun came up and he fired another crazy shot. She recoiled as he broke free. He swirled back around.

The white Muni bus bore down. She jumped back.

He was going to try and beat it to the curb, put it between him and her.

He charged in front of the bus as the airhorn blew.

The thump of his body hitting steel was followed by a raspy scream.

CHAPTER TEN

"Am I free to go?" Colleen asked.

"No," Inspector Owens said to Colleen. "You're still not telling me the whole story."

She sat at a table in a windowless interrogation room on the fifth floor of 850 Bryant, where she'd spent most of the day. Her torn jeans had been cut away at the knee, which wavered between aching and stinging. But the wound had been cleaned up and bandaged.

On the other side of the table from Colleen sat SFPD Inspector Owens, in a trendy brown suit with big lapels, big-knotted blue tie, red-and-white striped shirt with a long-pointed collar. When the disco look finally infiltrated Owens' wardrobe, its time had come. His Prussian crew cut, graying at the temples, was freshly trimmed. He shook his head, and his jowls shook slightly.

"There's not much more I can tell you," she said, leaning forward. She craved a cigarette. "I have no idea who the guy was—apart from the fact that he was working with the kidnappers." The little guy who had grabbed the gym bag full of money, which had somehow disappeared during the pursuit, had died in the ambulance on the way to SF General. He'd had an illegal .38 but no ID.

Owens continued: "You need to see how serious this is. A man killed running from an investigator who doesn't have her license . . . shots fired. And no gym bag containing twenty K anywhere." Owens eyed Colleen suspiciously. "Unless *you* grabbed it."

No, it was gone. "If I was playing games, would I even mention the twenty thousand dollars?" She had lost Moran in the terminal after he'd gone after the big guy in the duffle coat. She had left that part of the story out in her statement to Owens, not wanting to implicate Moran in something that could land him in hot water. She hadn't had time to follow up with Steve or Alex. They had been told to disperse if any trouble with the police arose.

So where *had* the money gone? The little guy either dumped it—or handed it off. Colleen recalled the roaring of a motorcycle when she chased the guy across 1st Street, by the Wagon Wheel Café. So the motorcycle was looking like a factor. She mentioned it to Owens.

"This shouldn't have happened." Owens tapped his pencil on a yellow lined pad. "When your client hired you to get his child back from a suspected kidnapper, you should have called SFPD immediately."

"I wanted to, believe me. But he and his wife were—*are*—adamant about no police. I tried to talk them out of it, but they wouldn't work with me if you were involved. So I decided to do what I could. I was planning to bring you in at some point."

Owens gave a frown, but it was one that said her comment made some kind of sense. "I'll ask you again: Who *is* your client?"

She shook her head. "Sorry." She imagined the little man, staring at her with terrified eyes as the life drained out of him when she got down on the asphalt and peered under the bus. Melanie was still gone. They'd outsmarted her.

"*Sorry* doesn't work," Owens said.

"Look, I want you on board. But I need my client's okay."

Owens frowned, tapped his pencil on the yellow pad. "If I book you for obstruction of a criminal investigation, how will that play with your parole?"

Colleen sat back, exhaling with frustration. "I *have* to honor my client's confidentiality. Give me a chance to talk to him." Her eyes connected with Owens'. "Give me one day."

Owens tapped his pencil. Let out a breath. Rubbed his face. "You've helped us in the past so okay. Talk to your client. Tell him how much trouble *he* could be in. And how much trouble you're in if I don't hear from you within twenty-four hours." Owens looked at his watch. "Tomorrow afternoon by five p.m. at the latest."

A trickle of relief flowed through her. She stood up, pushing her chair back with a squeak. Her knee throbbed, but she wouldn't let it slow her down. "Thanks."

"Don't thank me," he said, narrowing his eyes. "Just do it. Tomorrow by five. Or I'll have someone come and get you."

*   *   *

Downstairs in the lobby of 850 Bryant, Colleen called her answering service. Two messages, one from Moran, one from Alex. Both said they would check back later.

Nothing from Steve.

She called Steve from a pay phone. No answer. Where had he gotten to?

She called Moran's house and, as usual, Daphne answered, livid when Colleen wouldn't divulge where he might be, which meant he wasn't home yet. He lived in Santa Cruz, a ways away. She'd let Moran handle his own wife.

"Feel free not to call here anymore!" Daphne slammed the phone down. Colleen took a calming breath, called Alex in Half Moon Bay. Harold the butler told her Alex had come home, changed, and left. That's when Colleen remembered—they were supposed to go to Antonia's surprise birthday party that night.

"Please tell Alex I'm sorry to miss Antonia's party, Harold," Colleen said. "But I've really got my hands full right now."

Harold said that he would. She thanked him.

On Bryant Street, outside the Hall of Justice, gray fog hung low, the late afternoon air damp. Squad cars were double-parked, and people were coming and going, none of them smiling. There was never a happy reason to come to 850.

Tomorrow. She had until tomorrow to get back to Owens. There was a *lot* to do. Get in touch with Steve Cook—if he was still talking to her—then Moran and Alex.

Deal with the kidnappers. Find Melanie.

First thing she did was flag a Yellow Cab and head down to the Transbay Terminal. It was a short ride, but long enough to listen to most of "Afternoon Delight" on the radio, so it felt longer. She got a receipt for the fare and went into the station. Not as busy as that morning but busy enough, with evening commute approaching.

She went to the snack bar. No Moran. It had been a long shot.

She retraced her path down to 2nd and Mission, where the little guy had been hit by the bus. She scoped out trash bins, doorways, anywhere a gray gym bag with twenty K might have gone. She got some peculiar looks when she hoisted herself up onto a small dumpster and stood on a mountain of reeking trash, kicking garbage around. No gym bag.

She climbed back down, lit a Slim to mask the stench. She smoked, ran through the events of that morning.

The bag of money must have been handed off. She again recalled the sound of a motorcycle, the one she'd heard when she chased the little guy across 1st Street.

Steve Cook's daughter was still being held by kidnappers—if she was alive. On top of it, Steve now owed the wrong people twenty K plus interest that doubled by the week.

Hayes Confidential, she thought: when you really need to hose things up.

CHAPTER ELEVEN

A hot shower dispelled the lingering dumpster perfume and brought Colleen back to life. She plowed through a cup of black coffee fortified with brown sugar as she ran a brush through her wet hair. Then she dialed Steve Cook again while she sat on the warm waterbed in her underwear. Phone cradled to her ear, she dabbed mercurochrome on her gashed knee with the applicator from the bottle. It stung mightily and the skin around the wound turned pink red. Gently she applied a fresh bandage.

No answer. Where had Steve gotten to?

She hung up, pulled on fresh Levi's, white V-neck T-shirt, her white sneakers with the blue stripes. She called her answering service. No new messages. She was tempted to call Moran but didn't want to incur the wrath of Daphne twice in a twenty-four-hour period. She'd wait.

She dialed Steve Cook one more time. Thankfully, he picked up.

"Am I glad to finally get hold of you," she said.

She heard Steve sucking smoke. "So, nothing on Mel, I take it?" His tone was cool.

"The payoff was a no-go. The caller refused to let me speak to Melanie. So I said 'no deal.' As we agreed. I've just spent the day talking to SFPD."

"So what the hell happened, Coll? Last thing I heard on the news was some bloke being chased under a bus." She could hear him take a drag on a cigarette.

"That's pretty much what happened." She drew a deep breath. "He grabbed the bag. But he didn't have it on him when he was run over. He must have handed it off. I went back and retraced my steps. Nothing."

"Great," he said. "Bloody great."

"I didn't tell SFPD any more than I had to, Steve. Your situation with Melanie is still just between you and me. But we have to bring the police in now."

"No. I thought I made that clear."

Colleen waited a moment. Who could blame Steve for being angry? "Steve, SFPD have given me one day to tell them who my client is."

"Out of the bloody question."

"Steve, they can help. They *have* to be involved."

"I'm not going to be needing their help—or yours, anymore, for that matter. Send me the bill."

"Whoa," she said, brushing her wet hair back behind her ear. "Slow down. We need to talk."

"Talk about *what*? How you put my daughter's life in jeopardy? Went and lost twenty thousand dollars I now owe? Plus seven K vig?"

Seven K. Ouch. "Just for the record, Steve, Melanie's life was already in jeopardy." If Melanie was even still alive. "Do you really think you wouldn't have gotten ripped off, yourself? Sorry, but I wasn't just going to leave your cash in the middle of the Transbay Terminal and hope for the best. Call me cynical, but I tend not to trust kidnappers. All that would've gotten us was another demand for more ransom money."

"Well, at least you were right about one thing."

A surge of alarm hit her. "What? They called you again?"

"Yeah," he said, taking a noisy drag off a cigarette, exhaling in a blast of despair. She could hear his frustration, anger, worry, all in that one breath.

"How much?" she asked.

"Another twenty."

Kind of what she suspected. But it still knocked her sideways.

"And no update on Mel?" she asked.

"Nah," he said, his voice cracking. "Same electronic voice told me to shut up and listen. Said I better not pull any more stunts. Said you were to be out of the picture."

"How much time did they give you?"

"Till Monday."

Four days. They probably knew he'd need time to raise the cash.

"Don't go anywhere, Steve. I'll be right over. I live right up the hill." When he didn't protest, Colleen said, "Just wait for me. Don't go anywhere."

There was a pause.

"Yeah, okay."

Thank God for that.

"I'll be right there." She hung up, headed out, hair still wet.

Downstairs, early evening fog muffled the whir of elevated freeway traffic up Potrero Hill as she walked across Vermont Street to her Torino. She could smell the malty air of the Anchor Steam Brewery down the hill as she got in and fired up the engine, teasing the throttle to get it going. A tune-up and new set of rings was in order. Dark exhaust belched out of the twin pipes, filling the rearview mirror.

When the smoke cleared, she noticed someone sitting at the wheel of a white van a few cars behind. The windshield had two clear arcs, as if the wipers had been recently switched on, which

struck her as odd, unless he had just parked. But the driver was reading a newspaper. Or pretending to read a newspaper.

Watching her?

She unlatched the handbrake, threw the car into first, spun a tight
U-ey, and motored past a white Econoline van, banged up and rusty.
As she drove by, she leaned over to peer across the passenger seat
into the van.

The driver wore a dark watch cap and sunglasses. Sunglasses to
read the newspaper. In the fog. He didn't look her way.

At the corner she cut a hard left, gunned it for a couple of blocks,
spun a left, then another, and back up to Vermont where she turned
left again, driving past her apartment building.

The white van was gone.

She'd keep an eye out for it.

A few minutes later, she parked down the street from Steve's
driveway. For once, a parking place had opened up. No white van
had followed her.

In Steve's torn-down flat, tools were scattered everywhere. An air
of gloom lingered.

Steve still wore his work clothes from that morning and looked
like hell. He needed a shave. His bedroom eyes were ringed with
exhaustion and worry. He paced around, standing here one moment, there the next.

"You don't have any smokes, do you, Coll?" he said, hands in the
back pockets of his denims.

She dug out her box of Virginia Slims. "Can your masculinity
handle these?" She flipped open the box and he slid a long skinny
cigarette out. She got one for herself.

"*I've come a long way, baby,*" he said grimly, snapping the filter off
his cigarette, sticking the clean end in his mouth. Lighting hers first,
he lit his, took a deep suck.

She went over to the sofa, pulled the plastic covering off one side, sat on blue velour. She took a puff, blew it out.

"You talk to Lynda yet?" she asked.

He took a drag, let it plume out his nostrils. "Is 'talk' the same as getting screamed at?"

"Guess that was to be expected."

"Lynda is consistent, if nothing else," he said. "Yeah, she was here. Probably when you tried to call earlier. That was you calling, yeah?" Colleen nodded. "Gave me a ration and a half of shit. I had to throw her out. But she'll be back. She gave me an ultimatum."

"I bet Lynda's good at those. What was this one?"

"I could use a bloody drink," he said. "I'm out of booze. Out of smokes. Money. Luck."

Steve was down but still taking it in stride. But one look told anyone he was on the verge of cracking up. And he didn't need another run-in with Lynda to run things off the rails right now. Something felt wrong there, beyond the fact that Lynda was a bitch with a capital B.

Colleen dropped her unfinished cigarette into an empty beer bottle with a sizzle. She stood up.

"Let's go get a drink," she said.

They drove over to The Pitt even though it was within walking distance, because she didn't want to leave the Torino near Steve's place.

In the bar, the lights were dimmed, which helped ease the eyes. A band was setting up. Guitar twangs and random drumbeats. A few patrons propped up the bar and more entered as the workday ended and the band tuned up.

Colleen bought drinks while Steve fed the cigarette machine with change. He got a boilermaker and she nursed a longneck Olympia. Vernon, the owner with the biker gut, watched from the end of the bar as he leafed through some paperwork.

Back at the bar, Steve tapped out a Lucky Strike and lit up. He took a deep drag, picked up the shot glass, and downed the contents. He smacked his lips, thumped the empty glass on the bar, nodding at the barman for a refill. It came quickly and he gulped that down, too. His eyes were slitted, pained. He held up the empty shot glass for the barman one more time.

Colleen put her untouched beer on the counter, leaned back against the tarnished brass rail.

"What was the ultimatum Lynda gave you, Steve?"

"I need to get rid of you for one. Two, her old man will lend me the money to pay the kidnappers off. Keep it simple. Otherwise we risk losing Mel. If I don't play along, I can expect to be arrested for child endangerment. She'll make sure. Her lawyer will make sure." Steve turned to the barman, wiggled the empty shot glass. "Oi, mate, I'm gasping here."

The barman came over, filled Steve's shot glass with Wild Turkey. This time Steve took a measured sip, set the drink down on the ringed bar.

"Get the money from her father?" Colleen asked. Lynda had hit Steve with that before. "Why didn't you do that the first time? Instead of the people Al Lennox hooked you up with?"

Steve tapped ash off his cigarette into an ashtray. "Because Lynda's old man isn't just going to just give it to me."

"Doesn't he have it?"

Steve shrugged as he took a sip of his shot, followed it up with half an inch of beer. "He's a film producer, high profile, but it's feast or famine with that lot. He's lent me money in the past—money I've never been able to pay back. Back when Lynda and I were married, yeah?"

"But we're talking about his granddaughter."

"I've exceeded my credit limit. He wants something in return."

Nice guy. "Which is?"

Steve twisted his shot glass on the bar. "Sign over the Lost Chords catalog. Songs I wrote back in the day."

"As security? Until you pay him back?"

"No." Steve shook his head. "They'd be his—for good. I get to pay him back as well. Plus interest." Steve gave a wry look.

"What a pal."

"Yeah," Steve said. "There's a lot of bad blood between us. That's why I turned him down the first time and borrowed the cash from the leg breakers."

"Do those songs still generate royalties?"

He gave a bitter laugh. "They do. Just not for me. The catalog has been tied up in litigation more than ten years now, and I can't afford the lawyers anymore. So it's all in limbo."

"So you went with a shyster loan with no way of paying it back instead of your ex-father-in-law?"

Steve tapped ash. "Screw Lynda's old man. Mel is what matters."

Colleen realized how much those songs meant to Steve. "Who did you borrow the twenty K from, Steve?"

Steve took a hit on his cigarette. "Some guy Al Lennox knows."

"Yes, I know, but *who*?"

"Some cat named Octavien Lopes."

A chill went up Colleen's spine. "Al Lennox put you in contact with Octavien Lopes?"

Steve sipped. "Beggars can't be choosers."

Beggars might not live either. Even Colleen knew about Octavien Lopes, who headed up the M16 posse that ran the Mission. "That was a pretty drastic move, Steve."

"Those are *my* songs," Steve said. "Even though I never got a penny out of them. So yeah, I borrowed the money rather than give Lynda's old man my catalog."

Now Colleen understood. But if she was worried about Steve's financial situation before, her concern just went up a notch. Maybe two. Meanwhile, Steve's ex, who worked for a record company, was pushing him to borrow money from her father, in exchange for his songs.

If that didn't smell just a little bit off.

The band got onstage, a ragtag funk outfit with a mix of flashy clothes, jeans to spandex, and big hair. The singer was a ninety-pound woman with the cheekbones of a model and a bright red Rod Stewart shag cut. Her lithe frame looked the part in a slinky blue cocktail dress that glittered with sequins in the colored lights. Red embroidered cowboy boots highlighted the fact that she wasn't just any ordinary diva. Black mascara etched under her dark eyes stood out like war paint. She strutted up to the mic with a walk that generated a catcall and a whistle.

"Show us your tits!" someone yelled.

"So it's gonna be like that," she said in a raspy voice, unhooking the mic, shaking the cord like a tail. "This is 1978, you sexist mother. Get with the program." The drummer did a rim shot. The sax player, a black man who looked like a football player, grinned with gleaming white teeth.

Colleen was still trying to fathom out a man who would insist his ex-son-in-law turn over his catalog before he'd lend him money to save his granddaughter.

But she got it.

And Lynda fit right in.

She mulled over a few other factors.

And it made Colleen feel better about Melanie.

Because she was fine—wherever she was.

One. Two. Three. Four.

The band broke into an edgy version of "Respect," the singer strutting around the stage with the mic in her hand as she bellowed out the letters R-E-S-P-E-C-T. With each one she pointed an accusing finger at patrons who might be less than enlightened, which appeared to be quite a few. The song ended with a squealing sax and the crashing of drums, followed by raucous applause.

Steve turned back to the bar to order more drinks. Colleen showed her barely-touched longneck, but he bought her a shot anyway.

What the hell? The only way out might be *up*. She picked up her shot glass, clinked it against his with a little splash, and he gave her a grim look before he downed his.

The bourbon went down with a lingering afterburn.

"Hang tight, Steve," she said. "I think I've got a handle on where Melanie is. And I think she's just fine."

"You do? Clue me in."

"I need to talk to your ex-father-in-law first."

"Rex?" He gave a tight frown. "Lynda's not gonna like that."

Colleen sipped her beer. "She'll be plenty happy if you say you want to borrow the money from him."

Steve crinkled his face in confusion. "You reckon that's what I should do, Coll?"

"No. But that's what we're going to tell Lynda. But you've got to let me drive this."

"*Again?*"

"Again. I smell a rat."

"What rat?" Steve looked confused. He had just had about five shots and was exhausted. Plus, he didn't realize the power of betrayal within his own family.

"Two rats," she said. "I'll get back to you." She never shared info that wasn't 100 percent proven. "But, in the meantime, rest assured Melanie is coming home."

"How do you figure that, then?"

"Just hang with me for another day or two."

He squinted, perplexed. "I'll just pretend you know what you're doing, love."

Love. "I do. But if you borrowed money from Octavien Lopes, Steve, and you don't have it, things will get serious soon." Things had already gotten serious, but there wasn't any point in hammering the point too hard right now. "How long would it take to get the money from Lynda's father?"

"Not long. Overnight maybe."

"Funny Lynda hasn't got any money. Isn't she a big record producer?"

Steve shook his head as he smoked. "Yeah, but it's easy come, easy go there, too. We're talking the entertainment business. It's all limos and nose candy when the riding's high, but that's always on some band's tab. Lynda's broke at the moment. She just doesn't look it."

"Doesn't she own a house?"

"Oh, yeah. One that used to be ours—until the divorce. But it's mortgaged to the hilt. And, as she mentioned yet again today, losing Mel is my fault so I can just pay for the privilege of getting her back."

"Steve," Colleen said. "We need to go to the police."

He frowned, sipped beer. "Don't bring that subject up again, Coll, alright?"

"SFPD gave me until tomorrow to talk to you, Steve. Otherwise they're going to pull me in."

"Then tell them. But not with my blessing. And tell them they'll be wasting their time. Because I won't give them any info."

She sighed. "We'll talk again tomorrow."

The singer spoke into the mic while the guitarist tuned up a flat string. "I just found out we have a special guest here tonight." Colleen turned to see her looking directly at Steve, sipping his beer. "Steve Cook," she said. "At *my* gig. *Wow.*"

Steve held up his half-empty beer glass and toasted her.

She cleared her throat. "How about you join us on the next one, Steve?"

"No thanks, darlin'," Steve said. "You put me to shame."

The audience groaned.

"I know bullshit when I hear it," she said. "C'mon. Make a girl's dream come true."

"Sorry." Steve shook his head. "Long day."

The crowd grumbled in disappointment.

"Okay," the singer rasped. "I guess I can cry myself to sleep later."

But it wasn't enough for the patrons, who were now clapping and chanting. The drummer started a quiet drumroll, building anticipation. Vernon, the owner, came marching down the bar, glaring at Steve.

"Steve," he said, putting his big paws on the bar. "I been pretty patient with your girlfriend's band. I put up with her junkie guitarist. I let her keep her residency, even when you don't show up. And, quite frankly, *the band with no name* is no great shakes without you. I let you run a tab. A long tab."

"My daughter bloody disappeared, Vernon."

"Yeah, I understand. But one fucking song isn't going to kill you. You owe me."

"I'll owe you for a bit longer."

"No. How about this? You pay your tab and find somewhere else to drink. How about that?"

"You're all heart, Vernon." Steve drained his beer, slammed the empty glass on the bar, peeled his denim jacket off and handed it to Colleen. "Hold this for me, will you, love?"

Again, it didn't mean anything, but having her onetime fantasy call her sweet names made Colleen's pulse skip. She took the jacket. It smelled of workaday sweat and Steve's angst and frustration. It smelled real. And it smelled good, in a primitive way that made *her* respond in a primitive way. Steve was a survivor. One who needed help. And she was the one to do it. She'd left her own jacket in the trunk of the car, knowing she was coming into a bar, and she slipped his over her shoulders. It was still warm with his body heat. A very uncomplicated feeling reverberated through her torso and down below.

Steve rolled up his sleeves as he made his way to the stage. The crowd parted like the Red Sea. He hopped up to cheers and whistles. The singer was all nervous smiles but obviously thrilled. They conferred for a moment. The drummer thumped out a soulful four-four, just a little sloppy, the way a good drummer could play behind the beat and still keep time. The bass player throbbed along. Steve pulled a mic from a stand, shook the cable out like a whip, and got into a groove, moving side to side in sync with the singer, like they'd been singing together for years. A tight smile stretched across his face and you wouldn't have thought his daughter had supposedly been kidnapped and that he owed gangsters twenty-seven thousand dollars. The difference between a professional and an amateur. The band joined in, building up the intro like a big slow wave.

Steve and the singer gave each other a quick smile as they raised their mics in unison.

Chain chain chain . . .

Colleen found herself grooving to the song, just hoping it wasn't too prophetic. Because something sure wasn't right with Steve's situation. But she was going to get to the bottom of it.

She just didn't know exactly what she was going to do next. But she had a pretty good idea. She had four days. One day to deal with Inspector Owens.

CHAPTER TWELVE

Colleen and Steve left the bar late, Steve numbed by the drinks he'd had before and those that people bought for him after singing what turned out to be several songs with the band. On top of the worry and days awake, he was on the edge of consciousness. It wasn't a good thing, but under the circumstances, it wasn't a bad alternative. He was functioning.

Driving down Mission, Colleen spotted a Mexican hole-in-the-wall up ahead, the kind of place that had Christmas lights up year-round.

"I could go for an *enchilada verde*," she said. "Soak up some of that alcohol that was flowing so freely."

"Not really hungry."

"Have you had anything to eat today?"

"Can't remember." Which meant he hadn't.

"You need to take care of yourself. Otherwise things are going to get the better of you."

"I'll eat tomorrow." Steve rolled down the window, stuck his head out.

"I'll hold you to it," she said. "When was last time you slept?"

"The night before Melanie took off." Days. "I keep waking up. Wondering if it's all really happening. But now you say it isn't."

"Not the way you think it is, Steve. Stay calm. It won't be much longer. I know it's rough."

"No shite."

The phrase threw her, jarring a memory loose, recent, but unclear. She turned to Steve as she drove. "No *what?*"

"*'Shite,'*" he said. "Sorry, love—it's just the way some of us uncouth Brits talk."

She looked back at the road. "What does it mean?"

"*Shit,*" he said. "Pardon my French."

She'd heard the kidnapper use that very same word this morning, on the phone, garbled with voice distortion, when he'd lost his temper.

He was a Brit.

Steve nodded off.

Colleen turned right on 20th. Headed to Steve's place. A late model BMW 320i occupied the driveway.

Colleen drove by the house. In Steve's flat, light shone around the edges of the tarp over the window.

"Looks like Lynda's waiting for you, Steve," Colleen said.

"Christ," Steve said, waking up. "She said she'd be back. Good to her word."

"She still has a key, I notice."

"Needs it for when Mel stays over." His throat caught on the mention of his daughter's name.

"Get it back until Mel returns."

Steve turned, gave Colleen a smirk. "It's not that simple."

"Sure it is."

"You've never been married."

"Oh, yes, I have," Colleen said tersely. Steve didn't remember. He was exhausted and had been drinking.

Steve eyed her sideways. "Not anymore?"

"No."

"Mind if I ask why?"

"He's dead."

There was a pause.

"Oh, my God, Colleen. I'm bloody sorry."

"Don't be," she said. "I'm not."

Steve squinted. "That sounds worse. Was it an accident?"

"Something like that," she said, giving him a wry look. She turned a corner, out of sight of Steve's building, double-parked, flipped on the hazard lights, left the engine running. "Don't go anywhere. Wait here."

"You're not going in, are you? Lynda'll blow her top if she thinks you're still working for me."

"That's why I'll make sure she doesn't think that. I'll pretend I'm looking for you. But I need to scope things out." It was remotely possible Melanie had returned. *Remotely.* Colleen doubted it and didn't want to say so but needed to verify. And Steve didn't need another pointless fight with his ex right now.

Up on the porch in front of the door to Steve's flat, she tried to peer in. From the upstairs flat a squeal of a Hammond organ came from a stereo, too loud, someone playing Patti Smith. The gap was too tight to see anything. Taking a breath, she stood back, knocked.

Quick footsteps approached the front door. It opened and Lynda appeared, wearing a white bell-bottom pantsuit. Her blue eyes narrowed, and her mouth became a straight hard line.

"I do *not* fucking believe it," she said.

"Believe it." Colleen said.

Over on the sofa, where the plastic cover was pulled off completely and tossed on the bare wooden floor in a heap, sat a stocky man wearing thick-framed glasses. He looked like a boxer jammed into a light-colored linen suit that stretched across his arms and thighs. He had a thatch of brown hair and an unruly beard. He gave Colleen a friendly smile.

"Hey, there," he said in a southern accent. "How's it goin'?"

In the shadows, leaning against the far wall, Colleen saw the outline of a tall, slender man. His arms were crossed over his chest. From what she could tell, he was decked out in black leather from head to toe. The chains on his boots caught the light from the single bulb.

Lynda had brought a welcoming party.

"Is Steve here?" Colleen asked.

"What do you care?" Lynda said. "We no longer need your services."

"*We?*" Colleen attempted to step inside the flat.

"Uh-uh," Lynda said, standing in the way. Tall Guy stood up, arms hanging in fists.

Colleen moved back outside the door.

"I need to get paid," she said to Lynda. "That's why I care."

Lynda laughed through her nose. "After you went and lost our twenty grand? Fuck that. You should be paying *us*."

"Paying *you* money that was Steve's. That's good."

Lynda's nostrils flared. "Well, bitch, it makes no difference, because you are no longer part of the equation."

Colleen looked at the tall guy in the dimness flexing his fists.

"Can he talk?" she said.

She saw him cock his head to one side. Sneer.

"Don't mind him, kiddo," the stocky man said in a sociable tone. "But you might want to take a hint and be on your way."

Colleen nodded. "You make a nice group." She focused on Lynda. "Tell Steve to call me." She looked straight into Lynda's eyes, saw them harden.

"I'll get right on it, bitch."

Colleen waved goodbye over her shoulder as she stepped down the wooden stairs to the sidewalk. Upstairs, Patti Smith belted out "Because the Night."

Back at the Torino, smoke pumped out of the tailpipe. Steve was slumped over, passed out. Best thing for him.

She got in, threw the car into gear, set off. Turned right on 21st.

Steve woke up. "Where are we going?"

"My place," she said. "Lynda had a couple of thugs waiting for you."

Steve gave her an uncertain smile.

"You need to crash," she said. She looked at him with a straight face. "Don't worry—you're safe. I've got a guest room."

Steve rubbed his face as she climbed the hill, the big block V8 rumbling. "I'm not sure I like it, you protecting me like some schoolboy running from a fight."

"It's okay, Steve. You're plenty tough," she said. "But you don't need a run-in with your ex tonight."

"And you need to tell me what's going on with Mel," he said.

"Mel's fine," she said, pulling into the back of her apartment building, where there were a few off-street parking slots in a weed-infested yard. She edged the nose of the Torino up to a fence, killed the engine.

She turned, looked at Steve. His weary eyes met hers in the dashboard lights.

"Spit it out, Coll."

"I normally don't share working hypotheses with clients, Steve, until I have all the facts, but you're a wreck, so I'm going to break a rule: Melanie's safe."

He blinked at her in fatigued confusion. "Care to elaborate?"

"You've been set up like a bowling pin."

"What?"

"Your ex. Lynda. And her father."

"No." He shook his head. "Lynda's a thoroughbred ratbag, no argument, but she loves Mel to bits."

"Maybe she does. But you're still getting played. No fault of yours for not seeing it. You've been up for days and aren't thinking straight. And you're a decent guy who thinks other people behave in a relatively similar way. But I got news for you: they don't."

He dug out his cigarettes. "Alright . . . explain."

"Upstairs." She switched off the lights, pulled her keys, got out of the car. "Come on, Rock Star."

Upstairs, in her apartment, Colleen put the kettle on and went to the far end of the long living/dining room, devoid of dining table or chairs for the time being. She pulled the curtain aside to peer down at Vermont Street. No white Econoline van. Who'd been watching earlier? Someone connected to Lynda?

Steve stood in the living room, swaying, bleary with exhaustion and booze.

"Why don't you grab a shower?" Colleen said. "You'll feel better. I'll get some towels. Make some tea."

"No way," Steve said, collapsing onto the sofa. "I want to know why you think Mel's okay. Because I don't." He broke out a cigarette, lit up. Shook the match out, set in a clean glass ashtray. Rubbed his face.

"Fair enough." Colleen stood there, nodded. "When I looked in Melanie's bag at your place when I first came over, there were no overnight things. Why didn't Lynda make sure?"

He seemed to give that a thought, took a puff of his cigarette. "That's your theory? Mel not being packed?"

"It's the start. Lynda goes out of town on business, and Melanie gets dumped on you. And then Melanie gets kidnapped? Coincidence?"

He nodded. "Keep going."

"That night you played the gig at The Pitt—when Melanie disappeared? Did anyone actually see her go off with anybody?"

"No."

"Right, no one saw that."

"But the kidnappers called. You were there."

"Doesn't mean they necessarily have her."

Steve screwed up his eyes.

Colleen spoke: "There was an arrangement, Steve."

Steve gave Colleen a cynical look.

"On the phone," Colleen said, "the kidnapper referred to Mel as 'little Mellie.' Isn't that a family term for her? A nickname? How would he—or she—know that? Unless he—or she—or they—was in the know?"

Steve shrugged.

Colleen kept going: "You're being played, Steve. But you're not responding appropriately. You were supposed to take Lynda's father's money—in exchange for your catalog. But you didn't. You went and got a mob loan instead. That screwed up the intention of the 'kidnapping'—securing your catalog. It's not the ransom money the kidnappers really want."

"Twenty K is a fair amount of cash. And it managed to disappear just fine, didn't it?"

"Sure. But if I'm a kidnapper worth my salt, why would I target somebody who hasn't got any money? Like you? And Lynda is making sure you're the one on the hook for it—not her. And her father won't give you the money without you signing over your catalog."

"Okay." He pursed his lips as he seemed to think it over. "Keep going."

"Lynda wants you indebted to your ex-father-in-law. And Lynda—shy, blushing, demure creature that she is—is not acting like a mother whose daughter's been kidnapped."

"You don't know Lynda."

"I think I know enough. Anyone who's had a child in jeopardy doesn't act the way she does. She should be grateful for any help that comes her way. But, instead, she's making phony little speeches when you try to throw her out and won't tolerate her tantrums, and she's busy trying to get me out of the way because she reckons I'll figure her out. And she's rounding up thugs to pressure you for round two. She doesn't want the cops anywhere near this either. Why? Especially after a failed payoff? She should be desperate for the police to be involved. She wants you in debt to her old man. So he can own your catalog. Her father's in the movie business, right? Maybe it comes down to someone wanting those songs. Which I bet are worth a freakin' fortune once they get out of the courts."

Steve thought. "Close to a million quid, last time I checked. The lion's share will be eaten up in legal fees, though, if I ever even get it."

"But what if you aren't the lion?"

"How do you mean?"

"If someone else gets the royalties?" she said. "Maybe not so many legal fees for them. And, on top of it, there might be fresh demand for those songs."

She saw a light bulb go off over his head.

"Okay, but, why . . ." Then Steve's face changed color, from ashen to angry red as he put things together. He smashed his cigarette out, sat up. "Fuck. I don't believe it! I don't bloody believe it."

"It's not a happy development. But it sure beats the alternative— Melanie kidnapped. I bet you *a million quid* she's tucked away safe somewhere while your ex and her father scam you."

Steve shook his head. "My own daughter?"

Colleen took a deep breath. "She's a kid, Steve—and a pawn. She may not even know what's going on."

There was a pause.

"Christ!" Steve held his head in his hands. "Bloody hell!" He let go of his face, looked up. "But yeah, you're right. It beats the fucking alternative."

"I still have to piece it together, but my gut is telling me this—or something very much like it—is what happened."

She went to the linen closet where she grabbed a clean towel. In her bedroom, Colleen got her black-and-white zigzag-pattern kimono out of the stack of fresh laundry. It was roomy and would work.

She returned. "Help yourself to a shower. I'll make some tea. You need to crash." She handed him the kimono. "This is the best I can do, under the circumstances."

Steve stood, groggy but sobered by the news. He took the towel and kimono. "Yeah. Thanks."

He staggered to the bathroom, towel and kimono under his arm. She heard the water running.

She made tea with milk and found a bottle of brandy, the only alcohol she had, apart from wine. Steve might need one more belt to get himself to sleep. She set the tea, bottle of booze, and a glass on the glass coffee table, turned off the overhead light, turned on the lamp sitting on the floor by her new leather sofa. The spotlight pointed up to a section of ceiling, indirect. She sat down at one end of the sofa, kicked off her sneakers, lit a cigarette.

What a day. But she was getting somewhere.

The water shut off and Steve emerged from the bathroom a couple of minutes later, wearing the kimono. His hair was wet and ruffled. He had strong muscular legs and was more well built than she first thought. And she thought he'd been pretty well built to begin with. His chest was covered with dark hair. Even beat to shit, in a woman's kimono, he was worth a second look. Maybe a third.

"That was bloody brilliant." He sat down at the other end of the sofa, gave an inquisitive look at the cup of tea, eyed Colleen.

"I'm told Brits like milky tea," she said.

"It's in our genetic makeup." He took a swig of tea, uncorked the bottle of brandy, poured a good inch into his tea, took a deep draught. Then he sat back. "The problem is, Coll, is, what if it *isn't* the case? What if someone *has* kidnapped Mel?"

"I wouldn't tell you if I wasn't almost sure."

"*Almost.*"

"Ninety-nine-and-one-half percent. I didn't want to tell you but I can't stand by and watch it eat you alive."

"What about the half percent, Coll? What if you're wrong, love? What *if*?"

"Then we've got a little over three days to find out. But my gut is telling me otherwise. Loud and clear. I need to take a closer look at Lynda. And her father—Rex."

Steve drank his liquored tea. Set his cup down on the coffee table with a clunk. It seemed to hit him completely then. "Bloody hell."

"Does Lynda have a movie business connection? Besides her father?"

Steve shook his head. "She used to be an actress. Before we met. Not bad. Did half a dozen potboilers. Got out of it, though, after bad experiences with directors, if you know what I mean." He raised his eyebrows. "Then she got a shot with NewMedia, managing bands, something else she's good at."

"So she knows her way around the music and movie business."

"Oh, yeah. Works with her old man on a deal now and then."

That had to be it. But Colleen needed hard evidence.

Another look of rage crossed Steve's face again. "Fuck," he muttered, shaking his head.

Colleen took a breath. "I took a risk in telling you, Steve. I hate to share working theories. But you need to unwind. Just know Melanie isn't lying in a ditch somewhere. But you need to stay calm until I wrap this up."

Steve sighed. "Just my ex and my ex-father-in-law, along with my kid, playing me for a fool."

"The important thing now is to move forward. That means I can't have you going off half-cocked, taking it out on Lynda. Or her old man. Got that? You've got to promise me you'll hang tough with me for just a little while longer."

Steve looked up, eyes sunken. "At least I know Mel's alive."

"There you go," she said. "And right now, you need some sleep." Colleen got up as Steve poured more brandy into his cup. She went into the spare bedroom, turned on the light by the bed. There was the photo in a frame on the nightstand, Pamela at thirteen, before she went to hell. Taken when Colleen was incarcerated. Now she was up at Moon Ranch in Point Arenas, her pretty red hair butchered, wearing an orange robe and chanting bullshit with fanatics who kept the place locked down like a prison.

Someday Pam would change her mind. Someday.

And when she did, this room would be waiting for her.

Colleen turned the covers back, fluffed out the pillow, headed back out into the living room.

"Time to hit the hay, Rock Star."

Steve was leaning back on the sofa, head back, snoring at the ceiling. The kimono had fallen open, partway, barely covering his groin. She could be forgiven for stealing an involuntary glance. Her one-time idol, the crush of millions of girls, sacked out in her very own apartment, damn near naked.

A lesser human might have been entertaining some fantasies.

She was a lesser human.

She went over, reached down, touched Steve's arm. "Hey, Steve…"

He woke up, looked at her with sleepy bedroom eyes. "Thank you for setting me straight, Coll. I didn't see it."

"No need," she said. "That's what you hired me for."

He gave her a sly look.

She knew what he was thinking. Because she was thinking it, too.

"No," she whispered, brushing his cheek. "The timing couldn't be worse."

He gave a deep sigh. "You're right … I suppose."

She returned a sad smile. "Check back when this is all over, hey?"

He nodded, smiled. "Deal." He smiled again, slumped over, immediately started to purr.

She shook his arm.

No response.

She went to the linen closet, pulled a blanket, a leopard print flannel thing, came back, draped it over him, tucked it under his chin.

Let sleeping dogs lie.

In the bathroom she gathered up his clothes, took them to the laundry nook off the porch, threw them in the washer.

Then she went into her bedroom, shut the door, stripped down to her undies, being careful not to aggravate the bandage on her knee too much, tender as it was, and climbed into bed, pulled the sheet over her. The warm water sloshed under her, pulling her eyes shut.

She didn't yet know how to expose Lynda Cook and her father—yet. But tomorrow she'd start.

She fell into a deep sleep.

CHAPTER THIRTEEN

Early next morning, the sun not up yet, Alex stood at the door to Colleen's flat, decked out in a short paisley boho dress with a swirling dark red-and-purple flower pattern on a white background. Her outfit was accentuated by tan platform boots and a light brown floppy-brimmed felt hat. A matching handbag hung over her shoulder on a long strap. In contrast, Colleen wore a white fluffy bathrobe. Barefoot, she rubbed her eyes. She had just woken up to the doorbell.

"Hey there," Colleen said, giving Alex a peck on the cheek as she held the door open. "I was going to call you as soon as I got up. Where have you been? I haven't seen you since that fiasco at the Transbay Terminal."

"Antonia's birthday party last night." Alex entered the large living room. "Oh," she said, seeing Steve sitting up on the sofa, blinking himself awake, the leopard print blanket wrapped around him. She turned to Colleen with a frown. "Hope I'm not interrupting anything."

Alex had thought that she and Colleen might have been an item at one time. Colleen had contemplated it, given that her own history with men was a disaster—her ex in particular. Now her liaisons with the opposite sex tended to be occasional and brief. No strings.

She and Alex were close, and there was a level of intimacy and trust she hadn't found elsewhere. But ultimately Colleen's personal landscape was much too conventional. *Try boring,* Alex had said with a smile.

"Alex," Colleen said, "this is Steve. Steve—Alex."

"How do." Steve nodded. Alex said hello.

"I'll make coffee," Colleen said, heading into the kitchen, grabbing the kettle off the stove. Alex tailed her.

"I won't stay," she said. "Did Steve get his daughter back?"

"Not even close."

"I'm so sorry, Coll."

"I spent most of yesterday getting grilled by the cops."

"So he's having trouble with his wife and is staying with you?" She eyed Colleen.

"Alex, you have got your wires crossed. And it's his *ex*-wife."

Alex unhooked her bag, dug around, came out with a Polaroid photo. "I didn't actually come over to pry. I took this yesterday from the car when you were chasing that short character out of the Transbay Terminal. I was parked across Mission. That was the last I saw of you. I was going to give it to you at Antonia's party."

"I'm sorry I couldn't make it. I called, but Harold said you had left. Meanwhile, the kidnappers have made another demand."

Alex grimaced, handed the photo to Colleen. "Maybe this will help."

Colleen took the photo, studied it as she leaned back against the counter. A blurry picture of crowded 1st Street next to the Transbay Terminal. You could just see, partially blocked by a jaywalker, the little man in his Giants cap handing something—a bag?—to someone astride a motorcycle. It was hard to make out as the photo wasn't clear and the man wore a helmet. Colleen recalled again the popping of a motorcycle engine as she had chased the little guy out of the terminal.

"This is really helpful, Alex." Colleen held the photo up. "Thanks so much."

Alex reached over, gave her hand a squeeze. "Good luck, Coll."

Alex left. Back in her kitchen, Colleen examined the photo again.

No license plate. The driver took a risk with that, but no doubt didn't want to be ID'd. Colleen couldn't quite make out what kind of bike it was. It wasn't a Harley—too small. Too big for a Japanese bike. Colleen knew something about bikes.

But it explained the ransom money now.

She made coffee, took cups out for her and Steve.

Colleen pulled a Virginia Slim from the pack, lit it up, sat in the armchair, crossed her legs, took a sip of coffee. She pulled the Polaroid photo out of the pocket of her robe, leaned over, handed it to Steve. "Know this guy?"

He examined the photo, shook his head *no*. "Not much to see."

"Well, that's where your money went."

He gave the photo back. "Christ," he said. The tone in his voice was distinctly cool.

"Steve, about SFPD . . . we need to bring them in."

"Coll," he said, looking away. "I appreciate everything you've done . . ."

Colleen felt a "but" coming. She drank coffee. "You're not having second thoughts, are you, Steve?"

He drank some coffee, too, looked at her. "Now that I've had some sleep, time to think, I can see things a bit more clearly, yeah?"

She set her cup down. "And you've decided I'm making all of this up?"

"No, Colleen, but I can't afford for you to be wrong."

"Steve, I am *not* wrong on this. Bear with me."

He gave a frown. "I reckon I know Lynda a bit better than you do. And I just can't risk it."

Colleen smashed her cigarette out. "I *knew* I shouldn't have told you." She'd broken a cardinal rule, giving out information before it was solid. And now she'd pay the price.

"You were trying to make me feel better, yeah?" Steve said. "I appreciate it. But I can't afford to be wrong."

Damn it! "Well, we've got three days to see if I'm right. *Prove* that I'm right."

Steve downed most of his coffee. "No, I've got enough time to talk to Lynda's old man, borrow that cash."

"And lose your damn catalog."

He shrugged. "Easy come, easy go, eh?"

"Don't be a fool, Steve. Can't you see what they're trying to do?"

"Mel's my daughter, Coll. I've done nothing but let her down. I'm not going to let her down now."

"How can I talk you out of this?"

Steve drained his cup, put it on the glass coffee table, stood up. "Send me your bill. I'll pay it when I can. But I'm going to have to sort this out on my own. Thanks for all your help, Coll. Really."

"If you don't want me on this, Steve, I get it. But you need the police. Inspector Owens is the cop assigned to the case. He's a good guy. And I don't say that about cops in general. Let me get you his number."

"No," Steve said. "No police. And I appreciate you not telling him either."

She took a deep breath through her nose. "I can't promise that."

"Understood." He looked around. "Where are my clothes, please?"

"In the dryer." She stood up. "Steve, you really need to think this over."

Shook his head.

Christ. She went out to the porch, got Steve's clothes out of the dryer, shook the wrinkles out, stacked them. She brought the clothes back in the living room, handed them over.

"Thanks," he said sheepishly. He went into the bathroom to change.

He returned a few minutes later, dressed in clean jeans and work shirt.

"Have some more coffee," she said.

"No," he said, going over to his shoes by the door, stepping into them. "I'll be on my way. I've taken too much for your time."

"No, you haven't. Let me get changed and I'll run you home." She might be able to swing him back to her way of thinking.

"No, thanks, love. I'm good. It's only over the hill. I could do with the walk."

"I need to caution you about going back to your place. Watch out for anyone suspicious."

He nodded. He found his jacket, threw it on. "Send me the bill, please."

And then he was gone, stepping down the stairs to the front of her building. She heard the big old front door on the ground floor open and shut.

What a start to the day.

A slew of expletives flowed from her mouth, freely and without remorse. She went back into the kitchen, poured herself more coffee, got another cigarette, stepped out on the porch where the San Francisco morning fog hung like a gray cloud. She drank coffee and smoked.

If this was meant to stop her, it wasn't working.

In fact, she had a pretty good idea what to do next.

Colleen mashed her cigarette out, took the phone on its long cord into the shower, and set it on the black-and-white hexagonal tiles by the claw-foot bathtub, so that she could hear it in case somebody called. And then she got in the shower.

CHAPTER FOURTEEN

Colleen was parked in the Torino up on Colon Avenue in Westwood Highlands, half a block down from Lynda Cook's 1930s terra-cotta-color Spanish-style house that overlooked South City. This was a neighborhood of detached houses with front yards—not the norm by San Francisco standards. Lynda's was two stories and even had an ivy-covered brick wall around it. It was afternoon and the fog hadn't burned off all day. Gray mist hung along the hillside.

Steve might have changed his mind. But Colleen hadn't. She'd been staking out the house for a couple of hours.

Finally, a distant clanking confirmed the opening of the wrought-iron gate in front of the driveway. Colleen flipped the visor down, hiding her face, and straightened her hair in the mirror, pretending to freshen up.

A black BMW pulled out. Lynda's car. Colleen kept her head down as the car came down Colon and motored by. She caught a glimpse of Lynda at the wheel.

Colleen pulled her hair together with a fastener, got her white Pacific Gas & Electric hard hat off the passenger seat. The helmet came in handy now and then. She donned innocuous sunglasses, grabbed her large brown leather shoulder bag. It was heavy with her tools of the trade. She got out, tucked her ponytail up inside the helmet as she pulled it on. She looked the part in jeans, white sneaks, blue denim work shirt. It was too bad she had no one to cover for her, honk the horn in case Lynda suddenly came home.

She walked up the far side of the street opposite Lynda's house, checked around. The driveway behind Lynda's gate was empty. Crossing over, she ducked around the brick wall that ran along the property. Staying close to the wall, about thirty yards down she found a glossy green door that had been painted many times. The lock was an old Mortise lock, with a big keyhole. Surreptitiously, she looked around at Lynda's neighbor's house. No one at the windows.

She squatted down, stashed her clipboard, opened the flap on her shoulder bag, found her set of skeleton keys, along with her old leather gloves, thin and worn. She slipped them on and tried various keys on the lock.

No go. The lock was too old.

She tried her Dyna QuickPick but the lock was stiff. Probably hadn't been opened for quite a while.

She retrieved an eleven-inch pry bar and an old shop towel, the kind a gas station attendant might use to check oil.

The rumble of a car coming up the street caused her to stop, stand up, hug the door, making herself flat.

Lynda?

A blue Impala floated by. She breathed a sigh of relief.

Checking around one more time, she wrapped the tip of the pry bar in the towel and jammed the edge in between the door and the jamb next to the lock. She applied a good amount of pressure. There was a creak but the door held. She leaned into it with her hip. The door lock snapped, and the door loosened. Not too much damage around the wood.

She opened the side door, let herself in, pushed the door shut. A side door to the garage next to the house was locked. But it was a newer door and easy enough to pick. If she never got her PI license she might as well sharpen her cat burglar skills. Colleen entered, pushed the door shut quietly behind her. The dim two-car garage was devoid of cars. Lynda did not appear to be a very neat person. On the opposite side of the garage there was a kitchen door with windows. Colleen crossed the garage, one ear cocked. She tried the door. Unlocked. She opened it silently, peered into a large kitchen of burnt-orange tile. No lights on. All she could hear was the ticking of a clock. She was just about to step into the house when she noticed, sitting on the garage workbench to her left, a small red fabric suitcase with big white stitching. Next to it was an odd-shaped white case with a pink flower pattern, flat on the bottom. Both items of luggage looked suitable for a young girl.

Colleen stepped back, went through them. The unusual case was a helmet bag. Inside was a black equestrian riding helmet, size Youth M, along with a pair of junior leather riding gloves.

Inside the overnight bag were britches, a white blouse, and riding jacket, on top of a pair of riding boots that lay on their side amidst rolled-up socks and folded underwear. All the size a girl Melanie's age might wear.

Melanie was passionate about riding. Colleen recalled the photo Steve had shown her. Melanie was pushing for her own horse.

Interesting.

Colleen zipped the bag back up, set it back on the workbench, slipped into the house.

The kitchen did not adhere to Colleen's more fastidious style, with cups and bowls here and there and a half-eaten piece of toast on a crumby plate on the kitchen table next to an open *Chronicle*. Herb Caen's column was next to the Macy's ad.

The living room had high-end furniture, including a leather Chesterfield and a white canvas with a minimalist smear of black that was supposed to pass for art. A throw blanket was draped across one arm of the sofa, next to a copy of *Cosmopolitan*. A half-finished drink sat on the coffee table.

The walls were covered with gold and silver records and photos of Lynda over the years, posing with recording artists and movie stars, quite a few of whom Colleen recognized. No pictures of Melanie.

Colleen tiptoed upstairs.

At the top of the landing was a framed movie poster for *Deadly Blessing*, a potboiler featuring a buxom actress named Laura DuMond, wet hair dripping down a curvaceous body as she climbed onto the back of a motorboat in a skimpy red bikini that struggled to contain her shapely figure. One long-nailed hand held a smoking pistol. Her face was a sexy mean sneer and her eyes were slitted with intent. Laura DuMond was none other than Lynda Cook, ten to fifteen years ago. The tagline read: SHE PROMISED DANGER . . . AND DELIVERED.

Wasn't that the truth?

Ironically, the only two rooms upstairs that were not pigsties were Melanie's and an empty guest room, which was layered in dust. Melanie's room had all the accoutrements of a bedroom belonging to a young lady with a guilty parent, including her own Princess phone, a twelve-inch color Magnavox television, a Marantz stereo system with 8-track player, stacks of tapes next to it. Several equestrian trophies were lined up evenly on a shelf. There were the usual photos of teen idols, Leif Garret with his blond tousle and unbuttoned shirt figuring prominently.

What seemed out of place was a top dresser drawer left wide open. Underwear and socks that had once been organized appeared to have been rummaged through, some perhaps taken and placed in the bag downstairs in the garage.

Colleen dug around but found nothing out of the ordinary. No diary. No gray gym bag containing twenty thousand dollars.

Lynda's bedroom was the polar opposite of her daughter's. Again, high-end furniture, but clothes were strewn here and there, along with papers, letters, and more.

Colleen checked the nightstand. Opening the drawer, she found a loaded Smith & Wesson LadySmith revolver with a baby-blue handle next to a wicked-looking pink dildo. Lynda's weapons of choice. Colleen checked the closets next. Under the bed. Behind the bed. No bag of money sitting out in the open.

Keeping one ear raised in case the front gate clanked open, Colleen proceeded into the office, which was slightly more organized. She found a stack of work papers on an elegant mahogany desk.

She skimmed through the papers. Most were correspondence with NewMedia Entertainment, where Lynda worked. Toward the bottom of the stack, one note was from Sir Ian Ellis, chairman of Delco Records. The name rang a bell. Delco was Steve's old record company in the U.K., whom he said had robbed him and the band blind. The note was dated about a month ago.

She picked it up.

Lynda-

Simply lovely to see you again. But then, you are so easy to look at. Next time I'm in town, I'd love you to show me around.

Best, Ian

P.S. I think we've made some headway on SOS.

The note made Colleen cringe. Sir Ian was a dirty old man. All part of the rock and roll business. And Lynda was in touch with Steve's old record company. But what the hell did SOS mean?

She snapped a Polaroid of it.

She didn't have time to go through all of the correspondence. The top desk drawer was open, a cluttered mess. Side drawers were locked. She fished around, found Lynda's checkbook. She removed the checkbook register, lay it down on the desk. Too close for her Polaroid OneStep. She set her shoulder bag down, found her Olympus-Pen Fixed Lens Compact Viewfinder camera, loaded with black-and-white high-speed film. It was a little dark in the office, but she didn't want to fuss with a flash. She turned on the desk lamp, positioned it over the register, went through it, page by page, using a paperweight to anchor the edges, taking photos of Lynda's spending. That might lead to something. When she was done, she slipped the register back into the checkbook, tossed the checkbook back into the drawer. She turned off the desk lamp, repositioned it, along with the paperweight, to where they had been.

A filing cabinet was locked.

Colleen looked around, wondering where $20,000 might be hidden.

No safe visible.

But on an inner wall, she noticed a Warhol silkscreen of Marilyn Monroe, numbered and signed by the artist himself. It was slightly askew. She went over, lifted the frame.

And found a perfectly good SentrySafe wall safe behind it.

She didn't expect it to be unlocked and it wasn't. But who knew what the combination was?

She snapped a photo of it, just for good measure.

Colleen checked her watch. She'd been here less than ten minutes. She'd do another quick run-through.

The clanging of the front gate pulled her into the here and now with a start.

Colleen darted over to the desk and peered out the Venetian blinds. A black BMW sedan waiting for the gate to fully open. Lynda at the wheel, wearing sunglasses and a scowl.

Colleen's heart thumped.

She didn't have time to get out.

She rushed back to the guest room, which seemed unused, and the last place, hopefully, anyone would think to look. She shut the bedroom door behind her, slid the mirrored closet door open, pulled off her hard hat, stepped inside, slid the door shut. She took a deep breath and stood in the dark closet, breathing musty clothes smells.

The garage door clacked open.

She waited. Time had a way of slowing down in situations like this. Oddly enough, the car engine did not shut off. Colleen heard a car door open, someone get out—Lynda—then the trunk opening, then someone running around, throwing a couple of items in the trunk, slamming the trunk lid, getting in the car, and backing out of the garage.

The garage door clattered shut. The car backed out of the driveway and the outer gate shut as well.

Colleen exited the closet.

Time to go.

She put her PG&E helmet back on and tiptoed downstairs, and when she got there, the sound of a side door by the front gate opening caused her heart rate to ratchet back up. She ducked through to the kitchen, peering out. A mailman wearing a white pith helmet had unlocked the iron entrance gate next to the driveway gates. He held a bundle of mail in one hand as he approached the front door.

Colleen waited while he slid the mail in through the front door slot, turned around, left, pulling the entrance door in the brick wall shut behind him.

Colleen went to the front door. A pile of mail lay on a Persian rug in the entranceway.

She picked up the mail and went through it, keeping the correspondence and bills, leaving the magazines and junk mail behind. Stashing her haul in her shoulder bag, she exited the kitchen through the garage, surprised when she saw that the small red suitcase and helmet bag were now gone.

Lynda had come back to the house to pick them up. Must have forgotten them.

A sense of gratification flowed through Colleen's guts.

She had been right about Melanie all along.

Retracing her steps, she left, pulling the side garage door shut, locking it, exiting through the green side-door in the brick wall, checking that no one was watching her from the house next door.

She pulled off her gloves and walked down the path to Colon Avenue, checking her clipboard in a businesslike manner.

CHAPTER FIFTEEN

Colleen dropped her roll of film off at a one-hour photo on Mission, although there really was no such thing as one-hour photo processing. But she would get the pictures back later today.

It was well past lunchtime when she settled down at her office desk overlooking the city. Overlooking a blanket of fog would have been more accurate.

She proceeded to go through Lynda's mail.

A letter from Melanie's private school. Colleen plucked a letter opener from an empty coffee mug that said EAT AT JOE'S and opened it.

A bill. An expensive school, Colleen noticed. And a note from Sister Margaret. *Melanie is making progress but must still watch her language. Setting a good example at home will help immeasurably.*

Good luck with that, Colleen thought.

A birthday card to Lynda from someone in New Jersey. She read it quickly, feeling voyeuristic, and moved on to Lynda's Pacific Bell telephone bill.

Over $100 in long distance charges. A job like Lynda's no doubt involved a lot of phone time, and with NewMedia located in Los Angeles, that made sense. The bill cutoff date was last week. There were a number of calls to quite a few Los Angeles numbers.

She started dialing.

Most of the numbers ended up belonging to various executives at NewMedia.

But one heavily called number was unlisted. Colleen called it, got one of those fancy new telephone answering machines.

"This is Rex. You know what to do."

She hung up before the beep.

Rex Williamson was Lynda's father.

There were two more long-distance collect calls toward the end of the cutoff period, before Melanie disappeared, from Point Reyes, north of San Francisco. Another unlisted number. She dialed.

A woman with a Latin accent answered. Colleen hung up.

There were several calls to a location in the North Bay, Fairfax, around the same time. Directory inquiries told Colleen the number belonged to a business: Edenview Equestrian Center.

She was reminded of Melanie's disappearing riding gear.

And suddenly she got an *aha* moment.

She'd wait until the photos of Lynda's checkbook register came back before she continued. She wished she had just swiped the damn thing now.

She called Moran, in the hopes that he might be able to use one of his police contacts to track down the elusive Point Reyes number. But Moran's wife always got to the phone first.

"What is it now?" Daphne seethed.

"I was hoping to speak to your husband," Colleen said.

"Well, he's not here."

Colleen left a message, fingers crossed that it would get to him.

She ate cheese and French bread in the enclosed porch at a small table and washed it down with a wineglass of mineral water. Fog swirled outside. Inside it was relatively warm, as warm as an old San Francisco apartment with high ceilings got. Colleen counted her blessings. Not that long ago she'd been living hand to mouth in a condemned paint plant she was guarding for a client.

She would really have liked to speak with Moran, ask him to track down that Point Reyes number. But if she didn't have it today, it wouldn't stop her. Steve Cook's next payoff was due in a few days, and she had to nip that in the bud before he sold his catalog to his ex-father-in-law. But she needed hard evidence.

She called Inspector Owens.

"About time," he said.

"I'm going to need more time," she said.

There was a long pause. Office clatter and background conversations filled the line. "So, your client won't budge? Well, that's too bad."

"That's not the problem," she said. "I think I've found something."

Owens paused. "Something like what?"

"Something like *this is not really a kidnap*."

Another pause. "How so?"

"My client was set up. The kid is fine."

"You have proof?"

"I will," she said. "Tomorrow."

"Jesus."

"I'll get photos." She told him what she had in mind.

Another long pause. "Okay," he said. "One more day."

"Thanks," she said but Owens had already hung up.

CHAPTER SIXTEEN

Colleen crossed the Golden Gate Bridge at a painstaking twenty miles per hour, along with the rest of the evening commute traffic heading north out of San Francisco. Wet fog blew in from the Pacific through the red spans and cables. The Torino's windshield wipers slapped it away as the V8 grumbled in low gear.

She wore a smart black polyester pantsuit with a crisp white blouse and sensible heels. She'd made herself up and brushed her hair back in a businesslike manner, along with Pamela's silver Magpie earrings. When nosing around, it frequently helped to be well dressed.

Going through Marin wasn't much faster, but traffic picked up when she reached Sir Francis Drake. San Quentin prison loomed to her right by the bay, the tall lights of the perimeter sparkling in the moisture. She knew every person inside was counting off the days, just as she had done. She exited 101 and headed west, through the laid-back communities of well-to-do former hippies who had escaped the harsh realities of the modern world. Soon she was in countryside, climbing low hills where the fog fell away. Edenview Equestrian Center was tucked away in a secluded canyon.

She wound up on a narrow, well-maintained private road, lit only by her headlights, crossing a small bridge to a gravel parking lot.

Even at night, one look at Edenview revealed a prosperous stable. There were two arenas—one covered—an office, a tidy cottage, more living quarters behind the stables, all tastefully constructed of wood and painted in a rustic red with white trim. Colleen parked by the office next to a 4x4 pickup and an empty horse trailer. She got out, grabbing her trusty clipboard. Grass was watered and mowed. Hoses were neatly coiled. Water troughs were clean and full. Nothing looked out of place; nothing seemed wanting for maintenance. The country air was rich and pungent with the smell of wet earth and horse manure. In the distance, mariachi music floated from a building on the far side of the stables.

The office was closed for the day.

A light was on in the cottage, however, next to the covered arena. Colleen strolled over, stepped up on the porch. She could hear the braying of canned laughter. Someone watching TV. She knocked. The volume dropped on the TV. Footsteps approached.

The door opened and there stood a heavy but sturdy man about fifty years old with a white handlebar mustache and a gut pushing out a plaid shirt. He had a deep voice and was friendly enough, considering he'd been interrupted during what was probably his own time.

Colleen introduced herself as Carol Aird, insurance adjuster. She produced a card that claimed she was who she said she was, an identity she used to make unobtrusive inquiries.

"I'm sorry to bother you. Are you the manager?"

"Ed Brand." He didn't put a hand out. "What's it about?"

"I'm working with Pacific All Risk. I meant to get here earlier but got stuck in traffic." Traffic delays were a hindrance Bay Area people understood. She turned on the charm, making direct eye contact until she saw his brown eyes soften. She consulted her clipboard where she had scribbled some notes. "It's about an accident on

Canyon Road, week before last. Thursday. I believe you might know one of the alleged parties: Lynda Cook?"

She saw a flicker of recognition in his face.

"Yes," he said.

"Her daughter takes riding lessons here, I believe."

He gave a terse nod.

"Well, that's neither here nor there," she said. "But the other party is maintaining that Ms. Cook is responsible for the accident, up at the turn-off to Edenview. Said she pulled out in front of him on Canyon Road, didn't see him, didn't signal, caused him to hit the brakes, hit her rear bumper, made him veer off into a guardrail. Did quite a lot of damage to his car. He's putting in a claim. To be honest, there's no way Ms. Cook is liable, but I'm doing my due diligence and following up. Did you see anything unusual Thursday, week before last? Hear anything?"

Shook his head no.

"No one came down here to report an accident? Use the phone?"

Shook his head again. "I don't believe she brings Melanie here on Thursdays. I'd have to check."

"I'll double-check as well. Have you noticed anything unusual about Lynda's car since then? Like it might have been in any kind of accident?"

"No. Nothing out of the ordinary."

So Lynda had been here within the last week. Around the time of the "kidnap."

"And she didn't say anything about an accident?" Colleen asked.

Shook his head again.

"That's what I thought," Colleen said. She drew a deep breath. "I just love the air out here. You have a lovely stable. Do you mind if I look around? I've always wanted to take riding lessons. Ever since I was a girl. And now, just look at this place." She gazed around, smiled, shook her head. "It's so peaceful."

"Why don't you come back during normal working hours? I can show you a couple of the school horses. Introduce you to our trainers."

Damn. "That sounds excellent." She put her hand out. "Thank you so much for your time."

She got in her car, drove off.

On Canyon Road, she parked on the shoulder, over to the side, where it was secluded. She got her sneakers out of the trunk and switched shoes. While she was at it, she folded her suit jacket neatly, laid it on the back seat, threw on her leather bomber jacket. She slung her burglar bag over her shoulder, locked up the Torino, and headed back to Edenview, just shy of a jog, carrying her flashlight, leaving it off for the moment. The cool air was refreshing, and it felt good to unwind.

When she reached the gravel parking lot, she skirted the main area, ducking back behind the office where she might be seen from the cottage if anyone were looking. She made her way to the stables proper. The smell of horses was strong. She heard their gentle grunting as they slept. Laughter amidst the mariachi music floated from behind the stables. She suspected that's where the stable hands lived.

Quietly, she opened the half door to the stable and let herself in. Once inside, she turned on the flashlight, setting it on low.

There were a good two dozen stalls, all occupied, most of the horses blanketed. One or two were standing but most were lying down. Each stall had a name and an owner.

She made her way down, checking each name.

She passed a huge silver dapple Morgan that turned its head, gave a spirited whinny that reverberated. Colleen stopped, frozen, as the horse turned in the stall to stick its big head out. Gently, she reached up, stroked its warm neck. She had heard that horses did not like their faces touched. That seemed to do it. The horse calmed down.

Toward the rear of the stable she found a name she was looking for: Cook. The sign was not permanent but written on a piece of cardboard with a Magic Marker.

She didn't know much about horses, but she knew that the one in the Cook stall was a beauty, even with its rear end to her. It stood, a dark blanket covering much of a gleaming black coat. It had a long black mane that would have done a shampoo commercial justice. It turned its head and looked at Colleen with intelligent dark eyes and gave a soft headshake. It was a horse any girl would kill for. It turned in the stall and thrust its large head over the door, so close Colleen could smell its sweet breath.

She stroked it underneath its chin, and it responded with a friendly snort.

She directed the flashlight back at the temporary plaque. The horse's name was Ebony. It was written on a piece of paper and pinned underneath the temporary plaque. Ebony seemed to. be a new addition to the stable.

Underneath the plaque was a small chalkboard.

There were specific feeding instructions in Spanish. Underneath the instructions was a note that said: *Olema*, followed by a date. The date was tomorrow. It was circled. On the corner of the chalkboard, a clipboard hung on a hook that held a number of papers. She took it down, gave them a perusal. Veterinary instructions. State of California papers. The horse belonged to Lynda Cook.

It looked like Melanie might have finally gotten her new horse. Right about that time she was kidnapped. How tragic.

Or more than a coincidence?

What did *Olema* mean? There was a small town named Olema, right next to Point Reyes, on the coast. Maybe an hour's drive from here.

Colleen recalled the two collect calls on Lynda Cook's phone bill, made recently, from Point Reyes.

What was happening tomorrow?

Was Ebony taking a trip? To Olema?

Colleen knew what she was doing tomorrow.

CHAPTER SEVENTEEN

By sunrise next morning Colleen was sitting at the wheel of her Torino, nestled under trees on the uphill shoulder of Canyon Road, just before the turn-off to Edenview Equestrian Center.

Someone on KCBS news talk radio was explaining how aerosol sprays were destroying the ozone layer, contributing to something they were calling "global warming." World population had just passed four billion. No looking back, Colleen thought. Fog rolled down the hillside as daylight began to cast a gray pall across the remnants of the night sky.

After yesterday's visit to the stables, she had gone home, grabbed a nap, showered, and returned before dawn. No coffee. She didn't need a full bladder while parked by the road. She was stifling yawns.

She wore her most comfortable stakeout outfit: acid-washed bell-bottom jeans, soft as chamois, white V-neck T-shirt, her white Pony Topstars with the blue stripes, and her brown bomber jacket to keep her warm, despite what they said about global warming.

Little traffic had gone by. A beer truck, about half an hour ago. Now the odd car appeared in the opposite direction, the start of commuters into San Francisco. Callers into KCBS were currently venting about the rampant descent of San Francisco, thanks to the influx of gay men from all over the country. Guys dancing with each other all night at the Trocadero to Donna Summer didn't sound very dangerous to Colleen. She shook out a Virginia Slim, lit it up, rolling down the window. She'd cut down since Alex's father had died of lung cancer. She blew smoke out into the cool morning air.

She hoped she hadn't miscalculated coming back to Edenview. She had two days left before Steve Cook was due to pay Melanie's kidnappers another twenty K. She needed to show him he was on the wrong track. The note on the Cooks' stall last night said that Ebony, Melanie's horse, might be moved today.

Traffic was picking up.

Then she saw the nose of a gray Ford 4x4 pickup truck appear at the access road to Edenview. Right blinker on, it pulled out, turning right up the hill, towing a red horse trailer. The trailer was obviously loaded, swaying side by side.

Ebony, Colleen thought, putting out her cigarette.

The truck and trailer wrestled up the hill, out of sight around a curve.

She attempted to fire up the Torino and was met with the grinding of the starter motor that wouldn't catch.

She watched the truck and trailer crawl up the hill.

Several more attempts at starting the Torino met with a sluggish starter. She sat back, cursing, and waited.

A few minutes later, she tried again. Success, finally, as black smoke belched out the tailpipes, filling her rearview mirror. Ring job soon.

She shot up the hill, over the summit, down toward the coast. Heading out into countryside.

Without getting too close, she tailed the truck and trailer through the little town of Lagunitas, where the Organic Natural Café was opening for the day, into the pines and redwoods of Samuel P. Taylor State Park. Shadows through the trees flickered over the windshield. Ten minutes later, past rolling ranchland, cows grazed as the truck headed for Point Reyes. The coastal range loomed in the distance, hazy with wisps of windblown moisture. The truck turned south on 1, toward Olema. She did the same. A two-lane highway followed the coast.

Just past the little town of Olema, the pickup truck turned left, lolling side to side on a dirt road past a gas station that had closed down long ago. The red pumps still had regular at 31 cents a gallon, half of what it was now.

She pulled over to the shoulder, gave the truck and horse trailer time to get ahead, so as to not be seen following so close behind. She ate a quick bite of a sandwich she'd packed, wrapped it back up, put the Torino into gear, bumped left onto the dirt road the truck and trailer had taken.

In the distance she could see dust being kicked up.

She followed, at a distance. The truck and trailer disappeared over a slight hill.

When she got to the hill, she put the Torino into first, easing to the top of the rise.

A section of land fenced off with barbwire lay in the distance. The truck turned right, into it. There was a modest structure, a low barn, and a house trailer.

She slid back down the hill, pulled over, decided not to kill the engine in case it wouldn't start. Risky, but she didn't want them to see the car, and she needed to get closer. She got out, the ocean wind sharp on her cheeks, blowing her hair to one side. She opened the trunk, found her binos, went through her camera bag. Got her Canon SLR as well, slapped on a distance lens, hung it around her neck.

Peered through the binoculars.

The horse trailer was being unloaded. Ebony was led out backwards at the coaxing of a man in a cowboy hat. Two people had emerged from the trailer. One was a woman. Dark skinned, young, long gleaming black hair. A Latina.

The other was a girl.

Colleen zoomed in with the binoculars.

Melanie Cook, with a dark bob, wearing a green barn coat. Grinning as she nuzzled Ebony, who nodded in response.

A dark emotion flowed through Colleen's guts. She had known Melanie was in no real danger. Knew it.

The man in the cowboy hat shut the doors to the horse trailer. The woman who had come out of the house trailer with Melanie was chatting to him. He handed her something.

Colleen lowered her binos, jogged toward the rough-and-ready ranch on what was now a gravel road. When she was a hundred or so yards away, she stopped, got her SLR camera, moved around until she framed her shot.

Melanie Cook, sitting on Ebony, bareback. All smiles.

Colleen snapped a photo.

And another.

And one of the cowboy, who was none other than Ed Brand of the droopy white mustache, at the wheel of his truck now. And one of the nameless Latina.

Then, with a sense of alarm, she saw Ed Brand looking her way.

She turned quickly, headed back to the rise.

At the car, she put the camera away, got back in, did a quick three-point turn, headed back to Olema, bumping along the gravel road, just shy of kicking up too much dust and attracting attention.

She stopped at the defunct gas station, where there was a pay phone. She wiped the grimy receiver off with a handkerchief, called Owens. He wasn't in. She left a message, saying she had been right, and she would give him an update. She called Steve. No answer.

She got back in the Torino. At Highway 1 she turned left, stepped on it. It would be quicker getting back home this way. She needed to get this roll of film developed ASAP, show Steve his little girl was safe and sound. Maybe he would finally believe he was being scammed. She shifted up to third as the countryside blurred by, grabbing her unfinished sandwich as she did.

CHAPTER EIGHTEEN

"Proof," Colleen said quietly, not wanting to rub it in as she laid the photos down in front of Steve on the sheet of wallboard resting on two sawhorses.

Steve stood there, dumbfounded, the light from the single bare bulb catching the safety goggles on his face, the fine white plaster dust in his hair.

It was early evening and she had just come over after picking up the Olema prints from the drugstore.

Steve pulled his plastic safety goggles up to the top of his head, leaving raccoon eyes. He took a deep breath, lay his sheetrock knife gently down next to the photos, picked up one of Melanie riding Ebony, huge grin on her face.

"She looks so bloody happy," he said.

"I'm sorry, Steve."

"No—I'm sorry I doubted you, Colleen."

"The bottom line is that Melanie's okay."

"Right." He worked a soft pack of Lucky Strikes out of the pocket of his denim work shirt. Shaking one out, he popped it in his mouth. He patted himself down for matches. "And you're absolutely sure Lynda's behind it?"

"Just between you and me, I snooped around Lynda's place. That's when I noticed Lynda had gathered Melanie's riding gear together. It made me realize Melanie must be nearby. So I visited Edenview, where Melanie rides. Next day I trailed the owner delivering a new horse—whose name is Ebony—to Olema. I suspect the 'kidnap' is taking longer than expected, so Lynda decided Melanie could have her new horse in the meantime. A peace offering."

"Bloody bitch," he said, meaning Lynda.

"A hundred to one her father, Rex Williamson, is involved, too."

Steve found a book of matches, lit up his cigarette, leaning down into the flame. He sucked in smoke, blew it out. His eyes had assumed a hard squint. The expected relief of knowing his daughter was alive wasn't as apparent as she had hoped. "Rex is supposed to transfer the cash to my bank account tomorrow—once I sign and return the papers authorizing the release of my catalog. They're due to arrive any time tonight by special messenger. When I get the cash, I have a little under a day to pay the kidnappers." He took a drag, blew it out. "But it's all a bloody scam."

Colleen was relieved Steve hadn't pulled the trigger on the money yet. But she was concerned about his reaction.

"Well," she said, "now you're off the hook. No need to give up your catalog. No need to pay off 'kidnappers' anymore."

Steve nodded, but his neck was taut. Controlling the rage. He ran his hand through his dusty hair, hit the safety goggles, suddenly ripped them off, hurled them across the room.

"Fucking bastard! Damn bitch!"

Colleen saw new tension fill Steve's face as he came to the full realization of the betrayal. His ex-wife, her father, possibly even his daughter, had conspired against him, not only fleecing him for money he didn't have, but taking his music, his only legacy, and

putting him through emotional hell. "Lynda turned my own daughter against me!"

"Melanie's a kid, Steve."

"A kid who sold me out for a bloody horse!"

The apple didn't fall far from the tree, Colleen thought. "A kid
who's under the controlling influence of a very strong, manipulative
mother. Lynda doesn't take 'no' for an answer. Count your winnings.
Mel's okay. You keep your catalog. You don't have to go in hock for
any more money."

He gave a deep sigh, sucked in smoke, smashed his cigarette out
in the tuna can on the corner of the wallboard. "Talk about a mixed
blessing. But, yeah, you're right, I suppose—all in all, I'm up." He
looked at Colleen with a tired frown.

"Steve, it's time to call Inspector Owens. We might be able to get
that twenty K back."

"I'll take care of it. I'll bloody deal with them."

"Steve, I don't want you to confront Lynda on this." She nodded
at the photos of Melanie and Ebony. "It's not just Lynda. It's most
likely her father—and whoever else they've got working for them. It
could get dangerous. Let the cops handle it."

He gave a twisted smile. "I'd like to wring her bloody neck."

"Exactly why you should not talk to her for the time being. Stay
away. Change your locks. Don't let her in."

"I've never been in a situation like this before."

"Few people have," Colleen said. "You should get some sleep." She
really didn't want to leave him alone. He might go find Lynda.
"You've still got a lot on your plate. We need to deal with Octavien
before he wants his money."

"What's another day without sleep?" Steve laughed bitterly. "I'm
too bloody pissed off to sleep, love. I owe you a drink—or three.
You just got me out of a hell of a jam. You showed me that the

daughter from hell is still alive. It's ironic as anything but it's still a relief."

She smiled, glad to see some slight payoff. "A drink is always on my list of to-dos." She'd hang out with Steve until he cooled down. "It's been an eventful couple of days."

"You, madam," Steve said, "are the mistress of understatement. Give me five minutes to grab a quick shower, yeah?"

"I wasn't going to mention it," she said with a wink, although Steve smelled pretty good the way he was, in that primeval way. She was a sucker when it came to men and workaday sweat. When she liked guys, she liked the ones who worked with their hands. Basic: what you saw was what you got.

And this one could also sing like a soul-shouter extraordinaire.

"Help yourself to a beer," he said, heading off to the back of the flat.

She did just that, going back to an open kitchen that was only partially remodeled. She dug a longneck out of the fridge, popped it, looked at the pictures on one wall that hadn't been torn down to the studs. Steve had met just about everyone in music in 1966. John Lennon. Tom Jones. You name it, he was in a photo with them, with stylish mod hair and a world-at-his-feet smile. She had no idea he had been so big, to be honest. But it had sure come and gone in a hurry. Nature of the business, no doubt.

She worked her way down a narrow hallway off the kitchen, sipping beer, studying the memorabilia.

Steve's bedroom door was open. She peered in. The room, surprisingly, was neat, meaning the bed had actually been made and there were no clothes on the floor. He had a waterbed, too, from what she could see, and more goodies on the wall. She stuck her head in. A handbill from a concert. A photo of Mick Jagger in a white suit, leaning against Steve like he was a post, Steve with his arms crossed, propping him up, mugging for the camera. Another one, a grinning Keith Richards handing Steve a half-empty bottle of Jack Daniels. Marianne Faithfull in a headband looked on, bemused. Colleen saw a gold record on the wall. She fought the urge to go into the bedroom.

She wondered who else was involved in the faux kidnap. One guy was dead. But there were at least two others involved: Duffle Coat and whoever was on that motorcycle who most likely took off with the bag of cash.

The shower shut off with a squeal, and she stepped back into the hallway. The bathroom door opened. Steve appeared in nothing but a towel.

Muscular and trim, with deliciously tousled hair. She was proud of herself for not staring too much. What she did do was blush at snooping around.

"Sorry," she said, nodding at a photo of Steve sitting at a piano with Aretha Franklin. "Curiosity got the better of me. You should open a rock 'n' roll museum."

"No problem, love." He winked.

She did like being called that. He wasn't fazed at all. He'd probably been around hundreds of women barely clothed. And vice versa.

She headed back into the kitchen while he went into the bedroom to get dressed.

"You left your album the other night," he shouted. His bedroom door was open so they could talk while he dressed.

"I forgot it when your ex showed up, breathing fire," she shouted back.

"Well, she won't be doing that much longer," he said, coming down the hall.

That didn't sound right.

He wore a two-tone black-and-white short-sleeve shirt, nice tight jeans, smart black loafers, no socks. His hair was gelled, and he'd shaved. He looked a lot better.

"I know it's easier said than done, Steve, but you need to watch how you react to Lynda."

"What I meant was that she won't be getting away with any more bullshit," he said.

That sounded a little better. She sipped her beer. "We need to get your money back."

"One way or another."

The doorbell rang.

"Courier," he said. "Rex's papers."

He answered the door, and she set her beer bottle on the counter, and followed.

A guy in an expensive suit with slick-backed hair and a briefcase stood there, holding an official-looking envelope. "Good evening, Mr. Cook," he said, introducing himself as a lawyer representing Rex Williamson, Lynda's father. "I'm here to go over the paperwork?"

"Of course," Steve said, taking the envelope from him. "I can take care of it right now, if you like. I imagine you're in a hurry."

"I am, indeed." The man beamed. "I do appreciate that, sir."

Steve took the envelope, right on the doorstep, extracted the document, gave it a quick glance. Colleen looked over his shoulder. Legal papers. She saw the figure $20,000.

"Do you have a pen, mate?" Steve said.

He did. Steve took it.

And printed "VOID" in the signature box.

And wrote in big letters in a diagonal across the first page:
PISS OFF

Steve studied his handiwork, while the lawyer watched, mouth agape.

"Yes, I do believe that covers it," Steve said. He turned his head to Colleen. "What do you reckon, love?"

"Looks about right to me," she said.

Steve handed the document, torn envelope, and pen back to the lawyer. Before the man could protest, Steve shut the door on him.

He turned to Colleen. Their eyes met. His crinkled. She felt hers doing the same.

Both of them burst into laughter.

CHAPTER NINETEEN

The Pitt was what Steve called "heaving," meaning the bar was two deep with thirsty, noisy customers. Steve and Colleen were surprised to see *the band with no name* setting up on the cramped stage.

Deena, the drummer, in a tight Ramones T-shirt, short slicked-back raven-colored hair, tuned up a snare drum with a key while the guy with the blond ducktail and pompadour thumped a bass guitar and adjusted a Hiwatt amp. The ghostly-looking character with stringy brown hair and blue guitar stared into space. Steve was met with arm slaps and good-natured ribbing all round.

The mystery of Melanie's "kidnapping" might be behind them, but Colleen knew there was plenty of trouble left. They were still going to have to deal with Octavien's twenty-K loan, and there were people out there who had assisted in the scam. One was dead, but there were at least two others: the guy in the duffle coat and whoever had been on the motorcycle. But step one was to get Steve's money back. She'd pay Lynda a visit soon to start pulling that thread.

"Didn't think you could make it tonight," Vernon said to Steve from behind the bar, pouring shots for Steve and Colleen. He had a rare smile and it didn't look right on him.

"Neither did I, until an hour ago," Steve said, downing the shot as if it were water, then wiping his mouth with the back of his hand.

Colleen sipped hers. Wild Turkey. "So Deena's band is playing tonight?"

"Last-minute thing," Vernon said. "The regular band fell through. She said you wouldn't be able to make it."

"I've had a few things on my mind, Vernon," Steve said with sarcasm, setting his empty shot glass out for a refill.

"Understood, Steve," Vernon said. "But, now that you're here . . ." Vernon refilled Steve's glass to the brim, gave Colleen a friendly, questioning look as he wagged the bottle to tempt her. She shook her head no. Someone had to drive, and she wasn't done working. "House is more than half full, Steve—and they always dig to hear the guy with the gravel voice."

Deena hopped off the stage, came tripping over in her torn jeans and black high-tops.

"I did *not* expect to see you, Steve," she said in her nasal New York accent, giving him a look of concern. "What's up with Mel?"

"Mel's fine," Steve said, turning to acknowledge Colleen. "Thanks to Colleen here. It's a long story—one I'll explain later."

"Wow," Deena said, clearly impressed. "But Steve, that's—great."

"I'm still in shock," he said. "But it's the good kind—mostly."

Deena turned to Colleen. "You must be good."

"She is," Steve said.

Colleen said, "Like Steve says, it's a long story. One that's still in motion."

"But Melanie's definitely okay?" Deena said.

"More or less," Steve said.

"Cool." Deena smiled at Colleen. Then, to Steve: "I didn't call you about the gig tonight since I figured you had your hands full with Mel. But I couldn't afford to turn down Vernon, piss him off again, and lose our residency. And it *is* work."

"And work is work," Steve said. "Who you got on vocals?"

"Finn is going to fake it."

Steve raised his eyebrows.

"I know," Deena said. "If he only sang the way he looks."

Steve gave the bass player with the hair a thumbs-up. "Hey, Finn." Finn returned the same. "Get your ass up here, Steve!" he shouted.

"Well," Steve said to Deena, "I'm here now—if you need me."

She broke into a grin. "You don't have to ask twice." She slapped his arm. "Let's blow some fuses."

A flash of excitement filled Colleen. Steve was going to perform by the looks of it. He needed the distraction. It would be great for him and everyone else.

"Give me a moment to collect myself, yeah?" Steve said. "I'm a little fried."

"Deena!" Vernon shouted from behind the bar. He was holding up his wristwatch and pointing to it.

Deena gave him a dismissive wave and turned to Steve. "We'll wing the first one while you get yourself together." She trotted back to the stage, hopped up, got behind the drum kit, picked up her sticks, hit the high hat four times, and set the band roaring into a number with the bass player Finn doing his best to carry the vocals.

Shots came and disappeared. Vernon was applying liquid pressure. Steve had two. Even Colleen found herself downing one.

"Right," Steve said, as the song rounded into the last chorus. "Here goes nothing." He winked at Colleen, pushed himself off the bar. "Wish me luck."

"You don't need it, Steve," she said. "You've got more talent than the law allows."

"That'll do."

"I do have a request, though," she said.

He stopped. "Name it."

"'Shades of Summer.'"

He gave a smile. "I reckon you're the only one besides my mum who likes that one."

"It used to be my shower song," she said.

"You sang *my* song in the shower?"

She gave him a smirk and slurred, "Are you asking me about my shower habits, dude?"

"I think you actually brought it up. But now I'm curious."

Her face grew warm. How did one flirt with a onetime rock god? "So I did."

"Are you any good?"

"What? In the shower?"

Now it was his turn to grin. "*Singing.*"

"I'm hot," she said. And for some reason, that seemed pretty funny. They both laughed.

The band with no name's number came to a crashing end. There was adequate applause. Vernon was looking at Steve. The crowd was looking at Steve. Deena was looking at Steve.

"Get up there, already," Colleen said.

Steve slammed his empty shot glass on the edge of the bar. It fell off and crashed on the floor. Vernon scowled. Steve turned. "Out of my way, you bastards!" He pushed his way through the crowd, leapt up onstage like a cat, and did a staggering bow to hoots and hollers. He unhooked the mic and held it up to his glistening lips.

Deena pounded out an intro. And then Steve was leaning back, howling at the ceiling like a wolf.

The evening quickly turned into a blur. People bought Colleen drinks, seeing she was with Steve. The crowd was spending freely. Vernon was happy. She did her best to forget about getting Steve's money back. All in good time. She had the one and only Steve Cook singing for her.

A few songs in, Steve stopped, caressed the microphone. "And now, if I might beg your kind indulgence, I'd like to bring someone special up here to help us out with her favorite shower song."

Colleen froze.

"Come on, Colleen," Steve said. "Opportunity knocks."

She shook her head *no*.

"I think she needs a bit of encouragement, yeah?" Steve said to the crowd.

The audience started clapping.

What the hell. Colleen tossed back a Wild Turkey, set the shot glass on the slippery bar, making a point not to let it slide off. She turned, the room half a step behind her, and the sea of patrons parted as she negotiated her way to the stage.

Steve reached down, helped her up.

"This way." Finn the bass player stepped aside so she could use his mic. He gave her a friendly smile.

"You're in trouble now," she said.

"What key?" Finn asked.

"How the hell do I know?" Colleen said, noting the many people out there, watching. "Whatever the record is, I guess."

Steve turned back to the audience. "This is for all you punters out there who still think love has a chance."

And they broke into a song that had carried Colleen through some bad times. And when her part came to sing the chorus, she did just fine. She wasn't sure how it happened; it just did.

*   *   *

Colleen and Steve walked—*staggered*—back to Steve's, arm in arm, still humming, ears buzzing. The Mission was alive with people, the lights of little restaurants and bars twinkling in the alcoholic haze.

"Not half bad," Steve said.

"You were frigging great, Steve," Colleen said.

"I was talking about you." She squeezed his arm.

They passed an elderly Latina selling roses out of a plastic bucket on the corner next to a liquor store on 20th. Steve stopped to buy one, over-tipped the Señora who thanked him in Spanish.

He presented the rose to Colleen as they walked, in drunken lockstep.

She gave him a curious look, wondering if it meant what a rose usually meant.

"I always buy a rose from her," Steve said, seeming to catch her thought. "But tonight, there's someone to give it to."

She sniffed the flower as they turned down 20th, heading for Steve's apartment. The rose was sweet and rich.

Steve broke out a cigarette, lit it up. "No one special in your life, Colleen?"

"Who has the time?" she said.

"There's usually time for the right person."

"Then I guess I'm not the right person."

"I'm surprised men aren't beating a path to your door."

The only one who had been beating a path wasn't a man. But it wasn't right for her.

"I'm a loner," she said. "It's easier. Besides, isn't that the way it is these days?"

Steve exhaled. "You're asking the wrong person, love."

"Okay," she said. "Your turn."

"No one right now," Steve said, "if that's what you're asking."

She laughed. "Sorry. In my line of work, I'm just naturally nosy." But the truth was, she *did* want to know. She didn't like many guys, especially since her ex, but she liked guys like Steve. Along with a million other women, she bet.

"Deena and I had a brief thing, but nothing screws up a good band like musicians screwing each other. And a good drummer is harder to come by than sex. Thankfully, we both saw it at the same time."

She wondered if that was the case. "You have such a way with words."

"Yeah," he said, smoking. "I'm a regular Oscar Wilde."

"Since we're being so inquisitive, Steve, I've got another one for you."

"Shoot."

"What the hell happened?"

"What do you mean, love?"

"With your career? One day I'm a teenager of twenty-two singing 'Shades of Summer' in the shower, along with half the girls in the U.K., next day—*bam*—Stevie Cook is history."

His face lost its smile. "You're kidding me, right?"

"Uh, no. Not at all."

"You mean, you don't know?" A frown extended across his mouth.

She started. "Should I?"

Steve shook his head.

She sensed she had stepped in it. "I had a change of plans that seemed to take up my entire life around that time," she said. "I got pregnant when I was sixteen. Got married. *Had* to get married. My girl was about eight. My ex was intolerable. Guess I stopped reading *Tiger Beat*. So no, I don't know what happened to your career."

"Well," he said. "You're about the only one who doesn't."

She'd hit a nerve. The mood turned sour. She felt like a doorknob.

"I'm good at that," she said wistfully. "I'm always the last to find out." She was the last to learn about her ex. "Sorry, Steve."

"No biggie," he said solemnly as they walked. "Just something I'm not proud of."

As they got closer to his apartment, she was keeping an eye out for the driveway. As each car passed, she checked for a black BMW sedan.

They got to his doorstep.

"Well," Colleen said. "I'll leave you here. There's a lot we need to take care of—as far as your situation goes with Lynda and Melanie—but that can wait until tomorrow. But once they know that you know about their scam, which should be soon, we need to be on our toes. You've also got the moneylenders from hell to consider. I've got an idea there."

Steve looked a bit surprised.

"Come in for a drink, yeah?" he said.

She thought about it for all of one second. "Sure."

He dropped his cigarette on the sidewalk, stepped it out. "I'm not planning anything nefarious, love. But you did forget your album."

She felt like an idiot and covered it up with a laugh.

A few moments later they were indoors, jackets off, and he was pouring a couple of scotches in the kitchen. He came into the living room, handed her a drink.

The cheap little radio next to his toolbox was oozing some late-night Latin music.

They stood, clinked glasses.

"Thanks again," he said. "For Mel." His face darkened when he drank. The situation was still eating at him.

"I imagine Lynda's father's seen your paperwork by now."

"Rex?" he said. "Yeah, I bet he has."

"Which means Lynda probably knows, too."

He drank. "I'm hip."

"I hope you're ready."

"Oh," he said. "I'm ready, all right."

"What does that mean, Steve?"

"Nothing."

Nothing. There was no such thing, as far as she was concerned.

"Change the locks," she said. "Soon."

"Right," he said, sipping scotch.

She couldn't remember when she had drunk so much booze. She had reached some kind of strange level of enhanced drunken consciousness.

They stared at each other.

A little voice spoke to her: *go ahead.*

"Why are we standing?" She went to the sofa, pulled the plastic cover to one side, sat down, patted the sofa cushion next to her.

"All right, then," he said.

He sat down next to her.

She kicked her shoes off. Twiddled her toes.

Turned to look at him. Inches away. Gave him a little leer.

She said, "If I hadn't come in for a drink, what would you be doing right now?"

He took a sharp intake of breath. His eyes narrowed. "I guess I'd be thinking about you in the shower—singing 'Shades of Summer,' of course."

She finished her drink, set it down on the floor. She sat back up, unbuttoned the top button of her blouse. Her face was getting warm. Her groin was getting warm. She glanced at his. Yeah, he was, too. "You keep coming back to that shower thing."

"It's an image that just won't seem to go away."

"So you *were* being nefarious."

He gave a crooked smile. "It's not easy to lie to an investigator, is it?"

"It's certainly not wise. Now you owe me." She undid another button.

He eyed that motion, set his drink down on the floor, moved over to her, put his arm around her, stroking her hair, gently. His rough laborer's hands were calm, gentle. Just like the way he sang, tough and tender at the same time.

He leaned in, started nuzzling her neck. She could feel his warm lips, soft, but firm, as he drew her collar to one side.

She unbuttoned more buttons, pulling him down to her breasts, although it didn't take much encouragement. He couldn't seem to get enough of her as she arched forward, unhooked her bra, and that was just fine. And then she unfastened her pants, lifted her butt, slipped the jeans down, kicked them off on the floor while his workingman's hands roamed all over her, her hips, her thighs, on the outside of her panties at first, which were moist now, then inside, gently finding her spot. Applying sweet pressure. Hitting it just right.

*   *   *

She woke in the middle of the night in his bed, nude and exhausted in the best way possible. She looked over at Steve, facedown, head buried in a pillow, purring away. The sheet and blankets were twisted around his midriff. He had a hard, muscular build, maybe a pound or two to lose, but he carried them well. She had wiped him out in the sack and, for the first time in a week, she bet he was sleeping like a baby. She smiled at herself. She felt pretty damn good, too. Mission accomplished.

Her head was still buzzing. Music, drink, sex. She could get used to it.

She pulled the sheet up over him, climbed out of the sloshing waterbed. Nature called. Clothes were all over the floor in a tangle, leading up to the bed. She stepped over them, down the hall to the bathroom. Afterwards, she went into the kitchen, drank a long glass of water, ran another. She'd had enough drink to numb a small town and didn't need a hangover to match it. Her head was throbbing, but still in a nice way. She leaned against the cool tile edge of the countertop, feeling about as a free as a satisfied body without clothes can feel.

Time off for good behavior.

She raised the glass of water to her lips and drank.

And then, she heard a key slide into the lock of the front door.

CHAPTER TWENTY

In the darkened kitchen Colleen set her glass of water down on the counter quietly, listened to the front door unlocking, the sound reverberating through the house without walls. Her heart quickened.

The clock on the kitchen wall, visible in the moonlight coming through the window over the sink, told her it was past four in the morning.

Now her nakedness, freeing before, felt like a vulnerability, cold and prickly.

"Who's there?" she said, peering down the long hallway. But she had a good idea.

She saw the outline of a woman in a fluffy coat.

"What the *fuck*?" she heard Lynda say.

Colleen ducked into the hallway, into Steve's bedroom, quickly pulling on her bell-bottom jeans commando style. She threw on her shirt. Steve was still facedown, snoring, lights out.

She reached over, shook his shoulder. "Lynda's here," she whispered. He responded with an unconscious groan. "Get up!" Colleen headed back out, buttoning up her blouse.

Lynda appeared in the hallway to the bedroom.

"I might have fucking known," she said.

Colleen blocked her path, hands on her hips.

"I think you better leave," she said, adrenaline pumping her awake. "Now."

"Oh, you do, do you?" Something was in Lynda's hand. A hammer. She must have pulled it from Steve's tools.

It came at Colleen in a blur. Hit her shoulder. To say it didn't hurt would have been a lie. She stifled a yell, bounded off the wall. A photo in a frame crashed to the floor.

"You fucking *whore*!" Lynda shouted. The hammer came at her again.

Colleen deflected the hammer this time with an upraised forearm. That hurt, too. Lynda's enraged face swooped in.

Colleen recalled a fight she had witnessed in the showers in Denver Correctional Women's Facility. She spit into Lynda's face with all the force and saliva she could muster.

It had the desired effect. Lynda recoiled, dropping the hammer, which bounced off the floor as she grabbed at the spittle on her face. "Why, you *dirty* fucking *bitch*!"

Colleen lunged at her, grabbed a thick handful of blond hair with her left hand, yanked it like a rope, bringing Lynda's face straight into her fist. Not hard enough to break her nose, but enough to show she meant business. Lynda howled, and Colleen held onto her hair, pulling her down to the rough floorboards. All fights went to the ground. Another thing she learned in prison.

While Lynda was twisting, Colleen retrieved the hammer. She let go of her hair. A good chunk of it was loose and fell to the floor.

Colleen stood back. She set the hammer on an open joist.

Lynda gasped.

"Stay down," Colleen said. "I'm going to search you now. Don't move. Unless you really want to get hurt."

Lynda stayed down, sprawled, seething with hard breaths while Colleen patted her down. Clean. Colleen stood up and back.

"Can I fucking sit up now?" Lynda growled.

"Slowly," Colleen said, standing back, feeling her shoulder where the hammer had connected. She hoped nothing was broken. It didn't seem like it, but it throbbed with an ominous ache.

Out of the corner of her eye, she saw Steve in a pair of jeans, nothing else.

"What the hell, Lynda?" he said in a hoarse voice.

Lynda climbed off the floor, feeling her nose. "Bitch fucking tore my hair. *Bitch!*"

"What did you expect?" Colleen said. "Flowers?"

Steve had a cigarette going. Colleen wanted one herself.

"What do think you're playing at now, Lynda?" Steve said.

"'*Piss Off*'?" she said. "*That's* your answer? To Dad's agreement? After he offered to bail us out? Seriously? What are you trying to do? Get Mel fucking killed?"

Steve took a puff. "Your little game is up, Lynda."

"Fuck you." Lynda's face hardened. "Lucky for you, I spoke to Dad, and he's willing to give it another shot. It wasn't easy, believe me. But we're running out of time."

Colleen shook her head, amazed at the woman's ability to lie. Steve brushed past the two of them, headed into the living room, such as it was, flicked on the overhead light. He returned with a photo—one of the two Colleen had given him showing Mel on Ebony. He handed it to Lynda.

Lynda took it, looked it over. Colleen saw her face fall, but she recovered quickly. Lynda looked up at Steve, mouth open, appropriately shocked.

"It's Mel," Steve said. "On a horse."

"Oh my God," Lynda said, eyeballing the pic again. "Where is she?"

Colleen couldn't help but laugh out loud.

"What do you think you're laughing at, bitch?" Lynda snapped.

"You," she said. "You're good."

Lynda ignored her. She shook the photo. "Where is she, Steve?"

"Christ, Lynda—enough. You know where. You had Ebony delivered to some place in Olema, yeah? A little reward, was it? For playing along with the 'kidnap'?"

Lynda's face hardened. "If you know where she is, asswipe, you better come clean."

"I just told you," Steve said. "No one is holding her hostage. She's quite content, it seems." He raised his eyebrows. "Now, the question is, where's my twenty grand? Plus, the interest I owe."

Lynda stood there for a moment. Her eyes slitted. "Fuck you, Jack," she said, tossing the photo on the floor. "You haven't heard the last of this."

"That's funny," Steve said. "That's exactly what I was going to say to you."

Lynda shot daggers at Colleen as she turned for the door. "Is this how you work? Fuck your clients?"

"I think of it as a fringe benefit."

Lynda spun, headed for the door.

Steve spoke: "I expect Mel to be home, your place, safe and sound, by tonight, Lynda."

Lynda opened the door. She turned, glaring at Steve. "You sad, fucking loser. You could have had it all. You could have had John Lennon singing on your albums. But no, you had to go and kill that bimbo in a drunken orgy, blow it all to hell. Then you ran away. Threw it all away."

Steve's face dropped, the cigarette smoldering in his hand like an afterthought. "That's a low blow, Lynda. You know that's not the way it happened. It was a bloody accident."

"Your whole life is a *bloody* accident," Lynda said. She shook her head. "Dad tried to help you, but no. You had to cut your nose to spite your face. You think your music is something special? It's prod-uct, Steve, that's all it is, and you won't even leverage what little you've got left. You drove us to this. What we did with Mel is your fault. *Your* fault. Loser."

"Get out."

"I tried to rebuild you. Rebuild your career. Even married you, to pump up your little boy ego. Do you think I could ever love a sad sack like you? You just don't have what it takes. Even your own daughter laughs at you. You miserable piece of shit."

Steve's face was hardening on the outside but crumbling inside.

"That's enough," Colleen said. "What Steve says about Melanie being home tonight—that holds." She raised her eyebrows.

Lynda gave an angry gasp. "She'll be home." She turned to Steve. "But you'll never see her again. She'll be happy about that. So chalk up one good thing to come out of this."

Lynda slammed the door behind her, and they could hear her stomping down the front stairs.

Steve stood there, in just his jeans, staring at nothing. A desolate frown slackened his face. Colleen felt for him, humiliated and be-trayed by someone he had once loved, and still seemed to carry a torch for. He flicked ash off his cigarette onto the floor absentmindedly.

CHAPTER TWENTY-ONE

"We'll touch base later today, Steve?" Colleen said.

The sun was a hint of light in the east, creeping up Steve's kitchen window.

He nodded, blinking in thought.

"Good," Colleen said, placing her empty coffee cup in the sink. She felt both exhausted and fortified, not necessarily a bad thing, if you took Lynda out of the equation. It was just a shame that what had happened last night between her and Steve had to be marred by Lynda's visit. Her shoulder hurt but it wasn't enough to outweigh the sex.

What mattered most right now was straightening out Steve's money situation.

Steve leaned against the kitchen counter. He had dressed and composed himself and had recovered somewhat from Lynda's verbal tirade.

Colleen slipped on her bomber jacket. "Once we clean this up, the sooner you can put it all behind you, Steve."

"That's what I keep telling myself."

She gave him a cautious smile. Her times with men, since her ex, had been few. But each one had been special. Steve, especially. She came over to him by the sink, gave him a soft peck on the cheek.

"Call me if you hear something. If I'm not home, leave a message with my answering service."

"Will do," he said.

She raised her eyebrows. "We'll figure out your twenty K. Plus interest."

"Thanks, love."

There, he said it again. Just an expression to him. But not for her.

"*Ciao*." She turned, headed for the door.

"Hold up, Colleen." She heard him going to the back of the house.

She turned back, happy for the little extra time with him.

Steve came out of the hallway, holding an album.

"Hell, yes." She took the album, looked at a younger Steve, and read his dedication.

Colleen—Thanks for everything and more . . . Steve.

"Wow," she said, knocked a little bit sideways. "Can I retire off this?"

He gave a playful frown. "If you're planning on dying the next day."

"It doesn't matter," she said. "I'm never going to get rid of it anyway."

He gave her a tired but happy wink.

She went home, in high spirits, yet still conflicted. She didn't like the way Steve was brooding, although he had every right to.

CHAPTER TWENTY-TWO

The morning sun was glowing gray above the fog on Potrero Hill as Colleen turned right on Vermont, driving past her front door lobby, looking around for a white van, one that had been parked there the other day.

No van.

She drove around the block and pulled into the dirt parking lot behind her building. She locked up, grabbed her copy of *that album,* took the exterior stairwell up to her flat on the third floor. The old wood stairs creaked under her footsteps. She had mixed feelings about the separate entrance, which had been added long after the century-old building had been constructed; it allowed her a small deck off the kitchen and provided an alternative exit in the case of fire or earthquake but, by the same token, also afforded an extra source of vulnerability.

On the third-floor deck, she unlocked the door to the porch off the kitchen, let herself in. The flat was cold. She listened for a moment, as she always did, then checked the place out. Paranoia ran deep, especially nowadays. She flicked on the heat.

Last night with Steve was one to remember.

Leave it that way.

After her disastrous marriage, that was the way Colleen kept things with the opposite sex. Simple.

A quick shower rinsed off last night. Colleen dressed in fresh black 501s, purple turtleneck, sneaks, threw on her beat-up brown bomber jacket. She peered through the Venetian blinds onto Vermont Street and saw no van parked.

She needed to deal with Lynda, Lynda's father, and anyone else gunning for Steve. She'd start with Lynda. Try to see that Steve got his money back before he got his legs broken.

She called Lynda's house, got no answer. She wasn't surprised. Lynda might well be on her way up to Olema to get Melanie, now that the kidnap ruse was blown.

Colleen needed to make sure, though.

She grabbed her special hardback copy of *Pride and Prejudice*, took the back stairs down to the Torino, and headed over to Lynda's house on Colon one more time.

No one was home, judging by the single light in the living room.

She left the car running, got out, pressed the door buzzer outside on the brick wall, where there was an intercom.

No answer.

She went back and parked down the street a ways, where she could watch the house.

Hours later, midafternoon, up on Colon Avenue, she saw what she was hoping for: Lynda's BMW turning into the driveway. Colleen turned down KGO radio, picked up her binos.

Lo and behold, there was Melanie Cook, sitting in the passenger seat, face grim like she was going to a public hanging. Like mother, like daughter. But she was home safe, and that's what mattered. Colleen set the field glasses down on the passenger seat, picked up her book, checked around, rearview mirror, too. Nothing. It amazed her how little people actually noticed what went on in their own neighborhoods.

She opened the book, which had been hollowed out to hold the black Bersa Piccola .22 Moran had slipped her on a recent job. None too legal, but you couldn't have everything. She tucked the compact gun in the pocket of her jacket, got out of the Torino, locked it up. Headed up to Lynda's at a brisk pace.

The driveway gate was already shut. She pressed the door buzzer on the outside wall.

The intercom crackled.

"Who is it?" Lynda snapped over the tinny speaker.

"Colleen Hayes."

There was a pause while a click of static filtered over the speaker.

"I don't fucking believe it," Lynda said.

"Believe it. We need to talk."

"No, bitch, we most certainly do not."

"Then I guess I go to the cops instead, bring them up to date with everything that's transpired. How's Ebony?"

She waited for a moment. The gate buzzed open.

Colleen walked up the brick path to Lynda's front door, hands in her bomber jacket, one gripping the Bersa in case Lynda decided to go fetch the baby-blue LadySmith Colleen had seen next to her vibrator in the bedside table. She hadn't seen the house from this angle up close, having broken in through the side door by the garage, and it was smart. Mock Tudor. 1920s.

The front door opened as she stepped up on a brick porch.

Lynda stood there in beige toreador slacks and black flats and an angora sweater, fuming. But unarmed.

"Nice place," Colleen said, entering the rich hallway. The house had been cleaned up since the last time Colleen had "visited."

"Go to hell," Lynda said, shutting the front door with a push. She came into the house, stood in front of Colleen, legs apart, hands on her hips. "What do you fucking want?"

Colleen noticed Melanie, standing at the top of the stairs, in her green barn coat, black pants tucked into riding boots. She stared at Colleen with hard little eyes. Colleen felt for her, even though she might have willingly taken a horse over her father. Being Lynda's offspring would be a challenge for anyone, let alone a child.

Colleen nodded to acknowledge her, spoke to Lynda: "You sure you want her to hear what I'm about to say?"

Lynda turned to Melanie. "Go to your room, sweetie."

"God!" Melanie glared at Colleen for a moment, stormed off.

Lynda turned back to Colleen. "Spit it out."

"As you know, I'm working for your ex."

"More than working, from what I saw."

"You, and whoever you're working with, owe him $27,000."

Lynda smiled, not a nice smile. "How the hell do you figure that?"

"The twenty K 'ransom' that was collected, plus seven grand interest."

Lynda made a face. "Seven fucking grand? I know Steve isn't that fiscally savvy, but he's borrowing money from the wrong people."

"He didn't want to borrow it from your father and lose his catalog, so he went with some shysters. And they aren't going to wait for long."

"Sounds like Steve's got problems, then, doesn't it?"

"Well, his problems are yours now. That's why you're going to pay him back."

"Babe, I don't know how to tell you this—but you and Steve're shit out of luck."

"Don't tell me you don't have it."

"I do not." Lynda gave a sneer. "Maybe you can go ply your trade down on Mission . . . at ten bucks a pop it might take a while, but with your experience, you'll get there, eventually."

Colleen's hand came out of her jacket so fast it surprised even her. She smacked the side of Lynda's face hard, knocking her sideways. Lynda staggered, caught her balance, grabbed her face, looked at Colleen with genuine surprise. "Why, you goddamn *bitch*!"

Colleen thought about dragging Lynda upstairs, checking the safe. But that would be admitting that she was the one who broke in the other day.

If Lynda had the money, she'd return it.

Colleen got one of her business cards, set it on a sideboard, next to a cloisonné vase. "If I don't hear from you by noon tomorrow, I go to the police."

Lynda's face dropped. "I don't have it."

"Then get it from whoever does. Like your father."

Lynda's face went white as she took a deep breath. "He doesn't have it."

"Then who does?"

"It's complicated."

"Meaning what? The thugs who ripped me off ripped you off, too?"

Lynda looked at her with a plaintive frown. What a mess.

"Work on it," Colleen said.

"I'll try."

"It's going to have to be a little better than *try*."

"Maybe I can get the twenty."

That was a start. But now it was Colleen's turn to shake her head. "It's twenty-seven. You kicked off this little stunt so you can clean it up. And then I forget going to the police."

Lynda stood, lips pursed, blinking rapidly. Colleen looked at Melanie at the top of the stairs again, staring over the banister. She looked confused.

"Do you have any idea what's going on?" Colleen asked her.

"Leave her out of this," Lynda said.

Colleen turned back to Lynda. "Then pay Steve back."

Melanie gave a guilty look, stormed off.

Colleen turned, opened the front door, and left.

She was good and hungry now. But she'd stop at a pay phone first, call Steve, let him know the news.

CHAPTER TWENTY-THREE

"The good news is, Melanie's home," Colleen told Steve from the outdoor pay phone. The attendant was gassing up her Torino at the Shell station on San Jose Avenue, checking the oil. Premium was almost seventy cents. At this rate, the fill-up was going to cost close to fifteen bucks. Regular gas ran a dime cheaper, but the Torino struggled with it and No Lead, which they were pushing these days, made the big block V8 ping and knock. The writing was on the wall for muscle cars. A light drizzle fell into the afternoon air.

"The end of a painful episode," she heard Steve say. He sounded relieved, but there was still that measure of anger in his voice. She could understand. She just didn't want him to act on it.

"Next step," she said, "is your twenty K, plus interest. I'm working on it." The less Steve knew about the details, and her visit to Lynda, the better.

"What do I do, love?"

"Stay well away from Lynda until all of this is settled."

"You shouldn't have to shoulder everything."

"That's what you're paying me for."

"I keep forgetting that."

"Don't worry, I'll send you a bill when this is all done."

There was a pause. "I'd like to see Mel."

"She's okay, Steve. Take it from me. But heed my advice and stay away until the dust settles."

There was another pause. "Yeah," he said, finally. "Okay, then."

"And do me one more favor?"

"What's that?" he said quietly. She wondered if he was thinking what she was thinking. About last night. But, as they said, business and pleasure don't mix. Or, if they did, they probably shouldn't. Not too often.

"Get your locks changed today," she said.

"Another one of your brilliant ideas," he said. He had such an adorable way of talking, she didn't think she could stand it. But he was too *laissez faire* about things that could turn dangerous. She watched the attendant check the dipstick.

"Has Octavien Lopes been putting pressure on you for the money?"

"Let me worry about that."

"It blows me away how easygoing you are about getting your leg broken. This is serious, Steve."

"He called again. Well, one of his toadies did. Some charming little fella named Chepe. Actually, he dropped by. With some guy with one big eyebrow."

Her heart sunk. "Subtle."

"Ya." She heard Steve suck on a cigarette.

She took a deep breath. "Here's to getting it taken care of soon."

"Did you talk to Lynda or something?"

She thought about making something up but didn't want to lie to him. "I suppose I did."

"Without talking to me first?" His voice turned cold.

"I don't want to see you in traction at SF General. The less you and Lynda have to do with each other until this is all taken care of, the better. I'm the one who let the bag guy snag the money down at the Transbay Terminal, so I'm straightening this mess out." Including taking care of whoever else was involved.

She heard him puff on his cigarette. "I would've preferred being consulted about it first, though, yeah?"

"Next time." Maybe.

On the forecourt, she heard the attendant slam the hood of her car.

"Got to go," she said. "My car's blocking a gas pump."

She heard him take another drag. "It was nice last night. Until the *trouble and strife* showed up."

"It was," she said in a soft voice.

"I'd like to get to know you better, Coll."

"Likewise," she said. "But this isn't a good time—for either of us."

"Why?"

"Because, for the moment, you're still a client. With a number of balls in the air that need to be caught and dealt with. Besides, I'm not sure you know what you'd be letting yourself in for. I've got a skeleton or two in my closet."

"Join the club," he said. "But it doesn't make any difference to me."

A warm rush rolled over her. "That's the nicest thing anyone has said in a long time, Steve," she said, "and I should probably have my head examined for saying this, but can we leave it up in the air for now—like everything else in your life?"

He laughed. "Sure." Then, "By the way, *the band with no name* is playing The Pitt again tonight. And I've got a private eye to pay. I can put you on the guest list."

"Probably not. But thanks for the invite."

"Fair enough. I'll catch you later, love."

"Ciao."

She called Owens, explained the situation. It took some time.

"So, the whole thing was a ruse?" he said incredulously.

"To finagle Steve's catalog. Bottom line, Melanie Cook is back home."

"Well, some guy with no name is in the morgue because of it," Owens said. "So Lynda Cook and her crew aren't off the hook. Meanwhile I'm notifying Missing Persons to check on the kid. Close the report."

"You do what you need to."

Back home, Colleen found herself in that rare situation when working a case: time to kill. She wouldn't hear back from Lynda until tomorrow, if she heard anything at all. She couldn't call Moran without a good reason because there was Daphne to contend with. She hadn't heard from Alex and there were no new messages from her answering service.

She wouldn't go see Steve perform at The Pitt tonight; she needed to give things a break. But she did need to know more about his past. Why had he fallen from stardom so rapidly? What had Lynda been talking about when she let loose on Steve last night?

The main library on Van Ness stayed open late. Colleen drove down, parked by the Civic Center.

Once inside, she worked her way through the card indexes. Then she realized, one way or another, she was going to spend the evening with Steve after all.

CHAPTER TWENTY-FOUR

When Colleen sat down at a microfiche machine in the public library and read the article "Rocker Runs" from the London *Daily Mirror*, April 1966, things began to make sense. Once the shock passed.

At first, she found it hard to believe a man like Steve would run from a situation like that. But she got it. He was a kid at the time and the prospects of an underage girl dying in his hotel room bed—*nude*, as the papers kept pointing out—was not something the world took kindly to. Even so, nothing made Colleen feel he had done anything truly underhanded. His guitarist, and childhood friend, maintained Steve never used drugs and abhorred them. He was a boozer, and that seemed to be it. He was a decent guy. Any way one looked at it, the event was a tragedy for all parties involved, for the poor girl who died, her family, and Steve, who paid for it many times over. His career was eviscerated, and he became an outcast. All in one single night. He soon fled France, where he'd initially run, to Brazil. In Rio, he met a young American record exec on vacation by the name of Lynda Morris. The two hit it off, marrying on the beach after a whirlwind romance, allowing Steve U.S. residence. He had also established Brazilian citizenship so that he could escape extradition should he move elsewhere. He came to the U.S. with his new bride in 1967. The case in the U.K. had been filed as Death by

Misadventure, but the British authorities still wanted to talk to him. But he was safe enough if he kept his head down and didn't return to the U.K. Shame was his punishment.

His new wife, Lynda, made futile attempts to secure Steve a new recording contract. But no one would touch him. His money was gone. He worked construction. Melanie came along, but she wasn't enough to save Steve and Lynda's marriage. The two divorced. Lynda came into perspective as Colleen saw a woman who had believed in Steve, trying to revive his decimated career to no avail. And Lynda's anger at Steve, although certainly not justifiable, bore a slightly different context now.

Colleen put Steve to one side and did some research on The Lost Chords, Delco records, and even found a couple of minor articles in *Variety* about the ongoing lawsuit over rights to Steve's catalog.

That gave her an idea. She went to the periodicals section, dug out the latest copies of *Variety*.

There was an article at the bottom of page 17 of a recent issue that caught her eye. "Shades of Summer. Again." The song Colleen loved. A Hollywood director was quoted as saying it would make an ideal song for an upcoming RomCom—Romantic Comedy. Unlike the Chords' other songs, all firmly rooted in foot-stomping rock 'n' roll, "Shades of Summer" predicted the *Summer of Love* and sounded it, full of jangly guitars, phased drums, and ethereal vocals. Sure, it was just another pop song, but it was ahead of its time. Steve called it silly and downplayed it, but it was clear he had been growing as an artist, and it made his rapid exit all the more heartbreaking.

Now she understood why Steve refused to let his music go. Even at the cost of borrowing mob money from Octavien Lopes.

She drove home, feeling wiser but glum, and circled the block before she pulled into the lot, looking for a white van, or anyone out to do her harm. She found none.

Up in her flat, she called her answering service. No new messages.

This was what they called a quiet evening at home. She wondered what Alex was up to.

She poured a glass of wine, dimmed the lights, fired up the stereo, and got out her precious album, autographed by the guy who sang it, the same guy who was in serious trouble if his ex or her dad didn't come across with $27,000. She cleaned the record off with the disc-washer and put it on the turntable and set the tonearm down carefully on side two. Very few crackles for an album over ten years old.

She couldn't help but wonder what other connection existed between Steve's demise as an artist in 1966 and his current situation. Delco Records was hovering in the background. There was the news in *Variety* about an upcoming RomCom. Lynda's father was in the movie business. Coincidence?

She sat back, lit a Virginia Slim, and took a sip of Pinot Noir as the guitars chimed in the intro to "Shades of Summer."

CHAPTER TWENTY-FIVE

By late afternoon the next day, Colleen still hadn't heard from Lynda. She hadn't heard from anybody. At one point, she picked up the phone just to check for a dial tone, make sure the thing still worked. Her answering service, likewise, had no new messages. Outside, the fog had given way to soft rain.

She called Lynda's house. No answer.

How could Colleen have gotten it so wrong? She had really thought Lynda was going to come through with some money. There was the threat of SFPD.

So much for intuition. She slipped on her bomber jacket over a white T-shirt and jeans. She'd make one more attempt to convince Lynda to do the right thing.

She checked the window out front on Vermont. No white van lurking.

She got her junior burglar tool kit and headed over to Lynda's house on Colon Avenue.

No lights were on as she drove by. No car in the driveway. Odd.

She parked down on Monterey, got her PG&E hard hat, clipboard, threw on a plastic raincoat, headed up to Lynda's house with her bag of tools. Rang the front bell on the gate, just to make sure Lynda wasn't home. No answer.

The squeal of small wheels caught her attention. Colleen turned her head slightly to see a young woman in a scarf pushing a baby carriage.

"Problems?" she asked. She had a high voice.

"No," Colleen replied, looking at her clipboard. "Just a follow-up."

Damn. She waited until the woman moved by.

Colleen followed the same brick wall alongside the house she'd taken the other day when she broke in. She got to the emerald green door. No one at the window of the house next door. She slipped on her gloves.

The lock to the green door to Lynda's yard was still the way she'd left it, broken. Lynda either hadn't noticed or hadn't had time to make repairs. Checking around, Colleen let herself in. The side door to the garage was still easy to pick.

Lynda's black BMW was not in the garage.

Colleen entered the kitchen through the garage quietly, tiptoed in.

No breakfast dishes out, no box of cereal, no carton of milk. A couple of unfinished TV dinners sat on the yellow tile counter. A half-eaten Salisbury steak and a barely-touched Mac & Cheese. Colleen suspected Lynda had the former, Melanie the latter. Lynda Cook, master chef. And even though she owned a snazzy Kenmore dishwasher, none of the dirty dishes in the sink had made it that far.

A half-empty bottle of vodka sat on the kitchen counter, along with a near-empty can of Tab, next to a spanking new Radar Range microwave oven. The latest gadget. It didn't look like anyone had had breakfast, going by Lynda's fastidious kitchen habits.

In the living room, Colleen was surprised to see more disarray. The place had been neat enough yesterday when she stopped by. The stereo was lit, but no music was playing. The crocheted sofa blanket trailed across the floor. The brass floor lamp by the sofa lay on its side, the shade snapped off, halfway across the room, misshapen. A tall glass had spilled off the coffee table onto the rug.

Colleen got on her hands and knees and sniffed. Vodka and Tab would be her guess.

She stood up.

Did Lynda drink herself silly last night, stumble off to bed after trashing the living room? She might have had a rough night, dealing with the pressure of Colleen's twenty-seven-K demand.

Colleen headed up the stairs. And that's when she noticed the movie poster for *Deadly Blessing* lying on the floor of the landing. Glass was broken. Shards lay on the rug below. The frame was cracked.

Colleen heard the murmur of a television upstairs. Coming from Melanie's room?

Maybe someone *was* home.

"Hello?" Colleen said evenly. "PG&E. There was a gas leak reported. Anyone home?"

No response.

She headed up to Melanie's room.

The small TV was on at low volume. The bed was unmade, and clothes and shoes were scattered by the closet. A can of Coke lay spilled across the rug. Not like the room she had seen before.

Colleen went over, turned off the TV.

Something wasn't right. Her heart thumped with anticipation.

She crossed the hall to Lynda's room.

Lynda's bed was unmade, the covers pulled off to one side. No big surprise there, but the side table drawer was pulled open, the drawer that Colleen had opened the other day and discovered a baby-blue-handled pistol and dildo.

She stepped around the bed to investigate.

And jumped when she saw Lynda Cook, twisted and bent, face-down on the floor, in a silk dressing gown barely covering her naked backside. Her blond hair was matted with thick, congealed lumps of blood and brains surrounding an ugly hole in the back of her head. The blue shag rug directly below was a thickening crimson blotch.

Colleen had seen dead bodies in her time, but you never really got used to them. She let her stomach settle. It took a while.

Heart pounding, Colleen squatted down to check Lynda's pulse, knowing she was far too late. Lynda's wrist was stiff and stone cold, even through Colleen's gloves.

As much as she hated the thought, the first person who came to mind was Steve.

CHAPTER TWENTY-SIX

Lynda had been shot at least once from what Colleen could tell. Back of the head. Colleen lifted a lifeless foot. Stiff. Rigor mortis was a variable condition but reached the extremities roughly six hours after death and lasted for up to seventy-two hours afterwards. Meaning Lynda had been killed six-plus hours ago. Colleen had spoken to her yesterday. The state of the kitchen suggested dinner last night but no breakfast.

Lynda was killed last night.

Colleen checked the bedside table drawer, which was wide open. The dildo was still there. The baby-blue-handled LadySmith, however, was not. Some of the contents of the drawer, condoms, a jar of Vaseline, rolling papers, were scattered on the floor, around Lynda's corpse. Someone had retrieved the gun in a hurry. Had Lynda been surprised by an intruder, fought in the living room, run upstairs, knocked the movie poster off the wall on her way, gone for the gun? Had someone struggled with Lynda, taken the gun, shot her with it? Where *was* the gun that had been in Lynda's bedside table?

Lynda's right arm was contorted unnaturally above her head. Colleen got on her hands and knees, nose down to the cold, curled fingers of Lynda's right hand. Amidst the smell of lotion was that odor of burnt plastic with a sweet tinge to it. Smokeless powder. Had Lynda taken a shot at her attacker before she'd been overpowered and shot? With her own gun?

Colleen stood up, taking deep breaths, willing her heart rate to go down. She got out her Polaroid camera. Snapped pictures.

Again, her thoughts turned to Steve. He had been furious with Lynda. Understandably.

But this? Could he?

Standing back, she saw splotches of blood around the foot of the bed. She checked Melanie's room. One spot by the door.

She noticed more dark stains on the way downstairs but not around the sofa, where the initial struggle appeared to have taken place. That told Colleen the killer might have been shot, too, upstairs, on his—or her—way out.

Melanie was gone. Taken? Colleen's heart pulsed with the implications. No blood in Melanie's bedroom. Whoever had been shot might have helped take Melanie. It seemed a distinct possibility. But who? Her thoughts traveled back to the fiasco in the Transbay Terminal. The little guy who snatched the bag was no longer but the big man in the duffle coat was. As was whoever had intercepted the cash on the bike. And, of course, there was Rex Williamson, Lynda's father.

And there was always Steve.

Colleen checked the front door. Shut. No signs of forced entry. No bloodstains this way either.

But there was a chaotic trail of spots leading back through the kitchen, now that she was looking for them, across the wild burnt-orange pattern of the linoleum.

And out to the garage, now she saw, where Lynda's BMW had been parked, one sticky blot by where the trunk would have been, another two by the passenger door.

They had grabbed Melanie, spirited her away in Lynda's car.

Melanie Cook had finally been kidnapped. A deep chill ran through Colleen's guts. What had once been a hoax was now the real thing.

CHAPTER TWENTY-SEVEN

Colleen stopped at the gas station on San Jose Avenue, used the pay phone to dial the operator, asked for emergency police services. She covered the phone with her handkerchief, reported the location of the dead body, told them that Melanie Cook had most likely been kidnapped as well. Hung up.

Then she called SFPD at 850 Bryant, left a message for Inspector Owens. He was handling the John Doe case, the "kidnapper" who had handed the money off before Colleen chased him under a bus. That seemed like weeks ago now, although it was only a few days. Two dead so far. *So far*, Colleen thought, dreading what would transpire now that Melanie looked to be truly abducted. Not long ago, this episode had seemed to be almost over.

Now it was beginning again.

But she could trust Owens, as much as she could trust any cop. And she would tell him what she knew, in exchange for unofficial immunity.

It was around seven fifteen in the evening. She thought about calling Steve. But there was some news you didn't deliver over the phone.

And besides, she needed to see the look on his face when she gave him this particular news. Because maybe, just maybe, he wouldn't be too surprised. And, as much as she didn't like it, she had to accept that he might have had something to do with it.

She drove over to Steve's place, her heart in her throat.

CHAPTER TWENTY-EIGHT

Colleen stepped up onto Steve's porch and rang the bell. No answer. She tried again. Same. She put her ear to the door. Nothing.

She drove over to The Pitt on Mission. Maybe *the band with no name* was playing tonight. They were.

Finn, the bass player, with his signature pompadour and ducktail, was pulling his blue Rickenbacker bass guitar out of a tweed case. Boom, the roadie, was lugging a speaker cabinet onstage as if it were a basket of laundry. He wore his camo jacket and thick-framed glasses.

Steve and Deena were leaning over the bar, near the back hallway, having a tête-à-tête. Steve wore a tight black T-shirt and was tapping ash off a cigarette into a Budweiser ashtray. Deena's shock of black spiky hair stood up. She wore a black tube top, black denim mini, torn fishnets, and hi-top sneakers.

Colleen ventured over. Deena saw her before Steve did. She stood up and stepped back, a few inches away from Steve, as if distancing herself. She gave Colleen a cautious look. Did she know about Steve and Colleen's one-night stand?

Did she know about Lynda?

Steve turned from the bar, a look of surprise on his face. "Oh, hey, Coll. Come to see the show, have you?" He beamed. "Maybe we'll tempt you back up onstage, yeah?" It didn't seem he had any idea of what had transpired over on Colon Avenue.

"Steve," Colleen said, "—we need to talk."

He blinked in concern and flicked more ash into the ashtray. "Alright, love."

Deena rolled her eyes, possibly assuming the conversation was going to be boy-girl stuff between Steve and Colleen. "See you on-stage, Steve," she said with heavy irony, and disappeared.

A flash of awkwardness warmed Colleen's face.

"It's about Melanie, Steve," she said. "And Lynda." She watched his face for clues.

"What?" Steve's mouth grew stiff. It was hard to read. "What about Mel?"

"Let's go outside."

Out in the alley, in the soft San Francisco fog rain, the ever-present kid in the hoodie was nodding off by the dumpster. A couple of leather-clad girls smoking cigarettes and practicing for the Scowling Championships propped up a wall.

Colleen took Steve through the afternoon's events.

He stood, mouth open, dumbstruck.

The forgotten cigarette in his hand shook him awake when it burnt down to his fingers and he flung it loose. The butt bounced off the wet brick wall behind the bar in a flurry of embers.

"*Dead?*" he said in a loud whisper.

Colleen nodded.

"And Mel—*gone?*"

"Looks like for real this time."

"But—*how?*"

She watched his reaction. So far, so good. But stranger things had happened. "I'm guessing it has something to do with Melanie's first 'kidnapping.' I think things might have gone wrong when the scam was exposed. Maybe Lynda had a run-in with someone when it didn't go according to plan."

Steve grimaced. "Fuck, Coll," he said. "What did you do?"

"What did *I* do? Tried to get your damn money back. They were playing you, left you holding the bag with Octavien."

"I can't fucking believe this!" he said, holding his head in both hands.

The two scowler girls we're looking their way now. One smirked, obviously reading the situation as a romantic horror scene.

"Steve," Colleen said. "Get a hold of yourself."

"And you just walked out of there? After you broke in? Left her there, like that? Dead?"

"What was I supposed to do?" Colleen said as quietly as possible. "I called it in. I called Inspector Owens. But no, I wasn't going to stay and wait for the cops and implicate myself."

"Do you even know what you're bloody doing, Colleen?"

She took a deep breath, suppressing her aggravation. "Look, I've gone to bat for you, Steve. You were the one who was walking head-first off a cliff, with Lynda's blessing. You wanted your daughter back. You wanted me in on this."

"And what a boon it's been," he said.

"Okay," she said, staring him in the eyes. "I'm just going to say it. Look me in the face and tell me you had nothing to do with it."

He gawped at her in round-eyed shock. "Are you fucking crazy, Coll? Do you know what you're bloody saying?"

"Just do it." She pointed to her eyes with two fingers. "Look me straight in the eye, tell me you had absolutely nothing to do with Lynda."

He flinched, took another breath, looked away. "This isn't happening."

"Do it, Steve."

He composed himself, looked her in the eye.

"I did *not* do it," he said.

His look was steady, although his head was shaking. But who wouldn't be a wreck?

"If you *did* do it, Steve," she said, "I'll do what I can to see you get a fair shake."

"I didn't fucking touch her, Coll! Yeah, it might have crossed my mind when I saw those photos of Mel on that bloody horse, but I didn't do it. I swear."

She watched his pupils. She thought she knew people, she thought she had a good sense of intuition, but her ex had molested their daughter for close to a year, right under her nose, and she had been clueless. It had shown her that you never really knew what was going on in someone else's mind.

But Steve appeared to be telling her the truth. Appeared.

"Okay," she said.

"Okay? *Oh-bloody-kay?* You accuse me of murder, and I deny it, and that's all you can say now? You're a piece of work, Coll. Maybe you should just go your own way."

"No. It's going to be ten times harder to get Melanie back without you. And I'm getting her back, whatever you do."

She stared into his hardened face until he relented, taking a deep breath.

"Right," he said finally. "Right . . ."

"I found her once before, Steve. I'll find her again."

He frowned. "How do we start?"

"We bring Inspector Owens in."

"No. No way."

"Are you listening to yourself, Steve? Your daughter's gone."

"I hate the fucking cops. Worse, I don't trust 'em. Not with Mel."

"Well, join the club. But if you want my help, they're getting involved. I already called in the murder and possible kidnapping. There's no going back."

Steve frowned while he seemed to think about that. "Whatever."

"Good. Now, we head back to your place. The cops are going to want to talk to you at some point. I suspect you're going to get another phone call, demanding ransom. Or they might make you wait, sweat it out. And we don't even know who *they* are anymore." She made direct eye contact with Steve again. "Do you think Lynda's father is capable of this?"

Steve shook his head. "He's a hard-hearted old bastard, but killing his own daughter? No, I can't see it."

Worse things had happened. But maybe something *had* gone wrong with whoever was helping Lynda and her father extort Steve. Had Lynda stopped playing along with them when the hoax was blown and been shot for it? Maybe someone thought kidnapping Melanie wasn't such a bad idea, after all.

There was a lot she didn't know.

Yet. But right now, time was running out for Melanie.

"Cancel your gig tonight, and let's get back to your place, in case someone's trying to contact you," she said.

"Yeah," Steve said, scratching his head. "Right."

They went back inside The Pitt, wall-to-wall with customers now. Colleen waited by the bar while Steve talked to Deena, who was setting up her drums. Deena's face went from surprise to open-mouthed shock when she looked Colleen's way. Colleen wasn't sure how much she knew. She wasn't sure what anyone knew at this point.

Vernon, the owner of The Pitt, was the least happy about Steve's cancellation. Once he heard the news from Deena, he came swaggering over to Steve, who had rejoined Colleen. Vernon's gut preceded him in an RIP Lynyrd Skynrd T-shirt that poked out of an open leather vest. Three of the band members had died in a plane crash last year.

"Are you *trying* to fuck me up, Steve?" Vernon growled.

"No time to talk now, Vernon. Problems, yeah? Serious problems."

"I thought you were serious about this residency."

"Deena and the boys are going to rock the house."

"People aren't coming to see Finn sing, Steve. They're paying to see you."

"I'm sorry, mate. I'll make it up to you."

Vernon grimaced behind his gray mountain-man beard. "If you walk out that door, man, you're not coming back."

Steve leaned in. "Well, let me tell you something, *man*. I don't give a rat's ass. But if you fuck with Deena and cancel her gigs, you can be damn sure I'll be back to see you." He raised his eyebrows. "Yeah?"

"Is that some kind of a fucking threat, asshole?"

"Yeah," Steve said, pulling on his jacket. "That's exactly what that is."

CHAPTER TWENTY-NINE

Back at Steve's place, Steve checked with his neighbor upstairs to see if anybody had stopped by. One tenant, a young red-eyed Hispanic with a yellow watch cap pulled down tight over his head, reeked of marijuana but didn't recall hearing anybody ringing Steve's doorbell.

Downstairs, Steve paced back and forth, chain-smoking, waiting for the phone to ring. Colleen wondered if it was possible to rent one of those fancy new answering machines. She might just have to buy one and set it up first thing.

It was getting late. If wondering how Melanie was doing, if she were even alive, was eating at her to a point of desperation, what must it be doing to Steve?

She'd just have to compartmentalize, treat the child's disappearance like one more thing to deal with.

"I'm going home," she said to Steve. "I need to make some calls, and we have to leave this phone line clear in case they try to contact you. But you call me first thing you hear something. If my line's busy, call my answering service."

"Right." Steve smashed his cigarette out in the tuna can ashtray. He came over, held her at arm's length. "Don't bail on me now, Coll."

"No way." She still didn't know if she could trust him completely but finding Melanie was the priority and he was key. And, the fact was, she had feelings for him that had nothing to do with his current situation. Those few hours between the sheets had left an indelible imprint. "I'm only just up the hill. I can be over in minutes."

"Yeah," he said, letting her go, looking into her eyes.

"She's going to be okay," Colleen said.

Steve frowned. "Yeah," he said, but it didn't have the conviction she would have liked.

And, the truth was, she wasn't feeling it one hundred percent either.

Back home, Colleen called her answering service. A gruff message from Inspector Owens instructed her to return his call immediately, regardless of time of day. *Immediately.* It was close to ten p.m. She called. And heard the hustle and bustle of a busy office in the background after Inspector Owens answered.

"You're at 850 Bryant," she said.

"What did you expect? You called in a murder! And a kidnapping. And then you left the damn crime scene!"

"I had my reasons."

"Well, you can get down here right now and explain your reasons, or I can put out an APB to have you picked up. Your choice."

"I'm on my way." She hung up, headed back out.

Down at 850, in the same interrogation room she'd sat in the other day after the little guy was run over, Colleen faced Inspector Owens across the same Formica table, now littered with candy wrappers and paper vending machine coffee cups.

Inspector Owens looked weary. His gray crew cut needed a trim. He had bags under his eyes. But his outfit was alive: he'd obviously come in from home at short notice and wore a lime knit shirt with a little alligator on it, tucked into a pair of wild, orange checked flared pants—the checks four inches across. A wide white belt tied it all together.

"Explain," he said, tapping the eraser of a pencil on a yellow lined pad. "Don't leave anything out, or you can enjoy one of our fine community holding cells while we wait to hear from your milquetoast lawyer."

Colleen proceeded to explain the situation from the original call to Steve from the kidnappers up until this afternoon. She told him who her client was, everything.

Owens was stunned.

"I still can't believe you left the body," he said.

"I couldn't hang around. I'm on parole."

"That wasn't your call. This is a now a homicide, *and* a kidnapping, time critical."

Didn't she know it? Every hour Melanie was gone was another light-year. "Lynda was dead. I figured she would probably stay that way for a few more minutes. And that's all it was. Ten minutes, tops, until I called it in."

"You should have called it in immediately."

"Look at it this way: if I hadn't found her when I did, Lynda might still well be there, undiscovered." She raised her eyebrows. "Melanie's disappearance might still be unknown."

"Some might say that makes you look suspicious."

"If I didn't want to be associated with Lynda's murder, why would I even call it in to begin with? Why would I admit breaking in?"

"To cover your ass."

Colleen pulled her pack of Virginia Slims from her bomber jacket, shook one out, pulled it out of the pack with her lips.

"Don't," Owens said.

She paused, removed the cigarette from her mouth, slid it back into the pack. "Fine." She put the cigarettes back in her jacket, sitting with her hands in her jacket pockets now, hunched forward.

"I'm trying to quit," he said.

"I didn't know that," she said. "Sorry."

A moment passed.

"Have you been over there?" she asked. "To Lynda's?"

"My partner is there now. I needed to find out what you're up to while he does that."

Colleen nodded. She handed over a photo of Melanie on the horse at Olema. "Here's a recent photo."

Owens squinted at it. "Any ideas who might have taken her?"

"Someone involved with the first faux kidnapping is my bet. When it didn't pan out the way they wanted, they took over from Lynda and, possibly, her father. Hijacked it."

Owens pursed his lips, tapped his pencil. "Could Lynda's old man have killed her?"

She took a breath, thinking. "I haven't met him, but I'm told he wouldn't kill his own daughter. They were in cahoots, though, trying to steal Steve's catalog."

"The family that kidnaps and extorts together stays together."

"Maybe," she said. "But maybe things went wrong after Lynda pulled the gun, fired it, and was most likely overpowered herself and shot."

"How can you be so sure?"

"These." She pulled her Polaroids of Lynda facedown on her bedroom rug, laid them down, one by one, in front of Owens.

He looked at them, looked up at her, incredulous. "And when were you going to tell me about *these*?"

"I just did."

"You took time to take photos?"

"I'm a private investigator. Collecting information is what I do."

"By breaking into houses and taking illegal crime scene photos."

"Oh—so you don't want them?"

"I didn't say that!"

"I'm trying to help," Colleen said. "The main thing is, put out an APB for Melanie Cook. Anyway, if you look at the one photo, you'll see the disarray of the bedside table. I think Lynda ran upstairs, grabbed her gun, which is now missing, surprised the intruder." Colleen cleared her throat. "Your forensics team should find gunpowder residue on Lynda's right hand."

"Of course. You checked that out, too."

"If you can get a blood type from some of the blood splotches on the rug on the way out of the house, and the kitchen floor, and the garage, they'll be different from Lynda's. Might be the killer's. You can also run them against Steve's." Hopefully, they wouldn't be the same.

Owens examined the photos, nodded. He wasn't going to say "good work," but she could tell he wasn't entirely unhappy with the jump on the information. He sat back, tapped the eraser end of his pencil on the yellow pad. "You think Lynda's ex could have done this?"

"Steve?" She told herself she was past that suspicion. But she had killed her own husband. There were reasons sometimes. And Steve had his.

She shook her head *no*.

"That took you a while," Owens said with a smirk. "You one hundred percent sure about your client?"

"I'm sure. But get him to give you a blood sample anyway."

"Well, from what you say, Cook had every reason. His ex screwing him for money, his catalog, scaring the hell out of him by 'kidnapping' his own daughter."

"No argument there. But Steve is accustomed to Lynda's ways. He was more hurt than anything else at the possible betrayal of his daughter. And he knew I was trying to get Lynda to cough up the ransom money Steve borrowed from some loan sharks. Killing her would have nipped that in the bud. If anything, he'd kill her *after* he got his money back."

Owens grimaced. He knew the reason Colleen spent ten years in prison. "We both know that killing someone out of anger isn't always logical."

"If Steve did it, where's Melanie?" Colleen realized she was clarifying Steve's innocence for herself as much as she was for Owens. She couldn't let her personal feelings for him color things.

Owens gave a nod of confirmation. "Good question. But he could have his daughter tucked away somewhere. To throw off suspicion that he killed his ex."

Colleen thought about that for a moment, shook her head. "It just doesn't fit. He couldn't have done it against Melanie's will. He doesn't have it in him. Look at the effort he went to in order to get her back. And he doesn't get along with Melanie well enough to conspire with her. And where would he put her? No, she's bona fide kidnapped."

"We need to talk to Steve," Owens said. "If he calls you, tell him to stick around, not to take any unplanned trips. Got that?"

"Ten to one Steve gets a ransom call soon anyway."

"If he's telling you the truth."

She didn't answer that. She couldn't see Steve as a murderer, but she also knew she would tend to side with him. Whoever said men were simple creatures didn't know what they were talking about.

"We can put a trace on his line," Owens said. "But that can take a while and can be hit or miss. How do I get in touch with Lynda's father?"

"Rex Williamson. I've got his number." She got out her penny notebook, flipped pages, found Rex's number. She read it off. Owens wrote it down, set his pencil down, looked at her.

"You're welcome," she said, "for all the information."

"That's why I'm not booking you," he said with a wan smile.

"Wow. Thanks."

"You started all this, don't forget. By not coming to us in the first place. But that's done. Now I'm giving you a warning: stay out of this from now on. It's SFPD's case, not yours."

"I hate to lie to you and say 'yes.'"

Owens actually cracked a weary smile. "Are you always so easy to get along with?"

"Just being straight with you."

"Well, then I'll return the favor. If you *do* stick your nose in this case again, after I just told you not to, I won't be so appreciative. You're a PI without a license, and you're still on parole. You don't want a bad report card from me."

She nodded, stood up. "You can keep the photos," she said. "I imagine it will take a while for forensics to get you copies of theirs."

CHAPTER THIRTY

So much for doing the right thing, Colleen thought as she peeled off her jacket, hung it up in the hall closet of her flat.

But she understood Owens. He had come through for her before, and he would again. Just not this time. She kicked off her sneaks, poured a glass of wine, put *that album* on the turntable, set the volume low. Steve's teenage voice came in raw and throaty, like a Mississippi blues man forty years his senior, singing about a river that time couldn't stop. It was late, after midnight. She sat back on her sofa, lit the cigarette she had reinserted in the pack not long ago down at 850 Bryant.

As she smoked, she couldn't help but put herself in Melanie Cook's place. A child she barely knew was going through hell right now—if she were indeed still alive. Once again, Colleen had to pigeonhole that grim fact. Right now, she needed to get to the bottom of things so she could find her.

Steve had been adamant that Lynda's father wouldn't kill his own daughter. She didn't know Rex Williamson. But that's who'd she'd find next, first thing in the morning. He lived in Los Angeles so a trip to SoCal was in the offing.

The phone rang.

Maybe it was Alex. Even though the timing was lousy, Colleen kind of hoped it was. Alex was a good friend and they hadn't spoken in a while.

She answered.

"This is Deena." Her nasal New York accent was unmistakable. The clatter of voices and music filled the background. A bar, some-where like that. "I think I need to talk to you," she said.

It sounded important. "I'm all ears," Colleen said, taking a puff on her Slim.

"No. Not on the phone."

"Then I'll meet you," Colleen said. "Where?"

"All Night Donuts," Deena said. "On Noe." She hung up.

Colleen crushed out her cigarette, stood up, drained her wine. What could Deena want? Something to do with Steve? Colleen threw her jacket back on, left the stereo playing The Lost Chords. The turntable had automatic shutoff.

By 1:00 a.m. she was on 24th and Noe, where All Night Donuts presented a cast of characters who looked like they hung out in all-night donut shops: people sobering up, people grabbing a quick coffee or a snack before heading off somewhere else, people with nowhere else to go. Street people: more and more of them since Colleen moved to SF a year or so ago. The air was a blend of sweet-baked stickiness and warm bodies. "Stayin' Alive" bounced out of the jukebox. Rows of shelves displayed vintage toys, some going back to the 1920s.

Colleen found Deena perched on a stool at the counter, spooning a milkshake out of a huge metal malt cup. She envied skinny women who could eat like that, especially late at night. But then again, from what she knew, musicians ate sporadically. Deena wore the same outfit she'd worn earlier onstage: black denim mini, torn fishnets, black Keds, and now a black leather jacket dripping with chains, spray-painted with band names, none of which Colleen recognized. Colleen sat down on a stool next to her.

Deena spun to her, pulling the long spoon from her mouth. Her hair was still spiked, and her heavy eye mascara was dramatic, drawn to a point on either side of her face, like cats' eyes. But she pulled the look off with room to spare.

"About your phone call," Colleen said.

Deena stuck her spoon in the metal cup.

"It might be nothing," she said.

Colleen shook a cigarette out, offered one to Deena. Deena declined. Colleen lit up. It wasn't nearly as satisfying as a thousand-calorie milkshake.

"Is it about Steve?" Colleen set her spent paper match in an ashtray.

"I feel like a rat."

Colleen took a sip on her cigarette. "Does it have to do with Lynda?"

Deena nodded, looked away.

"Steve told you what happened to Lynda, right?"

Deena turned back, gave an awkward sniff. "Ya," she said, something catching in her throat. "Fucking unbelievable."

Colleen made eye contact. "Is it?"

"I'm not going to say Lynda had it coming," Deena said, "but she didn't do much to endear herself to people. But no, no one deserves *that*."

Colleen's ex had wound up with a screwdriver in his neck, on the kitchen floor, thanks to Colleen. And he had deserved it. "How much has Steve told you?"

"Everything."

"*Everything?*"

"About Melanie?" Deena said. "Her horse? The twenty-seven K? Oh yeah. Steve tells me things. We go back a ways."

"He confides in you."

"We used to have a thing," Deena said, giving Colleen a look. Rubbing it in? "Not anymore, though. But we still talk. Don't worry, you don't have me for competition."

"I'm not worried," Colleen said, wondering how much Deena knew about her and Steve. Deena might be his confidante, but she couldn't imagine he'd kiss and tell.

"Don't take it the wrong way. Most chicks who meet Steve want to go to bed with him."

"Okay," Colleen said. Deena wanted to take Colleen down a notch or two.

Deena patted Colleen's knee. "If you're going to hang with a musician, you have to learn to share."

"Got it," Colleen said, getting tired of the conversation. She tapped ash in the ashtray. "Back to your midnight phone call."

Deena spun back to the counter, looked down. "He went over to Lynda's last night."

An alarm bell rang between Colleen's ears. "Say what?"

"We'd just played The Pitt. I knew he was feeling a little better because Melanie was back home. Whatever that little cow and her mother did to Steve, he was relieved that she was okay. Normally, we hang out after a gig. But he called a Yellow cab, took off. He normally walks home so I figured he was going somewhere. He was very serious. I could see it in his face. More than upset."

Colleen took a puff, exhaled. Deena didn't think much of Melanie. "Do you think Melanie knew what was going on? With the fake kidnap?"

"Who knows? She treated—treats—Steve like shit. All she wanted was that fucking horse. She wouldn't ask too many questions if Lynda stuck one in front of her."

"So Steve was pretty angry with Lynda."

Deena looked up at Colleen, laughed. "*Ya think?* That bitch pretended his kid was kidnapped, got the little bitch to play along, and, on top of it, screwed him for a bunch of money. And was ready to go for more? Who wouldn't be furious?"

Colleen wondered how mad Deena was. She seemed to be carrying a sizable torch for Steve. "So Steve didn't hang out with the band afterwards after you guys played—like he normally does. He took off. In a cab."

"Yeah. After I have a drink with the guys, I stop by Steve's place—you know, just to make sure he was okay."

Just to make sure he was okay, Colleen thought. *Of course.*

"And Steve wasn't home," she said.

"Nope."

"So you went over to Lynda's."

"What if I did?"

"I'm not judging you, Deena."

"Sure, you are. But it wasn't the way you think. Steve can go to bed with anyone he damn well wants. I don't care anymore. We've been through that. Steve is like a brother to me now."

Deena sounded like a woman trying to convince herself of something. "So you drove over to Lynda's. And you waited outside. And watched."

"In the old days, Steve was always trying to get Lynda back. Mostly for Melanie's sake. He thought she needed a father around full-time—especially with a mother like that."

"This time, though, you thought he was going to have it out with Lynda."

"Wouldn't you?"

Maybe. "When did you see him leave Lynda's place?"

"About one fifteen maybe. Not long after I got there."

Right around the time Lynda was killed.

"Was he alone when he left?" Colleen asked.

"Yeah."

That didn't explain Melanie being taken.

"Did you hear a shot?" Colleen asked. "Shots?"

"Too far away." She shook her head. "I was up the street, on the corner of Mangels. I can see Lynda's house from there, but no one can see me. Steve knows my car."

Colleen wondered how many times Deena checked out Lynda's house, looking for Steve.

"Was Steve carrying anything?" she asked.

"What? Like a smoking gun?" Deena laughed. "Get real."

Someone made off with Lynda's gun. Or dumped it. "Could it have been in his pocket?"

Deena grimaced. "Do you really think he shot her? Come on! Steve's a prince."

Colleen nodded, tapped her cigarette. "Well, you obviously think he might have. Otherwise you wouldn't have called me."

Deena took a deep breath. "I can't believe he would. But he *did* go over there. That's all I know. And I thought you should know, too."

"I'm glad you did, Deena. I appreciate it."

"Now what?"

"I'll see what I can do. Do you know Lynda's father?"

Deena shook her head. "Some movie producer in LA. Steve says he's a slime ball, always pulling fast ones."

Wasn't that the truth? They looked at each other for a moment. "Let's keep this conversation between you and me, for the time being," Colleen said.

"No problem."

"It's important for Steve to tell the police the truth. They're going to question him."

"I know." Deena's face grew grim. "He needs to play it straight."

Not like the time he ran, in 1966, when that girl OD'd in his London hotel room.

"You've got my number," Colleen said, standing up, stubbing out her cigarette. "Please call if you learn anything new."

"Yeah, sure," Deena said, picking up her metal malt cup and stirring what was left with the long spoon.

Colleen left.

Poor Deena, she thought. Another female who fell by the wayside on Steve's path.

Would Deena have been angry enough to kill Lynda? No, she didn't think so.

But that didn't bother her. Not as much as wondering what Steve was doing at his ex's house the night she was murdered, if what Deena was saying was true.

CHAPTER THIRTY-ONE

Next morning Colleen woke early to the pelting of rain on her bedroom windows. Coming down strong. It was still dark. She wasn't going back to sleep. There was too much on her mind after last night's conversation with Deena. She got up, pulled on her kimono, padded out into the living room, flicked on the heater, and into the kitchen where she made coffee.

She poured dark roast into a cup and stirred in three spoons of brown sugar, took her coffee out to the living room, picked up the white Princess phone, dialed Steve.

To ask him why he went over to Lynda's the night she was murdered. And why he hadn't mentioned it.

She let it ring.

No answer.

Where was he, not even six a.m.?

Showered and dressed, she put another call in. No answer. Now it was bugging her.

She drove over, parked in the narrow driveway, stepped quietly up the stairs to the porch, peered in around the tarp as best she could.

Dark.

Maybe Steve didn't make it home last night. She hoped he hadn't done anything dumb. Like run. Like he did when he was sixteen. She left. It was raining.

*   *   *

A few hours later, she found herself back on Steve's porch, after more unanswered phone calls.

Still not home.

She swung by The Pitt, where nothing was going on that time of the day. No Steve. She used the pay phone in the back of the bar by the restrooms, where Melanie Cook had been "abducted" during her first "kidnapping." She called Deena, who wasn't home either.

Good and wet, Colleen went back home, made tea, poured a splash of brandy into it, cranked up the heater and dried out.

The doorbell rang.

She checked the blinds first.

An SFPD black-and-white sat in the middle of Vermont. Her heart thumped. What did the cops want now? She'd cooperated with Owens. She hadn't missed her meeting with her parole officer. She'd been keeping her nose clean. Relatively.

She buzzed the cops in, listened to heavy boots thump up the stairs. Opened the door to her flat, waited.

A patrolman appeared around a bend on the staircase. Young, with a sandy-colored feather-cut just down to his dark blue collar. Getting away with it. He had the beginning of a permanent sneer. He was going to be one of those cops.

She could tell he was annoyed having to climb three flights.

"Colleen Hayes?"

"Yes?"

"Get your jacket."

That didn't sound good.

"Am I under arrest?" she asked.

"Not really."

"Owens wants to see me?"

"You got it."

"He could have just called."

"He needed to make sure you came down, ma'am."

Ma'am. She went inside, slid into her bomber jacket, turned off the heater and lights, grabbed her smokes, matches, came back out, locked up.

CHAPTER THIRTY-TWO

"You're booking Steve Cook for murder?" Colleen asked Inspector Owens. She was surprised, but not too much. Her own doubts continued to be stoked by the fact there were things Steve wasn't telling her. Like why he went over to Lynda's the night she was murdered.

She was back in the grubby interrogation room on the fifth floor of 850 with Inspector Owens sitting on the opposite side of the Formica table. A cardboard evidence box sat to his right.

"We picked Cook up this morning," Owens said, tapping the eraser of his number two pencil on his ever-present yellow pad. Today he wore a white shirt and tie up to the collar.

That explained why Steve wasn't home when she dropped by.

"What made you decide to pick Steve up?" she asked.

Owens dipped his head slightly, as if sizing up how much to tell her. "A tip."

Interesting. "Care to say who?"

Owens shook his head side to side once.

"Was it a young woman?" Colleen said. "New York accent?"

"No," he said. "Who might that be?"

She smiled. He smiled.

"You show me yours and I'll show you mine," Colleen said.

"The call was to the anonymous tip line," Owens said. "Some kid, sounded as if he was outdoors, on a pay phone, reading it off a piece of paper: 'Steve Cook killed his wife. Check his place.' Someone probably paid him to make the call."

Colleen nodded.

"And yours?" Owens said.

"Deena Vanderhaven," she said. "The drummer with *the band with no name*. Steve sings in her band."

Owens squinted in apparent surprise. "She told you Steve waxed his ex?"

"No, but she did say she saw him leave Lynda's place around the time of the murder. Maybe a little bit before."

"And when were you going to tell me this, Colleen?"

"I only found out about it late last night. Deena and I met at an all-night donut place."

Owens wrote something down. "What is this Deena doing, watching Lynda's house at night?"

"Following Steve around. Not that she's jealous or anything." Colleen gave a wry smile.

"Ah," Owens said. "It's like that."

"They were involved at one time."

"Any reason to thinks she's lying?" Owens asked. "About seeing Steve at Lynda's?"

"That crossed my mind, but I don't think so."

"Well," Owens said, "she's telling you the truth."

Now Colleen *was* surprised. "You don't think Steve did it, do you?"

Owens gave a nod.

"He confessed?" Colleen couldn't believe that somehow. She realized now how much of her felt he was innocent.

"Just the opposite. But we are talking about the same guy who fled the U.K. when a nude girl was found dead in his hotel room."

Nude. The past never let go.

"You don't think this is all a little fishy?" Colleen asked. "Steve has already been set up by a fake kidnapping. Now this."

"I agree, it doesn't look good."

"Then let me ask again," Colleen said. "If Steve did it, where's Melanie? Deena saw him leave Lynda's about the time of the murder—alone. On foot. Everything points to Melanie being taken in Lynda's car. One of the occupants of that car was dripping blood. So where did Steve stash his own daughter if he didn't take her after he supposedly shot Lynda?"

"He could have come back later."

She shook her head. "And left Melanie there? With her mother—dead?"

"Maybe Melanie's not alive. We don't know."

A chill shuddered down Colleen's back. "That might be true, but if so, Steve had nothing to do with it. He borrowed money from the Mexican Mafia to save her. Lynda—he might have been tempted. But Melanie—no way."

"So how about this?" Owens said, reaching into the box, coming out with a plastic baggie. He set it down in the middle of the table.

A LadySmith revolver with a baby-blue handle.

CHAPTER THIRTY-THREE

Colleen picked up the baggie containing the LadySmith revolver, gave it the once-over. It looked like Lynda's. She set it back down. Pushed it back over Owens' way.

"Shouldn't this be on its way to ballistics?" she said.

"It will be." Owens tapped his yellow pad with his pencil eraser. "I wanted you to see it first."

To read the look on her face. "Why would you think I'd cover for Steve?"

"Because he's your client. Because you have a habit of not giving me all the info."

"I've given you everything I have," she said.

"Not right away."

"I have a responsibility to my client," she said. "But that doesn't include covering up murder."

"So you didn't know about the gun?" Owens nodded at the baggie.

"Not beyond what I told you. I first saw it in Lynda's bedside table when she was still alive. It was gone when I found her dead."

"Then someone took it."

"And you seem to think it was Steve. But Steve was on foot, alone, and she's gone."

"We found the gun in his flat."

An imaginary fist punched her in the gut. She recovered, quietly, forced herself to see sense. "Don't you think it would be incredibly dumb for Steve Cook to keep a murder weapon in his house?"

"From where I sit, he's not exactly Mensa material. And we did find it under a floorboard in the living room."

So the gun had been well hidden. But the cops could find anything. "Did your tipster tell you where to find the gun?"

"No. Just that he had it."

"Lynda had a key to Steve's place," she said, regretting that Steve never changed his locks. "I bumped into her there with two thugs a couple of days ago. Someone else could have easily planted the gun."

Owens shrugged. "This needs to be chased down and you know it."

"Did you get officers to canvass Lynda's neighborhood, see if anyone saw anything around the time of the murder? Shots fired, her car leaving, that kind of thing?"

"Been there. It's a sleepy neighborhood of detached houses. It was late. No one heard, saw anything."

"Not even a car leaving?"

"Not even."

"And what did Steve say about all this?"

"Just that he wants an attorney. So we had to stop questioning him." That was the law.

"Did he call a lawyer?"

"Not yet. He just asked for one. In the meantime, we can't question him on the murder until he gets representation. We put a call into legal aid, but that'll take time. And he can turn that down, too. He can sit it out and stall us until he goes before a judge and the judge can decide if he needs counsel. Seems he's pretty savvy when dealing with the police, wouldn't you say?"

"Can you blame him?"

"Of course not," Owens said, "especially if he's guilty."

Steve not talking didn't look good. But he was probably scared spitless and didn't know what else to do. But it wasn't helping to find Melanie. If anything, it was doing the opposite.

"Why don't you let me talk to him?" she said. "You can't question him anymore since he asked for representation, but I can. I might be able to find something. And, if Melanie is kidnapped, we can't afford to lose time."

Owens rubbed his chin. "It's worth a try. Otherwise we wait until he goes up before a judge. Which won't be until later today at the very earliest. But only under one condition."

"Shoot."

"You can't tell him about this conversation. And you don't warn him off, tell him to stay silent. None of that. The whole idea is to get information."

"No problem. When can I talk to him?"

Owens looked at his watch. "Visiting hours are over but we'll get you in there. And—" he gave Colleen a stare—"I'm going to be listening in."

That might make things tricky.

"He didn't do it," she said.

"Maybe not. But he's made for this and you know it. His ex pretended to kidnap his kid and screwed him over. The fact that his daughter is gone just might mean he's got her tucked away somewhere. It probably wasn't planned; he acted out of passion. But the motive is in flashing neon letters. If it goes to court, they better not put too many men on the jury because any guy is going to give him a pass."

She'd get a chance to talk to Steve. It could only help find Melanie. Time was pressing and having him sit in a cell wasn't doing anyone any good.

"I've got a condition, too."

Owens gave a weary smile. "And?"

"When you hear Steve, you consider letting him go. He won't leave town. You can always arrest him again later if things don't stack up. But we need to find Melanie. And he can do a lot more outside than stuck in here."

Owens seemed to think about that for a moment. "I'll give it my consideration."

That was probably the best she was going to get. "Deal."

CHAPTER THIRTY-FOUR

San Francisco County Jail #4 occupied the seventh floor of 850 Bryant. It was essentially a small town of four hundred unwilling citizens, which included a laundry, kitchen, emergency room, library, and other sundry facilities. The once-white walls of the visiting room were grubby gray now, with the odd scrawl of graffiti. Harsh fluorescent lights beamed down onto an antiseptic bank of nine Plexiglas windows along one side with backless visitor stools bolted to the wall below each window. A phone hung to the right of each visitor station.

No other visits were in session when Colleen arrived, being that it was late in the evening and visiting hours were officially over. The sheriff's deputy, a slender light-skinned black man in khaki with lace-up boots, showed her to window number one, at the far end of the room. Colleen noticed a ceiling camera pointed at them.

She saw Steve Cook's shadow on the other side of the glass before she sat down on the hard stool. He wore a wrinkled black T-shirt and needed a shave. He looked more pissed off than upset, which was the way to be. Colleen had spent close to a decade behind bars and despair didn't work. And, despite it all, he still managed to look good somehow. He was just that kind of guy. The one she had spent

the night with. It might have complicated things, but she didn't regret it. She hoped he wouldn't make her regret it.

She picked up the phone and Steve did the same. The guard stood
behind her against the wall with his legs apart and arms crossed.

"Imagine my surprise," she said. Owens was listening in. But she
would also do her best to communicate with Steve on her own
terms. The deputy watched her intently.

Steve gave a frown. "Looks like you found me, Coll."

She searched his face for clues. No one seemed to be a killer on
the surface. "I've been hunting all day. Been to The Pitt twice. Then
I learned you'd been arrested." She raised her eyebrows and nodded
at the receiver to her ear, to hopefully let him know the phone call
wasn't completely on the up and up. She saw his tongue moving
around his lower lip, as if weighing her look and words.

"I see," he said.

She gave an almost imperceptible nod.

They stared at each other through the smudged Plexiglas for a
long moment.

She'd just get it over with. "You know what I'm going to ask, don't
you, Steve?"

"I didn't kill her, Coll. I already told you." His eyes softened. For
a moment he looked fraught and weak. And for that moment she
believed him one hundred percent. He recovered.

"They found Lynda's gun," she said. "In your flat."

"Someone set me up."

"Lynda's father?"

Shook his head. "Doesn't bloody make sense. Rex is a complete
arsehole, but he is one of the few people who *didn't* want to harm
Lynda. No, I can't see it."

Defending Rex didn't help Steve. If he was looking for an out, he
could have jumped on it, pointing the finger at him. "So who?"

Steve shrugged. She saw that measure of desperation again in that little motion of his shoulders. "Like you said, someone connected to the fake kidnapping decided to take over when you blew their scam. Only now they kidnapped Melanie for real." His words took a sharp turn upwards in pitch, the worry about Melanie weighing heavily, most likely. She felt for him. Even more, she felt for Melanie, a girl she didn't even know. That poor kid was probably being held somewhere awful, in crummy circumstances—and that's if she was lucky.

If someone had hijacked the kidnap, that might explain why Lynda said she couldn't get her hands on the money. Whoever took Melanie probably had it and was after more. "But you never heard from anybody for more ransom money—did you?" she asked.

Steve shook his head *no* again.

They might be going to let Steve stew for a few days before they put in another demand. Make him sweat. Especially if they knew he was under arrest and in jail. Colleen looked Steve in the eye. There was still something she needed to know. It was digging at her.

"Steve—did you go over to Lynda's house the night she was murdered?"

She saw a flinch of surprise, not much, but enough. He was hunkering down.

"No."

Her heart sank. Unless Deena was lying. But Deena wasn't lying. Was she?

"I'm going to ask you one more time," she said, meeting his gaze. "The truth will help get your daughter back."

Steve looked away, slightly ashamed. Then he looked back at her with more resolve.

"Okay. Yeah. I did go over to Lynda's."

"Why, Steve? *Why?* I told you to stay the hell away."

He gave a helpless shrug. "Because I'm a complete fucking idiot, that's why. Because I couldn't believe a woman I'd married, one who'd had my kid, would fucking stitch me up the way she did. Because I wanted to see Mel. It was stupid on my part, yeah, it bloody was. But I didn't kill her, Colleen. You have to believe me." His eyes were pleading. But she remembered the look her ex gave her before she let him have it, and her ex had been guilty.

"So what happened, Steve?"

"Lynda wouldn't let me in. We argued at the front door. She told me to leave. So I left."

"What time was that?"

Steve looked up to the ceiling as he calculated. "After midnight? No, one o'clock. A bit after. I wasn't there long. I walked down to Monterey, caught the bus."

The time jived with what Deena had told her. And the fact that he was on foot, alone.

"Which bus?"

"Twenty-three. It was the Owl Service."

"You talk to anybody on the bus?"

Shook his head no.

"Remember the driver?"

Shook his head again.

"Where'd you get off?"

"Glen Park BART." Bay Area Rapid Transit was a new light rail system in SF and beyond.

"You took BART home from Glen Park?" she asked.

"BART was closed."

"What did you do? Take a bus over to the Mission? Call a cab?"

"Fuck, Coll," Steve said through his teeth. "I didn't kill her. Are you going to bloody believe me or not?"

"Just answer the question, Steve."

"I decided to stop at the bar—The Glen Park Station. My mind was full of shit, yeah? I had a couple of quick belts. Left, walked home. I walked home, yeah? I needed to unwind."

It was a decent walk, a couple of miles. "Talk to anybody in the bar?"

"The barman was some old codger with a comb-over."

"Think he'd remember you?"

"I don't bloody know."

Colleen took a deep breath through her nostrils, sifting it all out. "Okay," she said.

"That's it, Coll? *Okay?*"

"It means I'm working things out, Steve."

"Great," he said. "While you're working things out, someone's got Melanie. Really got Melanie this time. And I'm sitting in here, unable to do a fucking thing about it."

"Has Octavien been hounding you for the loan?"

"Yeah."

"Don't call him. It's better if he doesn't know where you are. You don't want anybody who works for Octavien finding you in here, either."

"That doesn't help Mel. I need to get out of here. I need a lawyer."

She wasn't supposed to bring the lawyer subject up. But Steve had. So she could play along. "I won't argue with you there, bud." She gave him wide eyes. Let him know the subject was open. *Keep going, Steve.*

He seemed to pick up her look. "Know any good lawyers? Can you help me out, Coll? The cops said they called the public defender but that sounds dicey."

Didn't it? Overworked and unlikely to give Steve their full attention. Especially for a murder and possible kidnap.

Who? Christian Newell, Alex's wimpy lawyer? Who had done a lackluster job helping Colleen fend off a frisky parole officer? No way, Jose.

"Let me look into it." She gave him another telepathic look. "Sit tight. I'll make some calls."

"Thanks, Coll. Thanks a lot."

"I found her once, Steve. I'll find her again."

"I'm counting on you."

"I'll be in touch. Tomorrow morning."

"Got any smokes?"

She cracked a smile. "Virginia Slims?"

He returned a smile. "Beggars can't be choosers."

She turned to the guard who was hanging on her every word. "I got a pack of cigarettes in my jacket. Can I get them out, and can you see that he gets them?"

Guard shook his head no. "Time for you to wrap this up."

Damn. She turned back to Steve. "Sorry, compadre."

"No worries, love. Virginia Slims might get me beaten up in here anyway."

CHAPTER THIRTY-FIVE

"You heard what Steve said," Colleen said to Owens, back at the Formica table in the interrogation room. She was beginning to feel an uneasy sensation of being in jail herself. After all the years she'd spent behind bars, being close to law enforcement and its trappings for too long put her on edge.

Owens tapped his pencil, gave her a cool look. "I heard what he said, but I'm not sure I heard the same thing you did." Owens had been listening in.

She felt her face warm. Owens still didn't believe Steve. "Do you really think he'd keep the gun if he shot his ex?"

Owens gave a smirk. "Seems to me you might be a little soft for your client."

"He's my client."

"Who lied to you about going over to Lynda's."

"He came clean when I pushed."

"Because he knew you had him." Owens grimaced, looked at his notes. "My recommendation is still going to be that we hold him, book him in the morning." He looked up at Colleen.

"You'll have to wait until he gets legal counsel. I'll get to work on a lawyer, but it will take time."

"The judge might wave legal counsel in our favor," Owens said.

"And he might not," she said. "And Steve's daughter has been kidnapped. The longer he sits in here, the worse it gets for her."

"*Maybe* his daughter has been kidnapped," Owens said. "Maybe he's got something elaborate going on."

"No. It doesn't make any sense."

"Well, charging him and holding him is one way to find out if he's up to something. And besides, your client has got 'flight risk' written all over him."

As much as she hated to admit it, she understood where Owens was coming from. He wasn't sure about Steve, who had a dead woman in his past, and a bad habit of fleeing the country. Charging him and holding him was a way to sit tight and apply pressure at the same time.

"We can always drop the charges later," Owens said.

"And you can always *not* drop them, too," she said.

"This is the way I'm going to play it. But, if it makes any difference, I don't think he *meant* to kill her."

Small mercies. She stood up. It wouldn't do any good to keep arguing. "I'll find him a lawyer."

"And you better not be actively working on this anymore." He raised his eyebrows. "Right?"

Sometimes it did not pay to tell the truth. "Right."

"I'll have someone run you home," he said.

"Don't bother."

"It's raining."

"I'll grab a cab." She'd had enough police for one day. The thought of riding home in a cruiser would only prolong it.

*   *   *

The next morning, the DA charged Steve Cook with second-degree murder, per Inspector Owens' recommendation, along with Child

Endangerment. The DA wasn't going to charge Steve with a kidnapping he couldn't prove. Not yet.

Colleen's heart sank.

If nothing else, it made her side more with Steve.

Outside, rain cascaded down her windows. Melanie Cook was still gone, and it weighed on Colleen. She willed herself to stay strong.

CHAPTER THIRTY-SIX

Colleen checked her answering service early the next morning, the rain pattering against the windows of her flat. She put in a call to a lawyer named Gus Pedersen, who had a reputation for getting people off of some tough charges. He lived in Stinson Beach, where he surfed and took the odd case.

She reviewed what paperwork she had, in particular Lynda Cook's phone bills.

There were numerous calls to Rex Williamson, Lynda's father, in Los Angeles.

She didn't buy that Lynda's father would kill his own daughter, kidnap his own granddaughter, but she hadn't met him. Stranger things had happened. Talking to Rex was next on her to-do list.

She called her travel agent. People's Express was running a ten-dollar flight from SFO to LAX. A little more than the cost of a cab to the airport.

A couple of hours later, dressed in a smart dark blue skirt suit with a white blouse and black pumps, hoisting her shoulder bag, she got off the plane in LAX. At a pay phone in the terminal she called Rex Williamson's house, and when he answered, she hung up. He was home. All she needed to know. She stepped out into the warm Los Angeles sunshine and flagged a Yellow cab. Rex Williamson lived in Manhattan Beach, not too far from the airport, so there was no need to rent a car.

*   *   *

By lunchtime she was standing in front of a sleek '60s modern two-story gray cement building not far from the beach on Highland Avenue, the Pacific Ocean twinkling beyond. The house had big windows and terraces.

She over-tipped the cabbie, a Vietnamese refugee in a crisp white shirt who spoke halting English, handing him a twenty-dollar bill and asking him to wait for her just up the street. She didn't think she'd be that long and would need a ride back to LAX. He accepted, returning a polite bow.

Rex Williamson had a wrought-iron fence, also gray, around his manicured yard. She rang the buzzer, the eye of the Vericon security camera over the gate watching her. Not too many people had these systems. It said something about Rex Williamson.

The gate buzzed open. That was easy enough, she thought, readying one of her business cards.

The front door opened as she walked up the flagstone path. A tall, lean man in beige slacks, red loafers, no socks, and a red cardigan over a beige shirt with a Nehru collar watched her guardedly. He had thick white movie star hair and wore light-blue sunglasses. His face was craggy and over-tanned. He was well preserved for a man in his sixties.

He raised his eyebrows questioningly.

"Colleen Hayes," she said as she reached the door. She saw no need for subterfuge at this point.

"Ah," he said.

She didn't see a great deal of surprise in his face. He shut the door, walked inside the house ahead of her. Colleen followed.

The lower level of the house was open floor plan, all whites and grays, giving out to the Pacific beyond a swimming pool that shimmered with midday sun. A color-coordinated modern art painting of nothing in particular hung over a black leather sofa. The house was immaculately neat.

Rex Williamson didn't ask Colleen to sit down.

Instead he walked into the sleek open kitchen that looked like it had never been cooked in, opened a drawer, picked something out of it, came out into the living room.

He stood, a small pistol by his side. He put his other hand in his pocket, rattling keys or change.

Her heart jumped. "There's no need for that," she said.

"I'm not sure I agree." He came up to her in measured steps, took her bag, tossed it on a black leather chair. He motioned for her to turn around.

"I'm not carrying a gun," she said.

"And I should just take your word for it." He patted her down with one hand, then, satisfied, picked up the bag, dumped the contents onto the chair with a clatter. Cigarettes, Bic lighter, lipstick, coin purse, hairbrush. Loose bills. But no gun.

He strode to the picture window, turned around, the gun lazily by his side. His face was completely devoid of a smile.

"What do you want?" he said tersely.

"To talk about your daughter. And your granddaughter. I can't imagine this is an easy time for you."

"Oh, that's good—considering you're one of the reasons Lynda's dead."

"You're saying Lynda would still be alive if I let you two get away with your scam? Pretending to kidnap your granddaughter? Putting Steve through hell so you could wrangle song rights out of him?"

"I'm not admitting to any of that."

"You don't have to. It'll come out."

"Perhaps you'd like to think."

"You orchestrated the so-called kidnapping with Lynda, in order to make your ex-son-in-law beholden to you. But you didn't really want the $20,000 he had to go in hock for. You wanted him to 'borrow' the money from you in exchange for the rights to his catalog. Question is, why? Or, more to the point, why *now*? Why not two years ago? Five?"

He nodded impatiently. "If you've got some proof of any of this, feel free to give it to the police. LAPD's been here all morning and they'd like to hear it. Oddly enough, they were more concerned about the fact that my granddaughter's missing."

Colleen cocked her head to one side. "I don't have any proof that implicates you—yet. Beyond the fact that you were eager to loan Steve the ransom money."

Rex Williamson gave a faux nod of confusion. "And where did you hear that?"

"I was there when Steve dealt with your lawyer."

"Oh, right—the man who's in jail for murdering my daughter." Rex gave a plastic grin, which immediately faded.

"*Variety* featured a piece that a director is looking at 'Shades of Summer' for an upcoming RomCom. That would be right down your alley, wouldn't it? Being an independent movie producer."

He gave a mean smirk. "Ah, yes. *Variety*, that veritable fountain of rumor and misinformation." He shook his head. "If you don't have anything beyond hearsay, I suggest you keep your theories to yourself. Otherwise, you will be hearing from my lawyers."

"Lawyer*s*," she repeated, accentuating the plural. "You've got more than one. I suspect you'll need them."

His chiseled mouth folded into a grimace. "I've got plenty of people when I need them." He raised his eyebrows. "You might want to remember that."

For all the vitriol, she could tell he didn't kill his daughter. But, rather than grieving, he was hiding behind anger. Anger and fear. He had a hand in this. Somehow.

"I didn't really come down here to accuse you of murder," she said. "Steve is in a lot of trouble. Why not help him out? He is the father of your granddaughter."

Rex Williamson gave another one of his light-switch smiles. "I'll get right on it."

"You know he didn't kill Lynda."

"Don't assume you know what I'm thinking."

"Steve is on the hook for $27,000—the twenty he borrowed to pay off the 'kidnappers,' plus another seven K interest. Thanks to you and Lynda. The people who lent him the money aren't going to want to hear excuses. So I can take it with me now, or you can get it to me soon, and Steve can pay off the loan sharks."

"Cojones, lady. You've certainly got 'em."

"You don't have the money? Then who does?"

"We're done here." He waved the gun lazily. "No sudden moves on your way out."

"Well, I tried." She went over to the chair, gathered her overturned bag, replaced the contents, slung the bag over her shoulder. She gave Rex Williamson one last look. "If you work with me, I can help get your granddaughter back. But I'm going to need the twenty-seven K to get Steve out of trouble. Someone you know has it."

He stood there for a moment and she almost wondered whether he was going to capitulate. Then he said, "Now she's trying to shake me down for ransom money for my granddaughter. I wonder what the police will think of that."

Colleen sighed. "If you have any info on who took Melanie, now would be a good time to tell me."

He shook his head, held the gun on her. "I've got nothing further to say to you."

"Okay, Rex," she said. "Have it your way."

Rex didn't know Melanie's whereabouts. And he was too scared to find out. Someone had gotten to him.

She headed to the door, walked down the flagstone path in the warm Los Angeles sun, let herself off the property. Out of the edge of the curb, she peered up the street, saw her Yellow cab waiting. She gave a wave and the car set into motion. She could hear the gulls in the distance circling over the beach.

*   *   *

Back home in San Francisco, a few hours later, it was still raining. She called 850 Bryant. Steve was still being held, hadn't been transferred. Visiting hours were over for the day. Gus Pedersen, the surfer lawyer from Stinson Beach, had returned her call. She called him back. They made arrangements to meet the next day.

Colleen sat down in her office and went through her case file. If only she had one more rummage through Lynda's place. She found the Polaroid of the note to Lynda from Sir Ian Ellis, President of Delco records, taken the first time she "visited" Lynda's.

Lynda-

Simply lovely to see you again. But then, you are so easy to look at. Next time I'm in town, I'd love you to show me around.

Best, Ian

P.S. I think we've made some headway on SOS.

The P.S. gave Colleen pause for thought. She hadn't made a connection the first time she read it. She got up, went into the living room, picked up the copy of *that album,* read the liner notes.

"When I first saw The Lost Chords play The Marquee, I knew right off I had to sign the band, right then and there. Signed them on the spot. I just knew. They've had their ups and downs—that's the nature of the pop music business—but The Lost Chords are the real deal. A *gas*, as their fans say. And I can say without a doubt that I'm bloody proud I signed them first. Like a proud father." . . . Ian Ellis, manager for The Lost Chords.

Made some headway on SOS.

SOS.

She looked at the track listing.

Side two, track one: "Shades of Summer."

SOS.

Colleen checked her watch. Good old SF Public Library on Van Ness was still open. She pulled on a raincoat this time, an SF Giants cap to go with it, and bounced down the back stairs to her car.

CHAPTER THIRTY-SEVEN

Colleen met Gus Pedersen early the next morning in the Rain Café on Haight Street. Appropriately enough it was raining. The café was steamy with moisture and half full of patrons. The radio played Linda Ronstadt, "Blue Bayou." It was rumored Linda was dating Governor Jerry Brown, who drove a beat-up Plymouth Satellite and was fondly called Moonbeam. Only in California.

When he pushed open the door, Gus Pedersen looked nothing like Colleen's previous lawyer, a nattily dressed young man with Ken-doll hair so neat it seemed to be painted on. Gus was football-player big, with a long unruly brown mane kept in place by a well-worn black cowboy hat decorated with an Indian beaded headband. His wide-set eyes were shielded behind tinted aviator glasses. He wore a long bushy mustache and sideburns. A fringed suede jacket was peppered with dark raindrops. Faded jeans and snakeskin cowboy boots completed the look. Gus looked more like he might be selling some of the products his clients got busted for out on Haight Street. Despite that, his manner was professional as he handed Colleen a business card.

"Thanks for driving down from Stinson Beach at such short notice in the rain," Colleen said. She wore a dark-red tracksuit with her Pony Topstars. She had dressed comfortably for the long trip ahead.

Her passport was in her pocket. Fortunately, where she was going didn't restrict her based on her prison record.

"You said you were leaving the country?" Gus said, sitting down on the other side of her table. He had a baritone voice.

"London," she said, getting her file folder out. "Today."

"Vacation?"

"No," she said. "It's actually for this case."

Gus ordered jasmine tea.

They went over the case so far.

"Does Steve Cook know I'm his attorney yet?" Gus said, elbows on the table.

"Not yet," Colleen said. "But I did let him know I'd line one up."

Gus checked his wristwatch, a Rolex Submariner with a black face. "I'll head over to the Hall of Justice after this, introduce myself. But it's going to be tough getting him bail, with his history of running from the law."

"He doesn't have any bail money anyway."

"Want a ride to the airport?" Gus said.

"No thanks," she said. "You focus on Steve. Try to find any weakness you can in SFPD's case."

"Wonder if they had a valid search warrant. A gun found under the floorboards is not in a location considered accessible by a normal, legal search, unless detailed in the warrant."

Colleen hadn't considered that. Gus was already promising more than her previous lawyer.

Gus eyed her from behind his sunglasses for a moment, as if weighing his words.

"Your client *is* innocent, correct?" he asked.

Colleen found herself mulling that over a little bit too long.

"Of course," she said. She stood up. So did Gus. They shook hands.

"I'll call you from London," she said. "It'll probably be collect."

"It all goes on the bill," he said, tapping his paper notes together, folding them, along with a check she'd given him. Colleen had paid Steve's retainer. It was a good thing she'd received an unexpected bonus on her last gig. She was plowing through it at a steady rate. But there was an eleven-year-old girl who was missing.

"That's fine," she said. "It all gets added to *my* bill."

If she ever got paid.

CHAPTER THIRTY-EIGHT

Delco Records' Head Office was located on Denmark Street, Britain's Tin Pan Alley, tucked away on the edge of London's West End. If Colleen thought San Francisco was foggy, she had just found a sister city in the United Kingdom, where thick vapor wafted down the narrow street, dampening all it touched, like soft rain. It was early morning and the three- and four-story buildings echoed with traffic. Wet sidewalks clattered with quick footsteps, punk rockers with Mohawks and chains intermingled with bowler-hatted businessmen. Colleen's head was light and hazy after her first international flight and she breathed in the wet morning air and blinked away the jet lag. She held a collapsible umbrella over her sensible blue business suit, having changed quickly at the bed-and-breakfast she had checked into that morning in nearby Tottenham Court Road.

She took a moment to get her bearings, taking in the iconic street with its 17th-century buildings that once housed London's well-to-do and was now the center for the U.K.'s thriving music industry. Every famous band that had come out of Britain had spent time on Denmark Street, wrangling deals with agents, recording in one of the many sound studios nestled cheek by jowl with music publishers and shops. The Stones. Bowie. Elton John.

The British Invasion began here. And, of special interest to Colleen, The Lost Chords.

She walked the length of the short street, past music stores, the legendary Giaconda Café, until she located a narrow limestone and brick entryway that would have been at home in a Dickens novel. Brass plaques listed the various offices in the building. Amidst signs for a Swedish film distribution company and Top Tier Modelling agency, she found what she was looking for: Delco Recording and Publishing Ltd, 2nd Floor. The words were interspersed with the engraving of a phonograph.

She made her way up lopsided stairs to a hallway of offices. Delco's were down the end of a long musty hall that needed a fresh coat of paint and new carpet.

The waiting room was in distinct contrast to the exterior of the building: muted tones, indirect lighting, and sleek modern furniture. At one end of a leather sofa sat a stocky man in his mid-twenties with short dark hair like a brush and heavy sideburns, and just a hint of eyeliner. He wore a purple shirt that bulged with muscles, two-tone pants, suspenders, and Doc Marten shoes with thick soles. He was reading a copy of the *Sun* newspaper.

At reception, behind a collection of telephones, sat an emaciated young woman in a sleeveless black top, with pale white skin and cropped peroxide hair. Gigantic black hoop earrings and mascara completed the look. She was audibly chewing gum. She gave Colleen a dour non-smile as Colleen approached the desk.

"Sir Ian Ellis, please," Colleen asked.

"Appointment?" the girl said in a sharp Cockney accent.

Colleen replied that she didn't have one.

"Sorry," the girl said in a tone that strongly suggested she wasn't. She plucked a business card from its holder and handed it over with an extended little pinky. "Demos go to the address on the card.

Don't include return postage as items will not be returned. If there *is* any interest, you'll hear from us. You will *not* be contacted otherwise." Her recited spiel suggested she had delivered it many times before. She snapped her gum.

"Oh, that's too bad." Colleen took the card, produced one of her own more creative business cards, listing her as Carol Aird, Artist Management Consultant. "I'm only in town for a day, on my way to Rome, and I was hoping to have a word with Sir Ian. I have a client interested in licensing."

The girl took Colleen's card. "Who did you say your client was?"

"I didn't. And I can't, at the moment," Colleen said. "But let's just say one of his movies was nominated for Best Musical Score." Colleen raised her eyebrows.

The girl's tone changed immediately. "One moment, please." She picked up the phone, pushed a button, turned her back on Colleen as she conversed in low tones. Colleen wasn't the best at deciphering subsonic Cockney, but the phrase *American film consultant* rang clear enough. The receptionist got off the phone, spun back around with a smile that was as genuine as the warm, nonexistent sunny day outside.

"Please take a seat, Ms. Aird. Sir Ian is just finishing up a call with a client."

Colleen thanked her, sat down, straightened her flared polyester slacks over her knee. The young man flipped a page of his newspaper, folded it back. A moment later, an inside line buzzed, and the young woman answered, hung up, stood up.

"This way, please."

She led Colleen down a creaky hallway lined with gold and silver records going back over the years, to a carved mahogany door that shone despite the semidarkness. The woman gave two gentle knocks, opened the door.

"Miss Aird, sir." She went in, set Colleen's business card on the desk, came out, showed Colleen in, shut the door behind her.

Colleen stood in a chilly room with a rustic beamed ceiling. The wood floor, covered in part by a red battered Persian rug, had probably not been level for centuries. The drapes were heavy burgundy velvet and the desk and furniture belonged in an antique store—or museum. Bookcases with impressively bound tomes lined the walls, along with more gold and platinum records, imposing documents, and photographs of Sir Ian Ellis over the years with many of Britain's entertainment elite. She spotted a young Paul McCartney in one black-and-white photo.

Sir Ian Ellis fit the room like one of the well-placed artifacts. In his seventies, his craggy red face and white handlebar mustache gave him a supercilious look that suggested a person born to privilege. His eyes were red and guarded, squinting behind wrinkles of skin. He wore what was most likely a school tie, dark blue with light-blue diagonal stripes, and a herringbone jacket with patches at the elbows. His desk was relatively neat, one or two folders side by side on his blotter, one open, which he closed as he stood up.

"Ms. Aird," he said in an accent as elegant and crisp as his French cuffs. He didn't come around to greet her, but waved Colleen to a leather guest chair. "Please."

She sat down.

"Filthy weather," he said.

She agreed.

"Where are you flying in from?"

"New York."

"I simply love your accent."

"Why, thank you," she said.

His eyes twinkled as she crossed her legs—the dog. He sat down behind his desk, nodded at a cut crystal decanter full of amber liquid on a sideboard. "A little something to ward off the chill?"

Not at ten in the morning. "No thank you." She continued to feed the smile.

He examined her nondescript business card. "And you are with . . . ?"

"I'm an independent agent, consulting with Jason Wood on a particular assignment." Jason Wood was a huge, worldwide talent agency, and it was safe to say one represented them. It would take an age to find out she wasn't. "My client is working with a small boutique production company through them. He has an interest in a song from one of your old artists for his movie—a musical set in London's swinging sixties."

"I see." Sir Ian's face registered *musical* as if she might have said *bubonic plague*. A step or two below his tastes, no doubt, which probably ran to Gilbert and Sullivan.

"May I ask who your director is?"

She gave a soft shake of the head. "All I can say is that he's a B-Lister knocking hard on the A door. Of course, if things gel, we'll all be the best of friends."

Sir Ian gave a crafty grin, sat back, and steepled his bony fingers. "And what song is he interested in for this—ah—musical?"

"'Shades of Summer,'" Colleen said, watching Sir Ian's face closely. "I believe it's by a group you once managed."

She met Sir Ian's stare, which became hard and icy.

She had hit a direct broadside. She was on the right track. She watched him recover.

"How interesting." Sir Ian gave a theatrical sigh. "But *that* might take some doing."

"I understand someone else might be after it, too. I've been asked to make enquiries."

Their eyes met again. "You *are* very well informed," he said. "Yes, there was a mention in *Variety*."

"I wanted to make a move before anything was finalized."

He continued, "Then you'll perhaps also know there's a copyright issue over 'Shades of Summer.' I'm actually in the process of straightening it out."

And had been for over a decade. "My client hinted I can go as high as six figures," she said.

Sir Ian raised his eyebrows. "Pounds?"

She gave a light laugh. "I believe it was dollars, but I'm sure the number is negotiable."

Sir Ian pursed his lips. She was surprised he wasn't drooling. "Where are you staying, Ms. Aird?"

"With some friends in Camden Town." She didn't need him calling her modest B and B or hunting around for some fictitious hotel.

Sir Ian adjusted the perfect knot of his tie. "Let me make a phone call or two. When do you leave for Rome?"

"Tomorrow. The 8:50 flight out of Gatwick."

"I'll call you tonight—if that's fine with your friends."

"I'm actually out with a client tonight. I'll call you as soon as I get back to New York—in a few days."

He gave a little nod. "Perfect."

She stood up.

Their eyes met again. His were cold, calculating. Malevolent.

Yes, he was one to keep your eye on.

*   *   *

When the American woman had left, Sir Ian stroked his mustache into place, then picked up the phone. Dialed the front desk.

Vicki, the receptionist, answered, smacking gum, as usual.

"Vicks," Sir Ian said. "That woman that just left here—Ms. Aird? Tell Reggie I want to know where she goes." Pause. "I know it's raining. Tell him to get after her now before he loses her. And stop popping that gum in my ear, please."

CHAPTER THIRTY-NINE

It was still raining as the black London cab dropped Colleen off across the Thames at The National Archives. She dashed inside and asked for the reference section. A soft-spoken gentleman pointed her across the tall round foyer under a glass and iron domed roof.

After a good deal of searching, she found Brenda Pike's certified copy of Entry of Death on microfiche, date April 15th, 1966. Two days after her body was found in Steve Cook's hotel room bed. Nude, of course. The EOD listed Brenda's home address as 2671 Ludlow Road, Church Stretton, a small town southwest of London. But what was curious was the cause of death, as determined by Doctor James Ledgwick, Member of the Royal College of Surgeons: pending investigation. That was twelve years ago. The status seemed to be lost in limbo.

The tabloids Colleen had read at the public library in SF stated Brenda Pike had died of a heroin overdose, supposedly delivered by Steve Cook. A single needle mark was found in her right elbow. She was right-handed, which suggested the shot had not been self-administered. No drugs or paraphernalia were found in Steve's hotel room, and he had been adamant that he never used drugs. One bandmate stated that Steve never used drugs and loathed them. "He had his hands full with booze and birds."

She recalled reading in SF that Brenda Pike's death was listed as "Death by Misadventure." The uncertain cause of death was a concern.

While she was there, Colleen researched articles on The Lost Chords, and former band members. One had died several years ago of an aneurysm, another lived with his aging mother in the town of Andover, and the drummer, whose nickname was Tich, now worked as a doorman in a London club. How the mighty had fallen.

Armed with a stack of ten-pence coins, Colleen left the National Archives, erected her folding umbrella against the rain, and found her way to a red London telephone kiosk.

She dialed Doctor Ledgwick's practice on Harley Street. A very polite young woman informed her that Dr. Ledgwick was on sabbatical in Southeast Asia and was expected to return by end of year. When Colleen asked about a death certification Dr. Ledgwick had signed off over a decade before, she was told no one would be readily available to help her. She was free to leave a message that would hopefully be returned eventually. She did, giving the number of her answering service in the United States.

She scratched that item off the list.

She called directory assistance, asking for Nev Ashdown's telephone number in Andover. Nev was the former guitarist with The Lost Chords who lived with his mother. But no telephone number was available.

She did the same for Dave Simons, aka Tich, the Chords' drummer who worked in London as a doorman. She got a phone number this time, a North London number, and called. The number had been disconnected. She sighed, crossed that out.

That left her Brenda Pike's family, if any, in Church Stretton. Once again, she called directory inquiries, got a number for Herbert Pike, Brenda's father.

She called. A woman with an almost inaudible, soft voice answered. She was so excruciatingly polite Colleen couldn't quite believe it.

Colleen explained she was doing research for an upcoming article in the *New York Times* and had a few questions.

"What kind of article, if I might ask?" the woman said.

"A story on the darker side of British pop culture in the sixties."

"Oh, I see." There was a discernible silence, broken by the clicking of the phone line as it measured out another few pence. "Well, if your article is related to Steve Cook, I'm afraid we're not interested."

Colleen swallowed, then responded. "I understand your reluctance, Ms. Pike, but I feel it's so important for our readers to get all sides of the story. And I'm not sure yours has been properly told. The tendency is to focus on the superficial."

"We are *not* interested," the woman said, more firmly now. "Please do *not* call again." And with that she hung up.

Colleen let out a breath, hung up, left the phone booth, lit up a cigarette. Blew smoke into the wet morning air.

Not much to go on. Except that Sir Ian was guilty of something and Brenda Pike's cause of death was technically uncertain.

Grasping at straws.

It took a while to find a free cab but when she finally flagged one down, she asked the cabbie how she might get to Church Stretton. He drove her to Euston Railway Station.

The train to Church Stretton meant changing at Crewe, on the way to Liverpool, and then heading south. It was a three-hour journey but, if nothing else, she could catch up on her sleep, perhaps rid herself of some of the jet lag.

*   *   *

"Church Stretton?" Sir Ian said, leaning back in his office chair, phone to his ear. "Are you sure about that, Reggie?"

"That's what I overheard the man at the ticket counter say. Change at Crewe. She's on the nine-oh-five return."

"I hope you don't have plans for tonight, Reg. I'll need you there at the station when Ms. Aird returns from Church Stretton. Follow her. Find out where she's staying. Don't lose her. Keep me posted. And be discreet."

Reg sighed on the other end of the line.

"It's what I pay you for, lad," Sir Ian said. "If she goes out later, I want to know where, and who she meets."

"Right," Reggie said in a voice that did little to mask its annoyance.

"I might need you to give her a little warning, Reggie."

That seemed to cheer Reg up. He liked that sort of thing. He grunted an acknowledgement.

"Good boy," Sir Ian said, hanging up.

CHAPTER FORTY

By the time Colleen's train arrived at Church Stretton, late afternoon had descended into rainy evening. No taxis were available outside the station. The small town may not have had that many to begin with.

It was like stepping back in time when she got to the high street, something out of a PBS Sunday night program where genteel characters lived their lives with a stiff upper lip. All that was missing was Winston Churchill on the wireless.

Colleen had learned that no taxis didn't mean there wasn't a ride to be had. She stuck her head into a red telephone kiosk outside the station and checked the cards pinned and taped on the wall above the phone. She found a local minicab, dialed the number. Someone would be there in five minutes. She went out, stood under her umbrella, smoked a cigarette, and waited.

It was more like fifteen minutes before a black Ford Cortina swerved up, blaring with punk music.

The driver was a man in his thirties with an orange crop that looked like he'd done it himself under medication. He wore grannie-style sunglasses even though it was dark and a jacket that dripped with chains and reeked of motor oil. The cassette player featured buzz saw guitars and a vocalist screaming about kicking out the Tories.

She gave him the address on Ludlow Road. She pretty much had to shout over the music.

"You want the Pikes, do you?" the cabbie asked.

"I do."

The driver hurtled through the picturesque town of Church Stretton, heading south, bouncing along a dark, rainy country lane, talking the whole time in a cluttered accent over the music.

"Can you turn that down, please?" she said, tapping his shoulder, making him jump far more than she thought warranted. The car jerked into a skid for a moment, before it righted itself.

He pulled up to a small pebbledash-fronted cottage. No lights were on and the driveway was empty.

Colleen paid the driver, told him to keep the change. "Please wait for me," she said. "I think I might need a ride back."

She rang the doorbell, got no answer.

She returned to the cab, where the music was blasting again. The government was apparently the enemy of the British workingman.

"Any idea where the Pikes might be?" she asked, after she got him to turn the music down one more time.

"I suspect they'll be at evening Mass, Miss."

"Know where the Pikes go to church?"

"St. Milburga's. Only Catholic church in town."

"St. Milburga's," she said, sitting back. "Try to keep this thing out of a ditch, please."

They barreled back into Church Stretton.

"How well do you know the Pikes?" she asked.

"As well as anyone does. And that means not well."

"They keep to themselves I take it?"

"That they do, Miss."

"Did you know their daughter? Brenda?"

He turned dour as they pulled up in front of a small, whitewashed church with a red tile roof and miniature bell tower. A few cars were parked outside.

"Here you are, love. Two quid."

She gave him a blue five-pound note, told him to keep the change. He liked that.

"You didn't answer my question," she said.

"It's not my place to talk about Brenda, Miss. Sorry. The family has suffered."

She got out and he thrashed off. So much for over-tipping. She walked down a neat winding stone path into a well-lit church with five rows of simple fabric-backed wooden chairs facing an altar that was so modest it resembled a shelf. Most of the chairs were empty.

A young priest in a white robe and burgundy stole was conducting prayer. He glanced up when Colleen sat down quietly in the last row, giving her a sideways look. Feeling sheepish, she scanned the churchgoers. There was only one older couple, seated by themselves in the second row. The woman wore a blue scarf and the man had a ring of white hair around a pink, bald pate. Both of them wore raincoats. Their heads were bowed. The other couple was younger, too young to have had a teenage daughter over ten years ago.

Out of respect, Colleen got up, exited the church, waited in the entry.

When service let out, she moved outside, in front of the church. The priest assumed a position at the door, quietly saying good night to the few people as they left.

He addressed the older couple, referring to them as Herbert and Maisie.

Brenda Pike's parents.

Colleen waited until they were walking down the stone path, Mr. Pike holding his wife's arm.

"Excuse me—Mr. Pike?"

He turned, eyed her furtively as he got keys out of his raincoat pocket.

"Yes?"

She introduced herself, using her real name. The American accent appeared to give him and his wife cause for concern. The woman's light-blue eyes scoured Colleen coldly. Her pale skin was aged, almost white.

"Are you the woman who called my wife earlier today?" Mr. Pike said with a tone of admonishment. He had a soft country lilt to his voice.

Colleen said that she was.

"We have nothing to say to the newspapers," he said. "We've had more than enough of that, thank you." With that, the Pikes turned, headed to the street, Mr. Pike taking his wife's arm. "Come on, love."

Colleen went after them.

"Please," she said. "I'm not really a reporter."

They stopped, turned, eyed her.

Colleen took a deep breath. "I'm working with Steve Cook."

Herbert Pike's face solidified. "And what on earth makes you think we would have anything to do with *him*?"

Colleen drew closer, lowered her voice. "His daughter has been kidnapped."

Shock registered on their faces.

"I am sorry to hear that," Mr. Pike said. "But I don't think it's any of our business."

"I've traveled all the way from the United States to try and get to the bottom of what happened all those years ago. I think there might well be a connection. Steve's been charged with murder, but I know he didn't do it. The same way I know he didn't cause your daughter's death."

"And how could you possibly know that?" Mrs. Pike said in her soft voice. Colleen had her interest.

Colleen cleared her throat. "The death certificate, for one. The cause of death is unclear, still pending. But, more to the point, I think it might have something to do with the record company he worked for."

"If that was the case," Mrs. Pike said. "Then why did he up and run? Flee the country? Like a criminal?"

"He was a teenager," Colleen said. "He was scared."

"Our Brenda never touched a drug in her life," Mr. Pike said. "She was a good girl. A *good* girl."

Mrs. Pike sniffed, blinking quickly.

"I believe you," Colleen said. "Surprising as it may seem, Steve Cook never used drugs either."

"It was that bloody roadie of theirs," Mr. Pike said. "I always thought he was the one who gave Brenda the drugs."

That was news to Colleen. "What roadie was that?"

"Some wastrel. Some tall lout. I don't know his name. But he was spotted with her in the bar the night before."

"How did you learn this?" Colleen asked.

"Herbert did his best to get to the bottom of things," Mrs. Pike said in her fading voice. "Brenda was a good girl. She went up to London to see the show with her girlfriend. They were picked up after the show by this roadie character, taken to the hotel bar. He promised the girls they'd get to meet the band, get them autographs. All rubbish. He was just trying to take advantage. Gayle—Brenda's friend—left but Brenda stayed behind." She shook her head angrily. "She was besotted with that silly pop star."

"There, there, love," Mr. Pike said, patting her arm. He turned to Colleen. "It was that roadie character who led our Brenda up to Steve's hotel room."

"Who told you the roadie took your daughter up to Steve's room?" Colleen asked.

"The drummer overheard them in the bar, then saw them staggering around on the fifth floor later. That roadie got our Brenda drunk, took her upstairs to supposedly meet Steve Cook. I reckon that was part of his job—finding girls for them. That's what they do, don't they?"

"Tich, the drummer, told you this?" Colleen said. "Dave Simons?"

"Yes, that was his name. I went up to that hotel when the police called about Brenda. Found the drummer chap in the bar. Drunk as a lord, he was, not even lunchtime. But he told me what he saw: our Brenda with this roadie character, up on the fifth floor, the night she died."

Steve's hotel room had been on the sixth floor.

"Did you report this to the police, Mr. Pike?"

"Of course, he did," Mrs. Pike said, louder now. "But they didn't want to know. They thought it was all Brenda's fault. They said girls threw themselves at Steve Cook. But our Brenda wasn't like that. She was a good girl."

Mr. Pike patted his wife's arm again, spoke to Colleen. "And a lot of good that did when Cook pulled a runner and fled the U.K. Basically admitted guilt, then, didn't he?"

CHAPTER FORTY-ONE

It was after 10 p.m. by the time Colleen's train rolled back into Euston Station.

Thankfully, the rain had let up, but the air was wet, with a sharp bite to it. Colleen found a ubiquitous red phone kiosk, looked up the Hot Box in Soho, where the last newspaper clipping she'd read said that Tich, the drummer for The Lost Chords, worked as a club doorman. That was some time ago, but she had nothing else to go on.

There were no taxis to be had so she grabbed the tube over to Leicester Square, where the young and drunk were staggering around, waving blue-and-white football scarves and chanting how they were champions. It was a short walk north of Piccadilly to the club scene. The Hot Box was on Firth Street, amidst clubs that were equally noisy. Rock 'n' roll thumped out of Ronnie Scott's as she walked by.

The Hot Box didn't enjoy the same status. A smattering of club-goers stood out front of the double matte black doors leading to a cellar, smoking or glaring at passersby. Industrial-strength disco music pounded from down the stairs.

Colleen's heart sank when she saw the doorman, a pale-skinned kid with acne and a spiky blond punk do. His shiny sharkskin suit was skintight, and his sneer was a warning. He would have been just starting primary school when The Lost Chords were top of the charts.

He gave her the once-over. She was pushing the age limit for a young scene. But she was female and well dressed.

"Two quid cover," he said.

"How much for a little information?"

"Ah. I see we have a *septic* in our midst."

"Say what?"

He eyed Colleen as if she were simple. "*Septic tank*—Yank."

"Cockney rhyming slang," she said.

"You got it, *pardner*," he said in a poor imitation of an American accent.

She held up a blue five-pound note. "I'm actually looking for one of your coworkers."

"Spit it out, then." He took the note. Pocketed it.

"Are you always so erudite?"

"Depends what bloody *erudite* means, don't it?"

"Tich," she said. "Dave Simons?"

The kid grinned as he rubbed his nose. "You're bloody kidding, right?"

"I wish. I heard he works here."

"Last year, he did. Before he got the sack."

"He was fired?"

"Yeah, that's what *the sack* means. Don't they speak English in America?"

"Not the King's English. Why did Tich get the sack?"

The kid made a quick drinking motion with his hand, extending his thumb and little finger.

"Drinking on the job," Colleen said.

"Comes with the territory, love. But Tich couldn't handle the punters when they got rough after he'd had a few. Which happened most days. It was more the other way around. So Tich got the boot."

"Any idea where I can find him?"

The kid looked her in the eye. "Possibly."

They continued to stare at each other for a moment.

"Oh, right." Colleen dug out another five-pound note, held it up surreptitiously. It disappeared.

"You're learning, darlin'," he said.

"So where can I find Tich? Not that I'm not enjoying this scintillating conversation."

"Pushing pints at The Queen's Head." The kid nodded to his left. "Round the corner."

When Colleen got there, she wasn't sure Her Majesty would appreciate having her name on the pub where Dave Simons, aka Tich, supposedly worked now. It might have been a fine place in its day, but a lot of beer had been spilled on the threadbare rugs since the turn of the century. The paint and woodwork were in a sorry state. You could smell the restroom from the front door. There were sparse upgrades, which included inane, ringing slot machines and a tinny jukebox, which was playing "Blondie." If you were to look up "dive" in the dictionary, a picture of The Queen's Head pub might well appear.

The same went for the clientele. Unlike other clubs and pubs in Piccadilly that aspired to being part of some sort of scene, The Queen's Head looked more like the last stop before A.A. Grim-faced drinkers, mostly men, lined the bar, no one looking too prosperous. Two questionable women sat at the end of the bar in miniskirts and high heels. One was black with a dramatic afro, the other pale white the way only English girls could be, with harsh red lipstick to contrast it. Ladies of the night. They gave Colleen a quick once-over as she entered, then dismissed her when they realized she wasn't competition.

But it was the barman that drew Colleen's interest.

He was the same man on the cover of *that album*. The one who once beat the skins with The Lost Chords. But that was about forty pounds and ten thousand drinks ago. Tich—Brit speak for "tiny," so named because he had been a large man to begin with—had lost most of his hair. Wisps of his once brown mane now curled a sweaty crown. His face was big, red, and puffy. He wore a nondescript white shirt that was tight on him and the sweat was more related to his body processing alcohol than the temperature of the bar, which was cold and damp. For a man who was about thirty, he was in poor shape indeed. He was drawing pints of foamy bitter, pulling a long wooden handle, which he set down in front of a couple of punk rockers who had to fish through their change in order to pay. He checked the coins and dropped them in a cash register that probably came with the place, slammed the drawer, and turned back around, where he picked up a smoldering cigarette from a full ashtray. He took a despondent puff that seemed to define his situation.

He noticed Colleen.

"Hello, love." He tucked his cigarette in the corner of his mouth and put his meaty hands on the bar. "What'll it be, then?"

It had been a long day. "Johnnie Walker Black," she said. "Make it a double."

He pursed his lips in admiration at her choice, turned to the suspended bottles where he squeezed out two shots from the dispenser. He set the glass in front of her with a remarkably delicate motion. "I assume you won't be wantin' to ruin that with ice."

"You got it," she said, getting out a red twenty-pound note that caught his eye. "Join me?"

Nothing like buying a drink for a drunk to cheer him up. "Don't mind if I do." He measured himself a double shot. He tapped his glass against hers. "Ta, love."

She sipped hers. His was gone in two quick swigs.

She fished out a cigarette. He lit it for her. She thanked him.

"You're American," he said, sipping from a pint of beer he kept under the bar. "No prize for guessing that." He gave a weary smile.

"And you're Tich Simons," she said.

"Whoa. I am no longer incognito."

"I've got your album."

He blushed, redder than the high blood pressure that was part of his makeup. "Not too many of those around anymore. Long out of print."

"It's too bad. You guys were great."

He gave a genuine smile now. "Thank you. Yeah, I reckon we were as well. But I bet there's even fewer copies of *that album* floating around the U.S. than here. We never really cracked America. Never got to tour. It was all over too soon."

"I've got the original Delco U.K. version. In glorious mono."

He nodded. "Nice."

"And personally autographed by Steve Cook."

He gave her a blink. "Get away."

"Steve lives in San Francisco."

"Yeah, I heard he moved there. After . . ."

She didn't bother to let him finish a sentence he wasn't going to. "He did."

Now he gave her a look of real surprise. "Do you know Steve, then?"

She nodded as she took a puff, followed it up with a sip of scotch. "I do. And now I know you—sort of."

Now it was Tich's turn to light up another cigarette, a stubby little thing from a blue and white striped box of ten. Player's No. 6.

"Well, you know more about Steve than I do, love. We never heard another bloody word from him after he pulled a runner on us." Tich shook his head. "Left us all in the bleeding lurch."

"He might have had a reason."

"Oh, you reckon? He could've stuck it out, taken his lumps. That would have been a way to do it."

"Maybe he wasn't thrilled with the prospect of going to jail."

Tich shook his head as he looked at her. "If he'd stood by us, we'd have stood by him. We had a rule as a band—we backed each other up, regardless. We were all in it together, even though Steve was the draw. But no, he scarpered off. I knew Steve since I was six years old. He didn't even say goodbye." He frowned.

"Feel like talking about what happened?"

"Not here, I bloody don't."

"What time do you get off work?"

"Fuck it, love. Water under the bridge." He walked away to serve the two ladies at the end of the bar, one who had been impatiently waving her empty wineglass at him.

"Cockney Rebel" came on the jukebox. Colleen downed her whiskey, held her empty glass up for Tich to see, since that seemed to be the way it was done. He ignored her.

At ten to eleven he rang a bell. "Last orders," he grunted. A flurry of activity at the bar kept him busy for the next ten minutes.

She held up her empty glass again.

"Bar's closed," he said.

"Come on," she said. "For an old fan."

He served her without a smile. "One pound."

She pushed two one-pound notes at him. "Join me."

"No," he said. "I'm fine."

"Now that surprises me."

"Well, nobody's asking you."

"Look," she said. "I'm sorry if I hit a nerve. But I really want to hear your side of the story."

"But you're not just some fan who's tripping down memory lane—are you?"

She sipped her scotch, relishing the afterburn. "Nope. I am not."

"What's the deal, then?"

She took a breath. "I'm trying to help Steve. His ex-wife was murdered. His daughter was kidnapped. He's in jail. Again. He didn't do this, either."

A look of round-eyed shock encompassed Tich's face. "Christ almighty."

"He doesn't even know I came over here. He never wants to talk about what happened back in '66."

Tich frowned. "Yeah, that sounds like Steve."

She checked her watch. "I hear there are some decent Indian restaurants around here. Where you can drink after hours, if you order food. I haven't eaten all day, unless you count two double scotches." She raised her eyebrows. "I'm buying."

He looked at her, gave a deep sigh. "Star of India, round the corner. I'll meet you there. I need to clear the place out, lock up, yeah?"

She didn't feel great about enabling Tich's drinking, but Melanie Cook took priority. And she suspected Tich would find his next drink just fine without her help anyway.

Half an hour later they sat across from each other in a small, dimly lit Indian restaurant amongst a boozy clientele downing curries and Tandoori and washing it all down with pints of beer. Indian music buzzed from shrill loudspeakers while a busy wait staff shouted orders to the kitchen. Colleen put away a lamb Vindaloo that scorched her tongue in a good way while Tich drained pints of lager. She brought him up to speed with Steve's case while she ate.

"So you think Steve's daughter—Melanie—was kidnapped by people associated with Sir Ian?" Tich said, incredulous.

"There's a connection," she said. "I'd bet on it."

Tich ordered another pint. "How so?"

"There's some kind of movie interest in 'Shades of Summer.' It was the reason Lynda's father was involved."

Tich's beer arrived. "Delco screwed Steve out of the songwriting royalties, to be sure."

"They've been tied up in court for years."

"Well," Tich said, drinking, "the rest of us didn't even have that. Steve wrote the songs. Sir Ian wasn't paying us either. And when Steve took off, The Lost Chords died a slow, miserable death."

"Sir Ian seems to be a piece of work," she said.

"An understatement." Tich ordered a scotch. He was done with beer. "Sir Ian screwed us and half a dozen other bands that made Delco rich. We'd play two gigs a day sometimes. I remember playing a telly program in Hamburg one afternoon, flying back to London for a concert that night. It went on like that for close to a year. All we saw out of it was a clothing allowance and living in posh hotels and all we could drink. No real cash. The real money never came. We were stupid, working-class kids who didn't know any better, thought we'd made it because we could order room service. Steve was the first to put his foot down. He and Sir Ian started fighting over money."

"So it began early, fighting with Sir Ian."

"Oh, yeah. But he had us in a contract we couldn't get out of."

Colleen measured her next sentence. "You never bought that Steve's behavior led to that girl's death? Brenda Pike?"

Tich shook his head and drank. "Steve never touched drugs. Hated them, in fact. None of us really got into them much. Beer and whiskey—that was our poison. We were working-class lads from Andover. There weren't that many drugs there when we started out."

"So Steve didn't give Brenda anything? You're sure?"

Tich drank. "Not his style. And he didn't have to, if that's what you're thinking. Birds threw themselves at Steve to the point of being a nuisance. He used to complain about it, if you can believe it. Said he never got a rest. None of us did." Tich laughed, then caught himself. "Sorry, no offense."

"None taken," she said. "I'm a big girl."

"Well, we were kids, weren't we?" Tich slugged half a scotch.

"Do you think Brenda Pike might have overdosed herself?"

Tich drank, gave a shrewd shake of the head. "I saw her and her friend in the hotel bar that night, hoping to meet Steve. A pair of shy ones from the sticks. You could see it. Deer-eyed. Overwhelmed by the big city. I bought them a drink, tried to chat them up. They ordered bloody shandies."

"*Shandies?*"

"Beer and lemonade—a kid's drink. No way was she using hard drugs. She was just a starstruck kid."

"So you bought them a drink?"

"Yeah, but I didn't stick around, to be honest, when I saw they were schoolgirls, up to The Smoke for the day. Wasn't my speed. I was a bit of a lad myself. Wasn't about to waste my time—not when there were plenty of willing ravers to be had. We had just played a big show. There were birds falling out of the rafters."

Colleen cleared her throat. "Someone said you saw Brenda Pike and her friend with the band's roadie?"

A look of shock pulled Tich's mouth open. "Who told you that, then?"

"I met Brenda Pike's father earlier today. He said he came up to London after Brenda was found dead, trying to find out what happened. Some story about you . . . seeing the roadie . . . with Brenda . . ."

Tich's face changed. She saw the shutters going down.

He drained his drink, stood up. He wobbled. "Thanks for the drink. *Drinks.*"

She put her hand on his forearm. "I'm not looking to get anyone in trouble, Tich."

"Right. Sure."

"No, I mean it. But if you saw something, you might be able to help me nail Sir Ian. Save Steve's butt."

Tich eyed her.

"Why let Sir Ian get away with what he did?" she said. "Screwed all of you over? What if he had that girl killed? To compromise Steve? Put him in his place? Get the rights to his music?"

Tich gave a heavy sigh. Sat down. Ran his meaty paw over his eyes. "Christ," he said. "Christ almighty."

She signaled the waiter for more drinks.

"It's time to come clean, Tich," she said.

Tich looked up. "Bloody Steve," he said. "If he hadn't bolted, I could've helped sort things out."

"You saw your roadie with Brenda Pike."

Fresh drinks arrived, a glass of white wine for Colleen and a double scotch for Tich. Tich waited until the empties were cleared away, then downed half his whiskey.

"Yeah. Saw them coming out of Ev's room, heading for the elevator."

"What floor?"

"Fifth, I think. Yeah, Fifth."

"What were you doing?"

"My room was on the same floor. I was just getting off the elevator with a . . . well, a young lady I'd met. Anyways, I see Ev with the one country girl—Brenda—stumbling into the elevator as I'm looking for my room key. I thought she was just drunk, yeah? But I was in a hurry to get to my little private party." He gave a frown of regret.

"Didn't think much of it at the time. I assumed Ev was taking her down to get a cab or something—you know. That's the way it worked: if the roadies couldn't get the girls in to see the band, they'd try and pick them up for themselves. Second best."

"How drunk was she?"

"Very. Ev had to help her stand up."

"On shandies?"

Tich looked up. "I know. In retrospect, I figure he might have slipped her something. She was smashed."

"Did you say anything at the time?"

Tich took another swig of his shot, shook his head, sadly. "Should have. But I didn't. Ev gave me a look though."

"What kind of look?"

"What they call a prison yard stare, yeah? One that was warning me to mind my Ps and Qs. And Ev could be a real bastard when he put his mind to it."

"Tell me about this Ev," she said.

"Ev Cole. Tall, blond, skinny. But mean. He and Steve came to blows, after Ev roughed up a female fan. Put her in the hospital. Fucking bully is what Ev was. Enjoyed it. Steve talked to Sir Ian, just the day before, told him he wanted Ev gone."

"Do you think Sir Ian talked to Ev?"

"I'm sure he did. Steve was adamant. But now, I wonder if Ev and Sir Ian had something going on."

Something jogged her memory: the night she had stopped by Steve's in SF, with Steve waiting in the car. Lynda had been waiting, along with two thugs. One was tall. It made her think twice.

"Steve's room was one floor up?"

"Right. Sixth."

"So Ev could have been taking Brenda to Steve's room?"

Tich nodded, glassy-eyed. "Steve was drunk as a lord that night. He'd had a big fight with Ian right before the show. Said he'd punched his lights out. We thought it was funny, but I could tell it was bothering Steve. Did a great show anyway but hit the bottle with a vengeance right afterwards in our dressing room. He got smashed quick, though. I remember that. Steve was exhausted. Well, he worked his arse off onstage, harder than the rest of us. We'd been touring for a year. He came back to the hotel that night, went straight to his room. Turned in early."

"So if someone were to sneak a girl into his room, he might not have even noticed."

Tich returned a glum nod. "Birds were always finding a way to get into your room. Especially Steve's. One time in Oslo, he said he found a bird climbing into his bed after he'd turned in, but he rolled right over, went back to sleep, he was that knackered. The excesses of rock 'n' roll."

"But in this case . . ."

Tich's eyes were red and watery. "Yeah."

"Why didn't you say anything?"

Tich shook his head sadly. "I actually did. I recall speaking to the girl's dad. Then I went to see Ian, yeah? But Steve had already bolted. Left the U.K. And Ian told me there wasn't any point in pushing it."

"Did you think of going to the police?"

Tich shook his head again. "Ian said it would hurt the band. Said he had plans to keep The Chords going, replace Steve. Never worked out, but that was the strategy, so he said. But you couldn't replace Steve."

"And your position was in jeopardy."

"I was the drummer. No one even knew my real name. I could be easily replaced, the way The Beatles got rid of Pete Best, hired Ringo. I'm a meat-and-potatoes drummer. As long as Steve was there, I was golden. We'd been mates since we were kids. But Ian could've easily found someone who could play rings around me." He gave Colleen the saddest of looks. "Playing with The Chords was the best thing ever happened to me. To all of us. It was all I had. Before we hit it big, I worked in a bloody butcher's. Never even got my O levels. I had nothing else. I was nothing without The Chords."

And Sir Ian leveraged the situation.

She felt for Tich.

"What about when The Chords failed to regroup?" she said. "Did you think about going to the police then?"

"What was the point? Steve was long gone, gone to Brazil, and Brenda Pike was still dead. We all went our own separate ways. I had to look out for myself."

She could see that. "What about Ev?"

"Ian did get rid of him—officially. But I heard he still used him for dirty deeds, off the books, yeah? There was always a need for someone like that in the music business. I heard Ev moved to the U.S., Los Angeles, working for various and sundry people."

That caught her by surprise. "LA? Really?"

"True enough."

Now it made sense. Ev had possibly been there the night she went to Steve's and found Lynda waiting. She'd left Steve in the car. Lynda had had two knuckle draggers with her. In plain sight.

She let the shock subside, took a sip of wine, pieced it together.

"Thanks so much, Tich," she said. "This has been a big help."

"Some bloody help. I was a coward."

"Well, you can set it straight, now. I can look into what it would take to get the case reopened. You can make a statement."

She saw him take a cautious breath. "You reckon?"

"There's no statute of limitations on murder in the U.S. It's the same here."

He gave a watchful look. "It would open up a can of worms."

"Think what it would mean to Brenda's parents. It would mean a lot to Steve." She took a breath. "It would mean a lot to me."

He gave a final nod, finished his drink in one gulp.

"You're right," he said, wiping his mouth with the back of his hand. "I should have bloody done it, twelve years ago. Well, better late than never."

*   *   *

"Bloody hell!" Ian's wife said as the phone rang on Ian's side of the bed. "Not again!" Her pear-shaped body turned over in a huff, away from him, yanking the covers over her head.

Thirty years of married bliss had not softened her.

Ian sat up as he fumbled the ringing phone off the cradle from his bedside table. He'd just managed to fall asleep. He squinted at the clock in the semi-darkness. Past one a.m.

"Can't you take that in the other room!" Eloise barked. Her pink curlers practically glowed in the night-light. *Captivating.*

Ian covered the mouthpiece of the phone with his hand. "It's work!"

She grunted as she yanked the pillow over her head. Hidden from view.

Small mercies, Ian thought.

He uncovered the phone, spoke. "This best be Reggie," he said.

"Some of us are still working." In the background, Ian could hear muted street noises, from outside the call box where Reg was obviously calling from.

"Just tell me what you've got, Reg."

"She just left the restaurant."

"What restaurant would that be?"

"Star of India. She's been having a few with your old pal, Tich."

Really, Sir Ian thought. "Tich Simons?"

"He's just left. She's flagging down a taxi as we speak."

So she managed to get hold of Tich. On top of the trip to Church Stretton, where the Pikes lived, the parents of that dead girl, Ms. Aird's little story of wanting to buy "Shades of Summer" was fast resembling pure fiction. If Aird was even her real name.

"Good work, Reggie. Follow her. Find out where she's staying. I want to know who she is. Really is. Don't be afraid to flex a bit of muscle to find out, eh?"

"Got it, chief," Reggie said, excited now. This was the kind of work Reggie did best. "She's just flagged a taxi." The phone clicked off, leaving a dial tone in Sir Ian's ears.

Ian nodded to himself.

"Are you bloody done now?" his wife said, raising the pillow. "I'd like to get some sleep—if you don't mind."

*   *   *

"Twenty-two Whitfield Street," Colleen said to the cabbie.

"Yes, ma'am," the driver said, turning off Tottenham Court Road down Goodge, taking the first left on Whitfield. A narrow side street. The rain had let up momentarily. The cab pulled over to the curb across from a small park, the diesel engine rumbling away. Colleen paid him, got out in front of her B&B with her folded-up umbrella. The cab trundled off down Whitfield.

A long day.

Which might become longer, she realized, when she heard the puttering of a motor scooter come around the corner off Goodge, down her street, otherwise empty now. Turning her head discreetly, she saw the driver, a man wearing a silver helmet, goggles, and big military parka with a fur-lined hood down around his neck.

The same guy who had been in the phone booth across the street from the Star of India when she left the restaurant fifteen minutes ago. The same silver Vespa he was riding now had been parked by the phone booth, the helmet on the seat. And she thought she had seen a comparable scooter leaving Euston Station when she returned from Church Stretton. She hadn't been sure then but now, late at night, on this desolate street, there was no doubt.

Her nerves jangled with apprehension.

Her thoughts traveled back to that morning with Sir Ian. She had told him she was staying with friends but hadn't said where. She recalled the young guy sitting in the waiting room of Delco Records, reading a tabloid. Same size and stocky build as the rider of this scooter.

She wouldn't go into her B&B now and reveal her location.

She turned instead, headed back up Whitfield, toward him. The racket of the two-stroke engine bounced off the buildings and reverberated across the park. He drew closer. She gripped the closed umbrella tightly, even though it was starting to sprinkle again.

He shifted down. Maybe thirty feet away. Watching her. Moonlight reflected off his goggles as he followed her.

The same guy who'd been in the waiting room.

She looked down, moved away, into the narrow sidewalk, as he passed her.

She picked up the pace.

Behind her, she heard him slow down, make a U-turn, stop for a moment, and she heard a clatter, then she heard him come back up behind her.

The plastic umbrella handle became slippery in her hand.

The *putt-putt-putt* grew closer.

She spun back around, facing him.

He was moving a few miles per hour. Something long was sticking out of the right side of the handlebars, held in place by his hand while he worked the throttle.

A tire iron.

"Excuse me," he said, coasting up to her. "Do you live around here? I'm a bit lost."

"I do," she said quietly, not wanting to give away her accent, although he no doubt knew who she was. But he didn't know she was onto him, most likely.

"Great."

Eat or be eaten.

She leapt out as he came to a stop, swinging the umbrella backhand. Not too classy, but she needed the advantage. His mouth dropped open, and he tried to veer away. She had him by surprise, though.

She connected, hitting him in the neck, just below the helmet. He shouted, trying to keep the scooter upright, but she hit him again, harder, getting him in the face this time, and his hands rose in defense. She kicked the scooter with her heel and the scooter tumbled, but he was quick enough to jump off and skitter back into the street, out of the way.

The scooter lay on its side between them, engine whining.

He raised the tire iron, ready, a grimace on his face.

"Right, then," he said.

She flipped the umbrella to her left hand, her right hand diving into her pocket, coming out with her keys, which she flipped between index and forefinger. Umbrella and keys. More than a match now. She stood sideways, one leg in front of the other, eyeing him.

The motor scooter continued to whine.

"Ian sent you," she said.

He said nothing, waiting for an opportunity to strike. His nose was bleeding. The engine continued to drone.

A front door opened down the street.

A fat man appeared in a robe.

"What the bloody hell's going on?" he shouted. "People are trying to sleep."

"This man tried to attack me," she shouted. "Call the police."

There was a pause. "I'm calling the police." The door shut.

Her attacker was growing nervous. He didn't want to run, leave his bike behind. She didn't really want to talk to the police. Not so far from home. Not with a record.

But she knew what she needed to know about Sir Ian. He'd had her followed. He was complicit.

"Have a nice day, asshole." She lowered the umbrella, crossed the street at an angle, leaving her attacker. She ducked into the park.

"Fucking bitch!" She heard the tire iron clang asphalt as he struggled to get the scooter back upright. It died on him when he did that and he started kicking it over. It wouldn't start. A front door opened again.

"I've called the police!" the fat man shouted.

Finally, the scooter started and whirred off up Whitfield in a wind-up of gears. And then it was gone.

Colleen exited the park, hurried down Whitfield to her guesthouse. She let herself in quietly, got to her room before the police could arrive. She peeled off her jacket, lay in darkness, her mind swarming with revelations. She now knew Sir Ian was involved in Steve's downfall, and the death of Brenda Pike.

As was Ev.

CHAPTER FORTY-TWO

It was raining at SFO when Colleen's red-eye descended through low night clouds to the city by the bay. A gust of wind buffeted the plane as they came in over the water toward the runway. Smeary lights flickered alongside wet asphalt as the 747 touched down, skidding until the plane righted itself. But her second international flight was easier than the first. Turbulence was a part of the process, to be expected. Just like life. She even managed to catnap. And having Tich's word that he would press ahead with his statement on what transpired the night Brenda Pike died helped settle her concerns, although there were plenty of unknowns left. Like Sir Ian's involvement. But she could call it progress.

Back home, on Vermont Street, she circled her block, looking for any sign of a white van, or anyone else keeping tabs on her. *Nada*.

It was still the wee hours when she sat down at her desk and checked her answering service. A call from Gus Pedersen, Steve's new lawyer.

*　　*　　*

Early the next morning she spoke to Gus. It wasn't looking good for Steve. He wasn't getting bail, which was not a surprise. But no word from the kidnappers. Gus had keys to Steve's flat now and was

checking in regularly and had installed one of those fancy new answering machines on Steve's phone as a long shot, knowing a kidnapper would not leave a message on an answering machine.

At 9:00 a.m. Colleen signed up for a visit on the seventh floor of
850 Bryant. She got down there slowly through SF commute traffic
and parked in a lot nearby that charged her three bucks. Parking
prices in SF were getting out of hand.

Just after ten, they brought Steve in. He sat on the other side of the
Plexiglas, wearing a faded orange jumpsuit. He hadn't shaved since
his arrest and a thick layer of stubble darkened his already moody
countenance. His eyes were sunken. Worry creased his brow. He was
about as unsteady as she'd ever seen him, and she felt for him. Even
so, he seemed to be holding up better than most people would.

This time he had a pack of Lucky Strikes. Gus had seen he was
stocked. He shook one out, lit it up, and picked up the handset. So
did she.

He took a deep drag. "Please tell me you've got some good news
about Mel."

Colleen took a measured breath. "I wish I did, Steve. But I am
closer."

"How so?"

"She's worth a lot more to the kidnappers alive. They're just waiting
to make their move. The longer you sit, the more they wear you down."

"I've got news—it's working." Steve knocked ash off his cigarette
into an abandoned Pepsi can.

"I met Sir Ian," she said. "In London."

He returned a sheepish look.

"Why didn't you ever tell me about Brenda Pike, Steve?"

He shrugged. "Why do you think, Coll?" He brushed some loose
ash off the countertop and looked away. "It's not exactly an episode
of my life I'm particularly proud of."

"But you were set up."

Steve squinted at her. "Nice to think so." Shook his head. "But no—I fucked up just fine all on my own."

"No," she said. "Sir Ian's got something to hide. Something big."

"How do you figure that, then?"

"Apart from the fact that he had me tailed in London?" she said. "Ev Cole."

"Strewth." A look of surprise crossed Steve's face. "There's a name from the past."

"Twelve years ago, he was seen in the bar earlier the night Brenda Pike was in your room—with Brenda. Along with a friend of hers. Her friend took off."

"How do you know all that?"

Colleen told Steve about her visit to Church Stretton, meeting Brenda's parents. Brenda's father going to the hotel, learning about Ev with Brenda. "He even mentioned it to the police. But by that time, you'd already left the U.K. So it was all back-burnered. The night before Brenda was found dead in your room, Ev was seen getting on the elevator with her on the fifth floor—his room was on the floor below yours. She was staggering, supposedly drunk. But she'd been drinking shandies in the bar. My money says Ev gave her something stronger, brought her up to your room. Where she died of an overdose while you were passed out."

Steve blinked in thought, obviously turning things over in his mind.

Colleen pushed ahead: "You'd had a beef with Ev a couple days before. He'd beaten up a fan. You told Sir Ian you wanted him fired. You had a fight with Sir Ian that night, too—before the show. You punched him. Threatened him over non-payment. So Brenda's death is shaping up to look a lot like revenge. Sir Ian is my bet. Maybe Ev. Maybe both."

"And how do you know all this, Coll? Ev on the floor below mine and such?"

"Tich," she said.

Steve did a double take. "What?"

"Tich lives in London, works in a pub, drinks too much."

Steve took a puff, exhaled. "Poor bloody Tich."

"He's the one who saw Ev and Brenda that night. You'd gone to bed drunk. After that fight with Sir Ian, you took it out on the bottle in your dressing room."

"I don't even remember going to bed. But, if that's the case, why didn't Tich say anything at the time?"

"He did—to Sir Ian. But you'd already taken off. And Sir Ian told Tich that if he wanted to be part of anything going forward, he'd best keep his mouth shut about what he saw."

"Christ." The cigarette sat forgotten in Steve's hand. "*Christ.*"

"'Shades of Summer' has been inquired about for an upcoming RomCom."

Steve looked up. "Rom *what?*"

"Romantic Comedy. It's in a gossip column in a recent *Variety*. Gil Johns, the director of *Sweet Sympathy*, is rumored to have been making enquiries into 'Shades of Summer' for a new soundtrack."

Steve thought about that. "Get out."

"'Flowers' went for over a million pounds," she said.

"I remember that tune. The Bang, 1965."

"Well, the guy who wrote it was working as a warehouseman in Liverpool before Hollywood picked up 'Flowers' for *Endless Love*, last year's romantic blockbuster. Guess what? He's no longer lugging boxes around the docks for a living. He won an Ivor Novello for the song after the movie was nominated and recently moved to the South of France. Now he's looking to buy a vineyard."

"No."

"And you were next, Steve. But your entire catalog has been tied up in litigation all these years. Sir Ian knows you won't deal with him. He's behind this. When I was in London, I met with him, pretending to make enquiries. He was most interested. I reckon he was able to talk Rex Williamson and Lynda into a fake kidnap, 'lend' you the ransom money in exchange for your catalog—get it at a bargain basement price. Both Rex and Lynda had the connections; both have worked with Delco Records. And NewMedia."

"Lynda's company. And Lynda went along. Promised Mel the bloody horse she'd been wanting." Steve shook his head, ran his fingers through his hair. "But it went wrong." He looked up. "Where the fuck *is* she?" His voice cracked.

"She's alive, Steve. When the faux kidnap was blown, my money says Lynda, and most likely Rex, bailed on going any further. Things were getting out of hand. But someone got greedy, shot Lynda, ramped everything up a notch, took Melanie for keeps. A *real* kidnap."

"Okay." Steve nodded. "But not Rex. He wouldn't kidnap his own granddaughter."

"But Ev Cole would."

Steve squinted. "Ev again. But he's over five thousand miles away."

Colleen shook her head. "Tich says Ev immigrated to the U.S., like a lot of Brits, when the economy went south in Britain. I'm told he lives in the LA area now. I now know he was the guy at your place that night when I stopped by. You were waiting in the car. Lynda was there, with Ev. And another guy. To pressure you into taking Rex's money. I think Sir Ian enlisted Ev's help for the dirty work." She pulled the Polaroid photo of the tall man on a motorcycle receiving a bag from the fateful ransom payoff down at the Transbay Terminal. She pressed it up against the Plexiglas. "Take another look."

Steve leaned forward, looked at it. "Could be Ev. But it's not a lock, is it?"

Colleen put the photo away. She described Ev to Steve as he had appeared that night when Lynda was at Steve's.

"That sounds like Ev, all right," he said. "Bloody hell."

"He was right in front of me." She shook her head in disbelief. "*Right in front of me.* Twice. Once on the motorcycle. The other time in your flat that night with Lynda."

A look of anguish took hold of Steve's face. "Ev was one of our roadies, back in '65–'66. He was mean and nasty then, and I have no reason to think he's changed. And now he's over here. There's plenty of old U.K. music people in LA. There's always a need for guys like Ev. They can collect payment for the gig when the manager at the Whiskey says he's short on cash and will send a check, work as a bodyguard, know where to get more nose candy when your promo party is running short." Steve gave Colleen a knowing look. "It's not all peace and love."

Colleen actually never thought any of it was. "My theory says Ev got greedy after the so-called kidnap blew up. He went over to strong-arm Lynda the night she was killed, sometime after you did. They got into an argument, he threatened her, she ran upstairs, pulled her gun, things got out of hand. He killed her."

Steve's eyes were empty. "And then he and whoever he was with took off with Mel."

"Couldn't leave her behind. Or they would have to kill her, too. Besides, now Ev had the most valuable bargaining chip in the world: your daughter."

The cigarette burned down to Steve's fingers, and he shook it loose, dropped it in the Pepsi can with a sizzle. "What if he killed Mel?"

Colleen's heart thumped. "There's no money in that. And money is what Ev wants. Melanie's worth a lot more alive."

"But there haven't been any more ransom requests."

"You haven't exactly been available."

Steve took a deep breath, let it out. "Trouble is, you've got to prove all of this, Coll. I'm stuck in here."

"I know. I will."

"How?"

"By finding Ev. I've got resources." Moran, to start with.

Steve hung his head. "If only I hadn't run back in '66."

"Brenda Pike wasn't your fault, Steve."

"I could have been awake and sober when she was brought into my room. I could have gotten her help. Before . . ."

"Ev gave Brenda Pike an overdose. He could have easily done something similar with you, slipped something into your bottle in your dressing room after that show. You got drunk fast, you went back to the hotel, straight to bed. Don't you think that's just a little strange?"

Steve looked up. "Perhaps. But that's not much comfort now. Ev was always around. No one would have thought twice about him being in the dressing room."

Colleen could certainly see that.

"Visiting time's up," the sheriff's deputy said behind her. "I already let you go over."

Colleen nodded. "Stay strong, Steve."

He gave a somber nod. "I owe you, love."

Love. They took a moment to look at each other, without sound. A decade had transpired between them in minutes. If there had been any lingering doubt about Steve's involvement in killing Lynda, it was gone. And Colleen's feelings for him were only stronger.

They both hung up their phones. And stood up.

A dark frown settled over Steve's face. Colleen saw twelve years' worth of regret and agony travel across it in a matter of seconds.

CHAPTER FORTY-THREE

"That's Ev Cole?" Moran said, squinting at Colleen's grainy Transbay Polaroid. He pushed his dark framed glasses up his nose as he studied the photo.

"That's the guy," Colleen said, flipping up the collar of her bomber jacket and hunkering down in the sharp wind coming in off the ocean. She and Moran were standing at the end of Santa Cruz Pier, the Boardwalk behind them. The roller coaster was silent. No riders today. A wet rainy midweek day. Whitecaps blew in on the rolling surf. "It's too bad our only real witness, the guy who probably handed him a bag of cash, is dead."

"Tell me about it," Moran said. He'd been there the day that Colleen chased the little guy under a Muni bus on Mission Street.

"I'm told Ev lives somewhere in the Los Angeles area."

The wind bent the Polaroid as Moran brought it closer. "What kind of motorcycle is that?"

"It's not American," she said. "Too small. Maybe Japanese. Maybe a 650. Or a 750. Ev's tall, about thirty years old now."

"And you're confident about this lead, Hayes?" he asked, handing back the photo.

She nodded as she pocketed the Polaroid. Wind blew her hair across her face as she filled Moran in on Ev's past, back in The Lost Chords' heyday.

"And you're sure he's got Melanie Cook?" Moran asked.

"If not, he knows a lot more than the rest of us."

"Have you considered that Melanie Cook might be . . ." Moran didn't finish the sentence.

"No," she said quickly. It was too grim to think about.

"Then why hasn't there been another ransom demand?"

"I don't know." Colleen shrugged, shuddering in the cold wind, and the turn the conversation had taken. "He's biding his time. Wants Steve to sweat it out. Steve hasn't been easy to get hold of, either, locked up."

"Okay." Moran nodded after some thought. "I'll buy it."

A surge of relief flowed through her. Moran's approval was a good sign although she could tell he had his doubts.

"Don't you have a contact who can run a trace?" she asked. Moran's connection was somebody at Santa Cruz PD. Someone with a link to FBI databases, other resources out of Colleen's reach.

"I'll see what I can find. But Los Angeles is a big place, Hayes—if he's even in Los Angeles."

"Can't be any harder than trying to get hold of you," she said, smiling.

"Sorry about Daphne. She worries about me. Which reminds me. I better be getting back."

"Please tell her I said 'thanks' for sparing you."

Moran gave a grin. "The less I say about you, Hayes, the better. How much of all this are you telling Inspector Owens?"

"Up until my trip to London, most everything. But after I was told in no uncertain terms to desist, I'm incognito, as they say. So, until I find Ev, Owens is not exactly at the top of my call list."

"Is that wise?"

"He had Steve Cook arrested. He could do the same with me. I'm not going to risk that until I have all of the information together— or, better still, Melanie Cook."

Moran gave Colleen a pensive look before he spoke. "Have you considered that your client Steve Cook might have actually killed his ex-wife?"

"For all of ten seconds."

"Sure it wasn't a little longer than that?"

"It might have been. But he didn't do it."

"And you're perfectly sure you might not be—ah—prejudiced towards him?"

Colleen blushed, her face warming. "Steve Cook was a teen idol. But now he's my client. And he didn't kill his ex."

"Fair enough. I'll let you know what I find out about Ev Cole. What's your next move?"

"Circle back to Rex Williamson," she said. "Lynda's father. He knows more than he's letting on."

"Be careful, Hayes. If this Ev Cole is what you say he is, and there's a connection to Lynda's father, you need to keep your eyes peeled."

She knew that. She was actually looking forward to bumping into Ev. But she also knew she needed to be prepared.

CHAPTER FORTY-FOUR

The phone rang in the middle of the night, pulling Colleen from a coma of sleep. Jet lag was catching up. She sat up, the warm water-bed sloshing underneath her bare butt, and blinked to focus. The sharp red digits of the clock read 2:19 a.m.

She had no idea how long the phone had been ringing.

Maybe it was Alex.

She answered the phone, brushing her hair back off her forehead.

There was a squeal of something electronic, followed by a tinny, familiar robotic voice, distorted.

"Good morning," it said. The sarcasm was heavy, even with the mask of hissing electronica. "Hope you weren't in the middle of something good."

"Who is this?" But she already knew.

"Do you really need to ask that?"

"We've spoken before. Down at the Transbay Terminal. Before you ripped my client off for twenty K."

"That was then," the voice said. "This is now."

"Why the hell are you calling *me*?"

"Round two."

As she suspected. More cash. "You've got Melanie?"

"You have a distinct knack for stating the obvious."

"Great. Put her on."

"She'd sound like Robbie the Robot. And I'm not about to un-hook my magic box and let you speak to her direct, love."

Love.

"So how do I know she's alive?" Colleen said.

"Of course she is. What do you think I am?"

"A murderer. You killed Lynda."

"Want me to hang up, bitch?" the voice snapped, irritated. She'd hit a nerve. Good.

"No," she said. "And neither do you."

"Then fucking apologize!"

She took a deep breath and bit down on her anger. "I apologize."

The metallic voice laughed. "That's better."

"But nothing happens until I have confirmation Melanie's alive."

"And you will. When you bring the cash. This is just a heads-up to start collecting it. Give you a day or two lead time. See what a wonderful person I am?"

"I never doubted it."

"Shut up!" the voice huffed. "Thirty thousand. Used bills. Nothing larger than a twenty."

Thirty K. Upping the bet. "Why are you asking me? Last time I checked, I wasn't Melanie's parent."

"Well, I think we both know your client isn't exactly available these days. So you'll just have to do instead."

"What makes you think I'm going to pay you? That I *can* pay you?"

"You want what's best for Steve—don't you?"

His mocking tone raised her blood pressure. But making her re-sponsible for the payoff wasn't as crazy as it sounded. She was, after all, the one who had been driving things from Steve's end. She couldn't very well walk away now.

"And what makes you think I won't go to the police?" Colleen said.

"You don't want to be responsible for Melanie's body being separated from her head."

She let that image sink in.

"Thirty K." He hung up.

Her ears buzzed. She was warm with exhaustion but knew she wouldn't be going back to sleep now. She got up, threw on her kimono, went out to the kitchen, drank a glass of water.

She sat on her leather sofa, in the dark, smoked a cigarette, and made plans.

CHAPTER FORTY-FIVE

An hour or so past midday, rays of sunlight flashed off the choppy Pacific as Colleen drove into Manhattan Beach. She pulled the Torino over at a gas station not far from Rex Williamson's house. She left the engine running while she hopped out, inserted a dime, called his house.

"Hello?"

She hung up. He was home. All she needed to know. She drove to his street, parked a ways down, shut off the engine, leaned back in her bucket seat, cracked out her back.

Less than six hours to drive to LA from SF. Not bad. It almost beat flying, when you took into account getting to and from the airport, waiting in line, checking into flights, hailing cabs. The drive had also cleared the crud in her carburetor, and the Torino was running like a rocket. A smoking rocket, but still.

And she might be down here for a while, would need her car.

And possibly her gun. Which she could not bring onto a plane.

She got the pistol out now, from the gym sock hanging under the dash. The black Bersa .22 Moran had given her on her last case didn't weigh much and didn't take up a lot of space. She slipped it into the side pocket of a dressy long black suit jacket hanging over the back of her seat. She straightened the flap over the pocket.

She wouldn't risk a visit to Rex's house. She might get shot, or he might call the police. She'd wait until he left and follow. Catch him off guard. She dug out her opera glasses, the fancy ones that came in an embroidered case.

About forty minutes later, the long nose of a two-door car bounced out of Rex's driveway. A lone driver sat at the wheel of a dark Chrysler Cordoba. Colleen peered through the opera glasses. Rex's lean, tanned profile came into view.

The car headed off down the street.

Key still in the ignition, she fired the Torino back up and headed out after Rex. She grabbed her sunglasses from the console and slipped them on for anonymity.

She trailed the Cordoba along Hermosa Avenue, the afternoon sun warming the inside of the car enough for her to roll the window down and take advantage of the balmy sea breeze. A break from the San Francisco and London damp. At Dockweller Beach, Rex's car turned inland, heading toward the airport.

She followed the Cordoba to a cheesy strip mall, where Rex pulled in, the car bouncing as it nosed into a spot. Colleen parked on the street, shut off the engine, leaned forward, watched Rex Williamson get out of his car. He wore shell-pink bell-bottoms, white loafers, and a snug floral shirt. For his age he was pushing it with the disco look. But he walked with a spritely gait directly into Amy's Oriental Massage.

The dog.

Well, she had wanted to catch Rex off guard.

This would be the place.

She smoked a cigarette, giving Rex enough time to disrobe and get comfortable but not enough time to get too far along with his massage. She climbed out of her car, stepped out her cigarette, slipped her jacket on over a paisley polyester blouse with ample lapels. The outfit was topped off with a pair of gray high-waist side-button flares, made of polyester as well, comfortable for the long drive from SF but dressy enough if she had to go somewhere where jeans and sneaks wouldn't cut it. She hadn't planned on massage parlors. No matter. She marched across the parking lot and into Amy's Oriental Massage.

The air inside wafted lavender. Indirect lights were pointed at the ceiling and plants, providing the suggestion of privacy. Hidden speakers played the sounds of waves lapping on a beach along with the call of tropical birds. It was almost enough to drown out the beep of a truck reversing out in the parking lot.

A middle-aged white woman with horn-rimmed glasses on a chain around her neck sat at a receptionist's desk, a magazine open in front of her. She wore a white lab coat over a bright floral top with a serious V-neck that revealed ample cleavage bordering on fat.

"Where is he?" Colleen snapped.

"Where is who?" the woman said in a Midwestern twang.

"Rex," she said. "The guy who just came in here."

She squinted. "Who?"

Of course Rex wouldn't use his real name.

"My husband, goddamn it!" Colleen said. "I just saw him come in."

"We do *not* divulge information about our clients," the woman said in a haughty tone.

"I see." Colleen pulled and flashed the security officer's badge she'd purchased at one of the police supply stores around the Hall of Justice in SF. It was housed in a leather case that was suitably beat-up and authentic-looking. "I'm assuming you'd rather have your license pulled?"

The woman's bright red lips fell open in shock. "There's no need to cause a fuss."

"So what room is he in?"

"Just a moment," she huffed, jumping up. She was round, despite her black stockings and high heels, and efforts to look alluring. "I'll go get him. Don't move. Wait here."

There was a hallway off to the left, where more low light filtered. Colleen blocked the woman's way. "I'll get him myself."

The woman sucked in a deep breath. "I don't want any trouble."

"Then just tell me what room he's in."

"*Avalon*," she sighed. "Last door on the left."

"Do *not* interrupt me. Or I'll shut this little slice of heaven down."

"Please be discreet."

Colleen stepped quietly down a narrow hallway, passing another room in session, the sounds of Latin music muffling a conversation between a man and a woman about the Dodgers.

At *Avalon*, the last room, the rapid squeaking of wood was muted by Bob Dylan's "Lay Lady Lay."

Colleen barged in.

Rex Williamson was arched on his back, naked on a massage table, being serviced by hand by a tall dark bony woman wearing a roomy pink bikini and a scowl. She looked up at Colleen, annoyed. Rex, for his part, was good and terrified. His erection quickly faded.

"You miserable louse!" Colleen said to Rex.

Rex eyed her, confused. Hadn't recognized her yet. Colleen flashed her badge at the woman. "Has he paid you?"

"Nice try. I'm not falling for that. We work for tips. And what we were doing was between two consensual adults."

"Yes, I'm sure you consensual adults are both meant for each other. But I asked you a question. Have you been tipped yet?"

"Uh, *no*."

Colleen went to the chair, picked up the pink pants hanging over the back, fished out a slim wallet, found two twenties. She threw the pants and wallet down on the chair, went over, handed the woman the money.

"Here's your tip. You're done here."

"Fine with me," she said, taking the money, straightening it. "Sorry, Luther," she said to Rex. "Better luck next time." She left the room.

Colleen went over, shut the door quietly, keeping Rex in her sight. He was busy pulling a towel over his dwindling manhood.

"Sorry about the unhappy ending, Rex," Colleen said. "But you and I need to talk."

"You!" Rex's mouth fell in recognition. "What the hell do you think you're doing?"

"Last time we met," she said, "I told you to call me, that we could work together. But you snubbed me, Rex. That hurts my feelings. So here I am. Hurt."

"This is about Melanie."

"I see the blood's finally returning to your head. Yes, of course it's about Melanie. Your granddaughter. I take it you know that Steve's still in jail."

Rex's face fell, as did his sagging body. He suddenly looked old and sad. "I would never, ever do anything to hurt my family."

Colleen stood, her arms over her chest. She studied him for a moment. "Do I think you kidnapped your own granddaughter after you killed your daughter?" She shook her head. "No. But you have an idea who did. And rather than act on it, you go out for a quick one off the wrist at Amy's Oriental Massage."

"I've been under a lot of stress." Rex sat on the edge of the massage table, his feet dangling. He looked at the floor. "There wasn't a damn thing I could do. You don't understand."

"Truly pathetic."

"Can I get dressed?"

"Not until you tell me where I find Ev Cole."

Rex looked up, doubly shocked.

There *was* a link.

Colleen continued: "I know Ev had a connection to Delco in the past and the music industry in LA now. I know he does dirty work for people. He's the one who helped set up the original 'kidnap,' isn't he?"

Rex took a deep, defeated breath. Then he nodded, reluctantly.

Colleen continued: "Let me guess: when the fake kidnap backfired, after Steve rejected your second offer to lend him twenty K for ransom in exchange for his catalog, you got cold feet and figured the ruse wasn't going to fly. But Ev kept the pressure up, took things into his own hands, went to see Lynda."

Rex sighed, eyed her sheepishly. "It went off the rails. I didn't want any more of it. I knew Ev was bad news. I'm no kidnapper. It was just a game."

"Some game. But you did nothing when Ev killed your daughter. Kidnapped your granddaughter."

A look of annoyance crossed Rex's face. "What exactly was I *supposed* to do?"

"Oh, I don't know—call the police maybe?"

He actually laughed. "You don't know Ev. Get on his wrong side, you're history."

"So you did nothing?" She couldn't believe it. "*Nothing?*"

"I don't think you know what's involved if you cross Ev—especially with something like this." His eyes were starting to glisten. "He's got friends."

"Poor Rex. So you let your granddaughter be taken?"

"Getting myself killed isn't going to help her one bit. Not. One. Bit. Besides, none of this was my idea in the first place."

"The fake kidnap."

"None of it."

"It was Sir Ian Ellis," she said.

Rex made a stone face before he returned a single nod.

"Because Gil Johns wants 'Shades of Summer' for an upcoming soundtrack," Colleen said.

"But Steve would never deal with Sir Ian, not with their history. So I was a natural middle man, with my movie connections, especially to Lynda and everything. But she said Steve would never go for it."

"So you arranged the bogus kidnap."

He shook his head. "Don't try to pin that on me. Sir Ian and Ev came up with that. Don't think I liked it—not one bit."

"But you went along with it."

"Steve was never going to get that royalty money anyway. He owed it to Lynda. And Melanie. *And* me. He owes me money, from when they first got married. Fucking bum."

Colleen shook her head at Rex's rationale. "I need to know where to find Ev Cole."

"I don't know. I haven't dealt with him since . . . the first Melanie thing."

"The phony kidnap."

"I met him during the first . . . thing. At a club in West Hollywood. Stig's. Another time at a coffee shop called My Cup on La Cienega. That's it. I don't know where he lives, but I'm pretty sure it's in the area. But I haven't talked to him since before . . ."

"Before he killed your daughter. Kidnapped Mel. Before he went out on his own."

Rex's eyes were wet. "Do you think any of this is easy for me?"

"No. That's why you have to seek comfort in massage parlors."

Rex looked at his dangling feet. "Go to hell."

"Do you think Melanie's alive?"

He gave a deep sigh. "I hope so."

"Why hasn't Ev called you? For ransom money?"

Rex looked down again, brooding.

"He *did* call you," Colleen said. "Didn't he?"

"I don't have it," he mumbled. "Thirty grand?" He looked up. "Come on! Everybody thinks I'm loaded. I'm in a dry spell. This is a tough business. And that's a lot of money. A *lot* of money. The only way I could get it would be through a deal."

"One where you could sell Steve's catalog."

"But we all know how Stevie feels about that, don't we?" Rex snapped. "But no, Steve's precious catalog has to stay in limbo for eternity, no matter who suffers, who dies. He could've dealt with this a long time ago. Lynda would still be alive. Melanie would be safe at home." He stared hard at Colleen. "Maybe Steve should be the one you're harassing. Maybe you should go bust *his* balls. She's his kid, after all, not mine."

Colleen shook her head again. "If Ev contacts you, you don't breathe a word of this. And you let me know if he does. Find out where he is. You call my answering service." She got a business card out, left it on the massage table, next to his flabby white knee.

She left him there, the door open, the mood music playing, and she walked back down the cramped hall, the sounds of a man grunting as she passed a room on her way out.

She found the tall bony woman in the foyer, in a turquoise blue silky robe, smoking a cigarette. She glared at Colleen.

The smell of lavender now had a tinge of sweat and desperation to it.

"Luther's ready for you now," Colleen said.

She left the massage parlor, went out into the LA afternoon.

CHAPTER FORTY-SIX

A visit to the My Cup coffee shop on La Cienega revealed that none of the staff remembered or knew Ev Cole. Next stop was Stig's, a rock 'n' roll club on Sunset that reeked of stale beer and mold. You could almost feel the lost brain cells swimming around on the damp floorboards. It was too early for any serious music or drinking yet—a little after 6:00 p.m.—and the only people on hand were staff setting up amongst the dim lights and an intense young woman with long hair, sandals, and acoustic guitar, singing something folky at a mic on a little stage. A spotlight shone on her earnest warbling.

Before she could finish her song, the manager, a weary looking guy with long hair and an early stoop, said, "That's enough. We'll let you know."

"Okay," she whispered, putting her guitar into a very beat-up case. She struggled with the latch.

Someone put on a tape. Queen. "We Will Rock You."

Colleen ordered a drink at the bar and a bartender in a tight leather mini, torn fishnets, and spiky hair set a gin and tonic down in front of her. Colleen over-tipped her and took a sip, lighting up a Virginia Slim to take the edge off the day, which had started with a pre-dawn departure from San Francisco, four hundred miles ago. The image of Rex Williamson's naked body on a massage table in the throes of passion was still fresh in her mind. But still not as potent as whatever Melanie Cook might be going through. Time felt like it was running away at breakneck speed.

She asked the bartender about Ev Cole.

"You a friend of his?" From her sideways look, it seemed that she wasn't.

"A friend of a friend," Colleen said.

"I see." The bartender plucked a maraschino cherry from a glass jar full of them, popped it in her mouth, chewed, looked off.

"Know where I can find him?" Colleen asked.

"What for?"

"I was just in town," Colleen said, sensing that the bartender might be wary to tell her.

She retrieved a pink can of Tab from under the bar and took a drink through a straw. "You need to be careful with Ev."

"I know," Colleen said, tapping ash into an ashtray. "Whatever you tell me is in complete confidence."

The bartender stowed her can of Tab back under the bar. "Ev used to crash at Deedra's place but they—ah—parted ways."

"And where can I find Deedra?"

"Right here," the bartender said, "in about two months. She's backpacking in India."

"Great," Colleen said, sighing. She took a slug of G&T.

The hippie girl with the guitar shuffled off behind them. The bartender gave her a lazy wave. "Good luck."

At a pay phone in the corner, Colleen dropped coins into the slot and dialed her answering service. A call from Moran. Yes! She slipped in enough coins to call Moran in Santa Cruz. For once Daphne wasn't too difficult. Colleen must have caught her off guard. But she still wanted to know what Colleen wanted.

"I'm returning his call—from Los Angeles."

"Hold on," Daphne sighed.

A few moments later, Moran picked up the phone, his calm voice a distinct contrast to his wife's.

"Sorry about that, Hayes."

"I'm the one who's sorry," she said. "For disturbing you. You left a message?"

"I did," Moran said, and she could almost see him pushing his glasses up his nose. "We actually got a DMV hit on your perp: Everett Cole."

A nice little jolt went through Colleen's midsection. "Cool." She had her pencil and penny notebook out, on top of the pay phone.

"He owns a '74 Triumph Bonneville," Moran said.

Triumph. "*That's* the bike in the Polaroid. So Ev did pick up the cash from the little guy at the Transbay Terminal."

"You caught him in the act, Hayes. Hang on to that photo."

"You know it," she said. "Do you have an address for Mr. Cole?"

He did. An apartment just past West Hollywood. Rex Williamson had said he thought Ev might live around the LA area.

"Thanks," Colleen said. "Sorry again about you-know-what."

Moran said quietly, "Daphne just worries I'll get bored with gardening and be lured back into police work."

Daphne didn't realize how much Moran was able to live the part vicariously by helping Colleen out and staying right where he was.

"Please tell her I appreciate her concern," Colleen said.

"Keep me posted."

Colleen hung up, checked her watch. Time to head over to West Hollywood.

Santa Monica Boulevard took her into the seedier part of the city, especially once she got off onto the side streets. Ev Cole's apartment building had probably been grand fifty years ago. Now it was a dry-rot special, with a cracked stucco exterior and a boarded-up window on the ground floor. A brilliant-green metallic lowrider sat outside the entrance in the middle of the street, several gang bangers sitting idle inside while music throbbed from bass speakers in the trunk. "The World Is a Ghetto."

Colleen drove down the block, parked off La Brea, where her car stood a better chance of surviving. She walked back to Ev's apartment building. The big Latino in the passenger seat wore a blue do-rag low down on his forehead and mirrored sunglasses that followed her.

"Looking good, mama," he said.

In the entrance, she scanned the numbers. Ev's was 301. She rang it. The intercom buzzed and spat.

"Yeah?" a young man's voice said in a hard American accent, nasal, with the hint of a slur. He might have been loaded. But he wasn't British.

"Is Ev home?" she asked.

"Who is this?"

"Deedra," she said, cupping her hand over her mouth, adding a sense of urgency. "I need to talk to Ev. Is he there?"

"Deedra?"

"Right," she said. "Is Ev home?"

"Nah. But *I* am, babe." A potential beau. Lucky her.

"I really need to speak to Ev."

"I thought you left town. What you up to?"

"I just got back from India. C'mon, let me in. These guys in the Monte Carlo are staring at me like I'm a pastrami sandwich."

He laughed. "C'mon up." The buzzer buzzed, letting Colleen into a grimy lobby that reeked of cat pee and was being overtaken by bags of trash and stacks of newspapers.

Ev lived on the third floor. She took the stairs, past floors of blaring televisions and stereos. People shouted at each other. Others laughed.

As she got to 301, she pulled the Bersa Piccola from her jacket pocket, flipped the safety off with her thumb, kept the small pistol down behind her butt.

Steve Miller was playing in 301. At least Ev's roommate had good taste in music.

She knocked on the door with her left hand, *shave-and-a-haircut*. Footsteps approached.

The door opened, letting a waft of stinky marijuana smoke out.

A big shirtless guy with a USMC tattoo on his fleshy bicep stood there, holding a can of Colt 45. He was white, in his thirties, with a Keith Richards shag cut, a shark's tooth earring, and a droopy porn star mustache. He needed a shave. He ponged of booze and sweat. He was muscular but had a band of hard beer gut around his middle.

His eyes flashed as he looked at Colleen in her dressy outfit, clearly not Deedra. His slimy smile faded.

"Wait—who are you?"

"Shut up," she said, bringing the gun up fast, pushing it into his gut. He backed into the room like a wind-up toy, dropping his beer. The can splashed onto the dirty orange rug.

She shut the door behind her.

The small living room was a mess, cans and bottles and an open pizza box on the sofa littered with half-eaten crusts. The TV, on the floor, flickered soundlessly. Wile E. Coyote was fastening an Acme rocket to his back. On the stereo, Steve Miller was singing about being a midnight toker.

There didn't appear to be anyone else in the small apartment.

"Who are you?" His voice shook. "What the fuck do you want?"

"Ev," she said.

"Not here." He shook his head quickly, gulped. "Ev's not here."

"Where is he?" She kept one eye on the hallway to the rest of the apartment.

"I dunno."

She pointed the gun at the TV. Fired. The TV jumped with the boom and a fist-sized hole appeared, ringed with cracks. The room stunk of burnt electronics.

"Jesus fuck!" he said. "Are you crazy?"

Colleen pointed the gun at the stereo.

"Let's try that again," she said.

"Sheep Hole," he stammered. "Sheep Hole."

"Ev's into sheep? What the hell is 'Sheep Hole'?"

"The cabin. East of Joshua Trees. Point that fucking thing somewhere else, will you?"

She pointed the gun down. "Details."

"Off Highway 62," he spluttered.

"Keep going."

"Highway 62. The Old Dale Road. Just past Bush. Amboy Road. The Pass. Sheep Hole Mountain Pass. On the right there's a ghost town. Ev is up the mountain."

"Up the mountain *where*?"

"Cabin. Up behind the ridge on the right. A couple old mining buildings. Hidden away."

"Is someone with him?"

"Don't know," he said. "Don't want to know. It's nothing to do with me. Nothing to do with me."

"Phone number?"

"No phone." He shook his head violently. "No electricity."

"When did Ev go to Sheep Hole?"

"Don't know. But he hasn't been here for a few days. He was up in SF before. He called me from outside Sheep Hole."

So Ev went to SF to work on the sham kidnap. Picked up some ransom money at Transbay, shot Lynda later on in a fight. Abducted

Melanie Cook? Seemed like it. Did he take Melanie Cook to Sheep Hole?

Ev would need someone to help him. It would be difficult to transport and keep tabs on an eleven-year-old girl on your own. If she were alive.

"Your wallet," she said, aiming the pistol at the big guy's gut, standing back. "Slowly."

One hand up, he reached behind him and pulled out a snakeskin wallet on a chain.

"ID," she said. "Get it out."

He fumbled out his driver's license and handed it to her with shaking fingers.

She stood back another step, the gun up, gave the license a quick read.

"And what part do you play in Ev's life, Vincent?"

"Roommate. We're not even friends."

"But you seem to know about his place in Sheep Hole."

"I do a favor for Ev once in a while, okay? So what?"

"And what favors have you done lately?"

"Ev called me. A few days ago. Had me drop some stuff off at Sheep Hole. So I went."

"*What* stuff?"

Vincent stared at his dusty python boots. Then he looked back up. "You're not gonna tell Ev I said anything, are you?"

"I won't breathe a word—unless you mess me around."

"His bag. He keeps it under his bed. He wanted me to bring it. I didn't even look inside."

"Sure you did. Especially if you drove it all the way to Sheep Hole."

"No way." His voice cracked. "You're nuts if you think I'm gonna cross Ev."

"Then I guess I give this license to the cops and tell them you're an accessory to kidnapping. Maybe even murder."

"Jesus! Is that what Ev's up to? I didn't know. *I didn't know!*"

"How much do you want to protect Ev now?"

He nodded and sighed. "There was a tape recorder in his bag. His English passport. An address book." He stared down.

Was Ev planning on running soon? "What else?"

"A piece."

"A gun?"

He didn't look up. "Sawed-off Rossi. A box of shells." Now he did look up. "Christ, you better not tell Ev any of this."

"No reason to," she said. "If you keep your mouth shut. Anyone with Ev? An accomplice?"

"I think so, yeah. Don't know who. Someone was there, though, walking around. But I didn't go inside. And Ev didn't ask me in. He just wanted me to give him his stuff and leave. And that was fine with me."

"Anyone else there? A girl? A young girl?"

A look of trepidation crossed Vincent's face. "There was a light on in the back room. So someone else might've been there, too. Like I said, Ev didn't ask me in. I just gave him his bag and left."

"Okay," she said. "Let's check out Ev's room."

"*What?*" Vincent screeched.

"You first. Turn around—slowly."

He did and she followed him down a cramped hallway to an austere room that contrasted with the trashy apartment. Neat. A single bed, the sheets stripped off, a chair, a pair of jeans hanging over the back. A desk, organized. Spare and basic.

Colleen went through the closet, bent down, keeping one eye on Vincent as she peered under the bed. A copy of *Penthouse* magazine. She stood up, pulled open the top desk drawer. Papers. Bills.

All neatly stacked. She rummaged through them. Nothing. She shut the drawer.

"Okay," she said, "back into the living room." She guided Vincent out.

She tossed his driver's license on the floor. "If you contact Ev, or he calls you and you give him a heads-up about this little visit, I'll be back." She raised her eyebrows. "*Claro?*"

"Yeah. Sure. Okay."

She left the apartment, the door open, headed down the stairs.

"Fucking *bitch*!" Vincent screamed, slamming the door behind her.

She slipped the Bersa into her pocket, pulled the flap over her tailored jacket, headed back out.

The green Monte Carlo was still parked in the middle of the street, blaring funk music.

The guy in the blue do-rag gave her a friendly smile.

"Sorry to see you go," he said. "But I do like to watch you walk away."

She gave him a smirk.

Back at the Torino she chased away a couple of teenagers eyeing the car. Inside, she got out her California map.

Joshua Trees was about 130 miles east of Los Angeles. Sheep Hole, a bare green patch on the map, was just northeast of that. The Mojave Desert. What looked like a mountain pass. Two and a half, three hours of driving. It was early evening.

She hadn't eaten all day. She didn't want to lose time, but she was starving.

She drove up to Pink's Hot Dogs on North La Brea and devoured a chili dog, standing outside by the walk-up counter, washing it down with soda. Grease and sugar coursed through her system, fortifying her.

Afterwards, she went inside to use the restroom and change. On the way she spotted a steak knife on the rim of a plate at a vacated table. A backup weapon. Without anyone seeing, she nabbed it. In the restroom she wiped off the knife, wrapped it in a clean paper towel, pocketed it, and donned jeans and sneaks, brushed her teeth and washed her face. She left, with her good clothes and shoes stashed in her bag. She filled up the Torino at a 76 station, buying a pack of mints, stopping at the pay phone where she inserted quarters, dialed Inspector Owens in SF. He didn't answer. After hours.

She dialed Moran one more time, taking a breath as she prepared for Daphne's warm reception.

"We're in the middle of dinner, Colleen," she said coldly.

"Your husband wanted me to keep him posted of something. It will only take a minute."

Moran came on the line.

"I'm not trying to ruin your marriage," she said. "But I have an update." She told him about Sheep Hole. "If you don't hear from me by tomorrow morning, call Owens. Better warn Daphne to expect another call."

"Tell me you're not going up there alone, Hayes."

"Just to check things out. I'll report back."

She heard him sigh over the crackle of the phone line. "Don't."

"Let me ask you a question," she said. "What would you do if you were in my place?"

Another pause.

"I'd check things out," he admitted. "Same as you."

"Then I'm learning from the best," she said.

"I expect to hear from you by midnight, Hayes."

She hung up, and headed east, getting onto Highway 10. She sucked a mint as she dialed in KROQ—the "ROQ of Los Angeles"—and cranked up Sly and the Family Stone.

Part of her said she needed help and was apprehensive of what lie ahead. The other part of Colleen asked *who?* Moran? How long would it take for him to get down here? Owens? He'd warned Colleen to stay well away from this case. Time was evaporating. Ev had his passport and might take off any moment. Melanie needed help *now*.

She'd go to Sheep Hole, scope out Ev's place, see what was what, then decide.

She had to think Melanie Cook was still alive. Had to.

CHAPTER FORTY-SEVEN

Miles of dirt road had jarred Colleen's kidneys loose by the time she finally approached the incline to Sheep Hole. In the cleavage of the mountain pass, the night sky blazed over the desert with brilliant stars unscathed by city lights. If Melanie wasn't looming in the back of her mind, it would have been a beautiful sight.

On the right, near the top of the pass, the outline of several low buildings darkened the hills. Colleen drew closer, stopped the Torino, its engine rumbling, and squinted into the dark. The buildings were old, wooden, faded. Windows were broken or boarded up. On one structure an old shake roof was collapsing. The shell of a rusted-out Model T, sans wheels, sat in the rocky dirt. One door hung open, sagging earthward. Next to the vehicle, a broken white toilet lay on its side.

Colleen fished around in her bag of tricks, got her binoculars. She fixed in for a better look. A crumpled wooden mine sluice lay over the rocks.

She put the Torino into gear, spun around, drove down the pass a couple of hundred yards and pulled into a turnaround she had spotted on the way up. There was no need to put her only transportation at immediate risk.

She got out the steak knife she had liberated from Pink's and, keeping the blade wrapped in its paper napkin, slipped it down her sock, taping the knife around her ankle with adhesive bandage, loose enough to move freely.

She checked the clip in her Bersa Piccola. Loaded up with eight short .22 rounds. The small black gun was lightweight and might look like a toy but fit nicely and was remarkably accurate.

She got out of the car, slipped the gun in the back pocket of her Levi's. She retrieved her five-cell flashlight from the trunk and put her bag of gear away. Locked up the car.

Ready to go.

A cold wind tunneled down the pass as she hoofed it up the road in the moonlight. It felt good to unwind after so many hours in the car and helped to ease the growing tension of what she might find.

At the dirt turnoff where the ghost town lay in shadows, she stopped, taking deep breaths, flashlight in hand, turned off for the moment.

She walked slowly by the long-abandoned Ford. Looking around, she saw what appeared to be fresh tire tracks. She approached the few empty wooden buildings built in the late 1800s. Uninhabited and dark. An open door creaked in the wind. A puff of dirt blew across the sagging porch of what had once been a general store, many years ago.

No one there.

Next door was an old garage, and workshop. The tire tracks led around back. She followed them. They disappeared under old-fashioned side-by-side garage doors. She rubbed the dirt off a grimy window with the heel of her hand. Peered in.

A black BMW sedan.

Her heart thumped.

She clicked on the flashlight, aimed it into the garage, at the car.

BMW 320i. Lynda's.

Suddenly, the sound of rocks rattling behind her made her jump. Heart pulsing, Colleen spun, reaching for the pistol in her back pocket.

Her flashlight beam lit up a huge bighorn sheep, bigger than a man, staring down at her curiously from a high rock. The curled horns on either side of the beast's head were the size of platters. She gasped, catching her breath, directing the flashlight beam down to the ground before turning it off.

The ram rotated, took off. Rocks clattered.

She stood, sucking in deep breaths as her heartbeats settled. Waiting, stone still, listening to the desert. Praying she hadn't alerted anyone. Up the hill, the animal trotted off.

In the distance, she heard a door open. She ducked behind a rock.

"Who's there?" a man's raspy voice said. He wasn't English so if Ev were there, he had company. As Colleen had suspected.

Was Melanie there as well?

She took several more calming breaths, raised her head, peered up the mountain into the darkness where the buildings sat.

A big man with a flashlight on the porch of the cabin. In his right hand, he held something. A gun. A short rifle or a long pistol. The sawed-off shotgun Ev's roommate mentioned? He looked familiar.

It hit her. The big guy at the Transbay Terminal. Duffle Coat.

He went back inside, shut the door. She heard muted conversation. Then silence.

She had a choice. Go back down the road, get in her car, drive the dirt road back to 62, head back to civilization, call Moran. And wait for help.

But something inside would not let her wait that long. Melanie might well be in that hut. If she were still alive. She couldn't waste another minute.

Time.

Colleen negotiated the rocky incline carefully in relative gloom. Her eyes had adjusted; shadows were distinguishable. She stepped carefully.

Up past an outcropping sat a multi-room cabin, next to a square, windowless cinderblock hut that had a sign on the door from the Bureau of Land Management informing the public to stay out. The hut was covered with graffiti and the door had been locked for some time, judging by the layers of corrosion on the lock.

She approached the cabin from the side, staying low along the rocks, hidden in shadows. There were fresh footprints everywhere, and she noted smaller ones, sneaker prints, small enough to belong to a girl Melanie's age. Her chest pumped with anxiety.

As she drew closer, she saw what looked to be a plastic bucket by the front door.

She heard a man snoring inside.

She stopped. Gathered herself together.

She went around the side, past a boarded-up window, to the back of the cabin. To an unbroken window. The glass was misted with condensation on the inside.

Someone was in that room.

Mustering her nerve, she slowly, *slowly*, slowly raised her head. Peeked in.

In the small, decrepit room she saw the outline of a wire bed-frame. The moonlight allowed Colleen a view of a young girl, her hands handcuffed over her head to the metal headboard. The girl lay on her back, motionless. A blanket had been thrown over her but her bare feet stuck out. A bucket sat by the bed, along with a milk carton and a bowl with a spoon in it.

No one else in the room. The door was shut.

The bedframe creaked as the girl moved, looking up at the window, sensing someone.

Melanie Cook. Her face was dirty. Her dark pageboy was disheveled and matted, but it was the same girl. Colleen caught a glimpse of her haunted eyes before she ducked back down below the windowsill.

"Help me!" Melanie cried. "Please *help* me!"

CHAPTER FORTY-EIGHT

Colleen's chest pounded as she squatted under the window to Melanie's room. Inside the girl continued to shout for help.

"Help me! Please—*help me*!"

Colleen's heart went out to the poor child.

Inside the cabin, two men conversed in hurried voices. Footsteps pounded the floorboards. On the far side of the cabin, the front door screeched open.

Someone coming out to investigate. Colleen's nerves ratcheted up.

Crouching, she drew her Bersa, turned to face the corner of the cabin. Waited.

Heavy boots came her way, thudding on the ground. The big man.

Meanwhile, she heard the door in Melanie's room inside fly open, hit a wall.

"What the fuck are you up to now?" an Englishman growled. He had a Cockney accent. Ev. She detected the light from a handheld lantern shifting.

The boots coming along the side of the cabin toward Colleen slowed as they drew closer.

Colleen readied her pistol. Flicked the safety off. Her hand vibrated with tension. In her other hand, she gripped her flashlight.

The big man's heavy breathing was close by.

"Who's there?" he said.

She held her breath, ready. Her left thumb was on the flashlight switch.

Inside the room, Ev struck Melanie with a blow that made Colleen flinch. "You want the gag again, do you? You know how much you enjoyed not being able to breathe."

Melanie cried out.

"I should just let you bloody die!" He slapped her again. Melanie screamed, making Colleen's wrath boil over. "Shut up!" he yelled. "Shut the bloody fuck up!"

Melanie whimpered.

"Be quiet or I'll let the wolves have you!"

Melanie fell silent.

A large shadow darkened the corner of the cabin where Colleen squatted.

She saw the outline of the sawed-off shotgun.

She brought the Bersa up fast as she flipped on the flashlight, aimed the light into the eyes of a melon-size head full of grizzled stubble. The man squinted.

She fired just before he did.

He flinched back as his shotgun went off, up close, deafening, but thankfully, off-kilter. Even so, her left arm took a good portion of the blast, sending her to the ground with a thump. The flashlight tumbled away, the shaft of light rolling off into darkness.

She righted herself, head swimming, shut one eye, kept firing.

Each subsequent snap of the .22 caliber pistol made the big man balk, one bullet hitting him in the cheek, another taking out his right eye. Screaming, he reared back, shotgun flying off into the shadows. He clawed at his face like an enraged bear and fell to the ground with a wallop.

Wounded arm buzzing, Colleen scrambled to her feet. Her head reeled from the blast. The big man lay facedown, motionless in mortal surrender. She looked over in horror at her left arm. The leather sleeve of her bomber jacket was torn away. Blood soaked through. Her arm was warm and numb.

She sucked in steady gasps, reclaiming her sense of equilibrium.

She had to get Melanie out of there.

"Stop right there!" the Cockney voice said.

She turned, saw a tall skinny man with cropped blond hair, shirtless, wearing leather pants, barefoot. Maybe in his thirties. The same guy who had been at Steve's flat that night. With Lynda.

Ev Cole.

He was holding a very large revolver, aimed directly at her. His bicep was wrapped in a sloppy, amateur bandage where Lynda must have shot him. It didn't seem to slow him down.

He gave a sneer.

"Lose the bloody pop gun." He motioned at the Bersa in her hand. "Now."

CHAPTER FORTY-NINE

Heart thrashing, Colleen dropped the Bersa. A puff of dust erupted at her feet. She still had the knife taped to her ankle.

Inside the cabin, she heard Melanie crying anew.

"Hands up," Ev said, gesturing with his gun.

It wasn't easy getting her left arm up. She managed it halfway. It throbbed with a deep ache. Warm blood sopped inside the padded lining.

Ev came over, looked at the big man on the ground, stone still.

"You fucking killed him." He turned to Colleen, seemingly incredulous, before his mouth twisted into an ugly grimace, and he swiped the pistol at her. She got her left arm up, which took the brunt of the blow, but he still managed to catch her ear. It stung. She went back down, curled up in a half-crouch, covering her head with her numbing hand as he swung at her again. Now she felt a warm trickle run down her chin. Her ear buzzed.

"You're that bloody bitch!" he shouted. "The one working with Steve."

"People know where I am," she panted. "Let Melanie Cook go. Let her go and you've got a chance to avoid the death penalty." California had just reinstated the death penalty that year.

"And what makes you think you're going to bloody live?"

He lashed out at her with the gun, catching her head one more time, despite her hand curled over her skull. A jolt of pain shot down one side. She thought she might lose consciousness.

He started kicking her with his bare feet.

She rolled into a ball as he kicked and grasped her right ankle. The side of his foot connected with her back. The pain soaked into her, making her shout out uncontrollably.

Pulling up the leg of her jeans, she grabbed the plastic handle of the steak knife, yanking the knife free from the adhesive tape while he swooped in again with the gun, striking her on the shoulder.

"You cunt!"

Rolled up in a ball, she gripped the knife in both hands between her knees while he beat and kicked, discreetly pulling the protective layer of napkin off the blade. She felt the blade slice her finger like a razor.

He came in with his foot again, aiming for her head.

She dodged the kick, rotated around his foot in the dirt, quick, coming up like a cobra, the steak knife in both hands.

She brought the knife down on top of his bare foot.

A stomach-turning crunch of bone and gristle culminated in an air-piecing scream as she put all her weight down into the blade, twisting, pinning his foot to the ground.

He dropped the gun, howling, trying to pull his foot free from the dirt.

She scrambled for the gun, a big revolver, heavy, got hold of it.

Hopping up, she jumped back, disoriented with pain, her fragmented equilibrium rocking her vision from side to side. She was warm with blood. It dripped off her gun hand.

Ev finally yanked his foot free from the hard ground. The blade stuck out of the sole as he hopped, blood flying in an arc, splattering her. He turned, limping away on one good leg, the toes of his pierced foot like a demented ballet dancer. His grunts kept a gruesome cadence to his hobbled movements.

She pulled the hammer back with her thumb, aimed with both hands, squinted, gritted her teeth before she shot him in the back of his good leg. The boom of the big pistol reverberated off the nearby rocks, across the mountain pass, then faded.

Ev went down, screaming. He clutched his wounded leg.

She stood up, head spinning, went over. She'd blown out the back of the knee. She aimed the gun at his other knee.

"No!" he screamed. "Please! *Please!*"

Holding the gun with both hands, she squinted.

"Where are the keys to the handcuffs?" she growled. "The ones holding Melanie to that bed?"

"In my . . . pocket," he wheezed.

"Get them out. Anything funny, you're crippled for life. Got that?"

He shook his head in a thousand yesses as he struggled to get a hand into his pocket. He fumbled the key out. She took it, slimy with blood.

Throbbing with pain, she stumbled over to the dead man, hunted around his motionless corpse until she found her Bersa. She slipped it in her back pocket. She located her flashlight, turned it on. Eventually, she recovered the sawed-off shotgun. She tossed it off into the rocks, where Ev couldn't get to it. She went back to Ev, moaning as he clutched his leg. Blood had pooled in the dirt underneath his knee, glinting in the moonlight.

He wasn't going anywhere.

"Make a move and I'll come back and take the other knee," she said. "You'll never walk again."

"Got it!" he gulped, clutching himself. "*Got it!*"

She turned, dizzied, staggered to the house. Sleeping bags were rumpled on the sofa, and on a blow-up mattress on the floor. Cans and bottles were scattered everywhere. A hash pipe sat in an ashtray. Colleen stuck the big gun down the front of her jeans. It was heavy and awkward and warm.

She could hear Melanie whimpering in the back, amidst the hissing of a lantern. She followed the lantern light into the back room.

Melanie looked up at her like a frightened animal.

"It's okay, sweetheart," Colleen said, hobbling over to the bed, setting the flashlight down. "It's okay now."

She unlocked the girl's trembling wrists from the restraints and Melanie immediately curled into her arms, rocking. Colleen immediately recalled Pamela, her own daughter, the day she found her after her ex had abused her.

The day she had killed him.

This day felt similar. But this day would be different. Melanie would recover. She would make sure.

"It's okay, now," Colleen said, stroking the girl's greasy, limp hair, kissing her sticky forehead. "It's okay."

CHAPTER FIFTY

"There's your father, sweetheart," Colleen said.

It had been a little over a day since Sheep Hole.

She and Melanie stood with a social worker who had a long gleaming black braided ponytail hanging over the back of a blue jacket that read SF COUNTY CHILD CARE AND FAMILY SERVICES, at the top of the steps on the wide entranceway to 850 Bryant. It was after 11:00 a.m. and the sun was fighting to get through the clouds.

Steve had just emerged through the doors, fresh from jail. He wore the same jeans and T-shirt they had arrested him in and a week's worth of beard. But a broad smile punched through it when he saw Melanie.

He came striding over to where she stood between the social worker and Colleen.

"Hello, Mel!" he said, bending down in an attempt to meet her gaze. Melanie turned her face to the cement. She wore turned-up denims and a large gray-hooded sweatshirt with a big front pocket, an outfit courtesy of the City. She was still pale and emaciated from her days of confinement. The cuts on her wrists from the handcuffs were bandaged.

"Don't you want to say hello to your father, Melanie?" Colleen said, earning a glare from the social worker.

Melanie stared at the ground. "Hi," she whispered.

"Hello, love," Steve said. "It's bloody good to see you." He ruffled her hair.

The social worker shot Steve a hard stare.

"Sorry," he said, pulling his hand back.

"She's been through an incredible ordeal," the woman said.

"I know." Steve's hands went up in a motion of appeasement. "But she is my daughter, yeah?"

The social worker frowned at Steve. "We can leave whenever you want, Melanie," she said, keeping her eye on Steve. "There's no pressure."

"Okay," Melanie said.

"Do you want to leave?" the social worker said.

Colleen wanted to punch the woman's lights out. Steve was being treated as a pariah because of his time in jail, and his perceived failure that led to Melanie's kidnap. But arguing the point here and now would not help Steve and Melanie's situation. And her wrist and hand throbbed with pain from protecting herself from the pistol-whipping. Her left arm was heavily bandaged under a denim jacket, her old beloved bomber jacket bloody and beyond repair from the shotgun blast that—thankfully—had not shattered bone. Her bruised face was bandaged along the left side of her jaw and mottled with cuts and abrasions. A lump on the side of her head pulsated. But she was alive. More than. As the song went, she wasn't looking too good but feeling real well.

"How are you holding up, Mel?" Steve said to Melanie.

"Okay," she said to the gray cement.

"I'm proud of you, yeah? For getting through that nightmare. It's going to get better from here on. Everything's going to be fine. You'll see."

Melanie did not look up.

An awkward silence was broken by the constant rush of traffic on Bryant. An ambulance screamed.

"I think that's enough for today," the social worker said.

"What?" Steve said. "I was hoping we could grab a bite."

"I don't think so," the social worker said.

Steve sighed. "When do I get to see her again?"

"We have to schedule it."

"Can we have a bit more time next time?" Steve said. "Perhaps go to lunch?"

"We'll see."

"Make sure you allocate plenty of time," Steve said. "Mel eats quite a bit."

Melanie looked up with a glower, then gave a weak smile.

Steve winked at her. "Thanks for coming to get your old man out of the nick, Mel."

She stared at the ground again. "Yeah. Sure."

The social worker led Melanie down the stairs.

Steve cupped his hands around his mouth. "Love you, Mel!"

The two stepped down and into a white Crown Victoria that read SF CITY AND COUNTY on the door.

They drove off.

"Fuck it," Steve said, frowning.

"She's just a kid, Steve," Colleen said. "She's feeling sheepish about what she did to you." Colleen hoped she was, anyway. "She probably feels partially responsible for her mother's death, too."

Steve nodded. His eyes were glistening. "Got any smokes?"

Colleen dug out an unopened pack of Lucky Strikes, handed it to him. "I didn't think you could handle Virginia Slims. Your prison buddies might see you."

"Ta, love." He ripped the pack open, pulled a cig into his mouth, tore a match, lit up. "Thanks for organizing Mel's visit."

"Sorry it only lasted about thirty seconds."

"As the bishop said to the actress."

Colleen laughed, checked her watch. "It's 5:00 p.m. somewhere. Want to get a drink? Or two?"

"I've been in the nick for days," Steve said. "What do you bloody think?"

"That I should have sold my Budweiser stock? But then I remembered, I don't own any stock."

"There's only one problem," Steve said. "I'm skint. Flat broke."

"No, you're not," Colleen said.

"How do you figure that, then?"

"I found a gray gym bag in Ev's cabin," Colleen said, smiling.

Steve's eyes rounded in surprise. "My twenty K?"

"Most of it," she said. "Nineteen thousand, three hundred and forty dollars." She gave a crafty smile. "I forgot to mention it when I made my statement. I've got it safely stashed away. Now you don't owe Octavien nearly so much."

"You, madam, are a bloody miracle."

*   *   *

"Ah," Steve said, setting an empty pint glass down on the bar. He eyed Colleen, stirring her double gin and tonic with a plastic swizzle stick. "Ready for another?"

"I only got this one about ninety seconds ago," she said. She took a sip. Ice cold, loaded up with Gordon's. Perfect. She savored the pain-killing effect.

Noon. The Pitt was still near empty. Gray light filtered in and neon beer signs prevailed for ambiance. The jukebox played "Hot Blooded."

"You might need another, love," Steve said, sipping from a fresh pint as he gave her a sympathetic smile over the top of his glass. "You look a bit torn and frayed."

"You should see the other guy," she said. "*Guys.*"

Ev was barely walking, his knee shattered, as he recovered down at the Arrowhead Medical Center under 24-hour guard. And Ben James, the big man who had been his accomplice at Sheep Hole, Duffle Coat, was flat out in the morgue.

And then there was the little guy, who lost out to an SF Muni bus. Lynda Cook was the fourth victim.

"I don't know how you did it, Colleen," Steve said. "But you did. I'm forever in your debt. You saved my daughter. Even if she never speaks to me again."

"She will," Colleen said, sipping. "It'll just take time."

"I need to work on a few things."

"It's not going to be a breeze, but you'll get there."

Steve drank an inch of beer. "I knew Lynda was a hard case, but I never expected that."

"Lynda didn't expect a lot of things, either. Ev going rogue, taking over, and kidnapping your daughter for real."

Steve shook his head. "Ev was a bad apple from way back. When he was our roadie. You reckon they can prove what he did . . . to Brenda Pike? In my hotel room?"

"Some news about Ev," Colleen said. "He confessed to spiking your bottle of whiskey that night in the dressing room of the Hammersmith Odeon. He's pinning it all on Sir Ian, of course. Singing like a bird, as they say. He's staring down extortion, murder, and kidnapping charges."

"So that's why I got so bloody pissed that night," Steve said.

"Now you know it wasn't your fault, Steve."

"It was enough of my fault," he said with a sigh. "I ran from it once. Not again."

Maybe someday he could forgive himself.

"Tich says he'll provide a statement," Colleen said. "Inspector Owens has contacted Scotland Yard. Gus Pedersen says Sir Ian is an accessory to multiple crimes, if not more. And then there's your ex-father-in-law. Rex is going to be facing more than a few charges: extortion, kidnapping, child endangerment."

Steve frowned. "All the bloody trouble I caused."

"You were set up, Steve. Yes, you did the wrong thing by running but you know you weren't responsible for Brenda Pike."

"All the misery I set into motion?"

Colleen knew all about regret. Killing her ex in a fit of rage. She had lost nine years in prison, time that could have been spent with her daughter. Time that had driven a seemingly permanent wedge between them.

"You haven't seen anything, Steve," she said.

"Well, it's Mel that matters now."

"There you go. What are you going to do about Octavien? Your mob loan? We need to get SFPD vice involved."

Steve gave a single shake of his head. "No. I borrowed that money fair and square. Thanks to you getting that gym bag with most of the ransom money back, I can get enough short term to pay Octavien off. Gus is going to help me get the rights to my catalog back, which will be a whole lot easier now that Sir Ian has been exposed. Once that happens, I can cover my legal fees, pay you, and have enough left to focus on raising Mel properly."

It would be a while before she got paid. But she had no doubt she would be.

"Whoa, dude. That catalog is your lifeblood. Now that you're off the murder charge, aren't you in line to inherit Lynda's house?"

He gave a desolate laugh. "Lynda didn't leave a will. Everything'll go through probate. Gus tells me Lynda's old man is her next of kin, so he'll probably get whatever she has—including that house."

A small wave of sadness washed over Colleen. "But you've held onto those songs all these years, Steve. They're *your* songs."

"They were everything to me once, but all they've done is cause problems for me and anyone who got near them." He drank a cheerless draft. "Time to let them go. Mel is what's important."

Colleen sipped her drink, more than a sip. Maybe Steve was right. "No one will ever sing them like you anyway. They'll always be yours, no matter who owns them."

CHAPTER FIFTY-ONE

"Ladies and Gentlemen, I give you *the band with no name*!"

The crowd that was jammed into The Pitt broke into a roar as the band churned into a '60s rocker, Deena's drums thumping away, the bass throbbing, the guitar dialed up to a meaty crunch, all of which set an infectious groove. Colleen felt the beat deep in her guts, primitive and basic.

Steve stepped up to the mic, clean-shaven, hair freshly shorn, nice and tight to the sides, looking like a young bull as he pulled the microphone off the stand and flipped it up into the air, caught it in his other hand, generating shouts and cheers. He wore a crisp white shirt with the sleeves rolled up, the buttons halfway down, snug-fitting 501s that showed off his workingman's build, slimmed down by a week in jail, and a confident grin that said he was back in his element.

He put the mic out to his lips.

"This one goes out to that lovely lady standing right over there at the bar. Buy her a drink; she's the reason I'm up here today."

People turned to Colleen and cheered. Someone slapped her shoulder and said, "Yeah!" Someone else, "Go girl!"

And she never felt quite so pleased with the outcome of a case.

Steve started singing about being in a frenzy. The Lost Chords first number one hit.

Colleen set her drink down on the bar and clapped along. Despite her beat-up appearance, she was decked out in a leather mini, platform shoes, tight lace top.

And for a few wonderful minutes, she was free.

CHAPTER FIFTY-TWO

The Torino's windshield wipers slapped away wet late-night fog as Colleen turned right on Vermont, her ears still buzzing with the ravages of *the band with no name*. It was well past two thirty in the a.m.

Her head swam with the drinks people had bought her, and the kiss Steve had planted on her in the alley behind The Pitt that went on for delicious seconds.

"Fancy comin' back to my place, love?" he whispered, holding her in a warm clinch. His eyes crinkled.

As tempting as it was, she needed some alone time. To process.

"Not tonight," she said.

"Fair enough. But I'm holding you to a rematch."

"Play your cards right and we'll see," she said, winking.

Now she drove by the front door of her apartment building.

And then she noticed, with a start, the white van, parked across the street.

No.

No.

Her patience disappeared. She stopped the car, middle of the street, the motor running while she fished around under the dash, grabbed the gym sock that contained the Bersa. Freshly loaded.

The light pistol had killed at least one man and now felt much heavier in her hand as she flung open the driver's door and climbed out in her miniskirt, gun down by her side.

Her platform shoes clomped on the asphalt as she crossed Vermont in a diagonal, heading for the white van. The windshield was smeared with moisture but behind the wheel she could make out a figure in a dark jacket, wearing some sort of hat.

She got closer.

He was wearing a knit cap. The same man as before.

He sat up, mouth open when he saw her coming straight for the front of the van.

The engine fired up, coughing moisture. The windshield wipers cuffed away two sister arcs, revealing a man in his late twenties, early thirties.

He moved to put the van into gear.

She stopped in front of it, brought the gun up, pointed it directly at the windshield, straight into his frozen face.

"If you move," she said, loud enough that he could hear her over the engine, through the glass, "I fire."

He put the gearshift back into neutral.

"Put your hands up where I can see them," she growled.

His hands went up.

"Turn the engine off with one hand," she said. "Then get out of the van."

"You're insane!" he shouted.

"Yep," she said, moving the gun to the center of the windshield, away from his head, squeezing off one shot. The *pop* was followed by a small, neat hole punched through the glass. The rearview mirror shattered. He flinched as glass tinkled around the inside of the cab.

It only got easier, she realized.

"Hands up," she said. "Up! Up! Up!"

He did. They trembled.

"Get out of the van," she said. "*Now*."

The van door creaked open. He stepped out. She held the gun on him, moving between the parked van, onto the sidewalk.

"I'm unarmed," he said, shaking visibly. "Unarmed!"

He was heavy and wore orange baggy silk pants that ballooned at the ankles. He had sandals on his big feet.

"What?" she said, surprised, realizing where he'd come from. "Lose the hat."

He pulled the knit hat off with a shaking hand. His head was shaved.

"You're from Moon Ranch," she said. The commune in Point Arenas. Where Pamela was staying. She'd joined the sect and Colleen had been issued a restraining order when she tried to intervene.

"Please don't shoot."

"What are you doing here, watching me?"

"Aadhya," he stammered.

Aadhya was Pamela's name at Moon Ranch.

"Her name is Pamela," Colleen said. "*Pamela*."

"Sure," he said. "Sorry."

"What about Pamela?" Colleen said.

"She's gone. Ran away."

A bolt hit Colleen, running up her spine. Her daughter, once brainwashed, had finally run. *Yes.*

"And you're looking for her," Colleen said. "And you thought she'd come here."

"Yes." He gulped. "I was only following instructions."

"That's why you've been watching me. To see if she came home."

He nodded quickly.

"When did Pamela run away?"

"Last week," he said.

A jolt of excitement flowed through Colleen's guts.

Pamela. Pamela was free.

Colleen lowered the gun.

"Okay," she said. "Leave. Go."

He jerked in surprise. "Okay."

"But tell your masters if I see any of you again, I won't be so kind."

"Yes," he said. "Thank you. *Thank you.*"

He hopped back in the van, heaved the door shut, fired up the engine. She stood up on the curb as he threw the vehicle into gear, cut the steering wheel tight, peeled out into the street in a taut 180, squealed off down Vermont, skidding. Then gone.

Colleen stood there, ears still buzzing, gun by her side.

Free. Pamela was free.

But where?

EPILOGUE

The unmarked cream-colored Rover sedan pulled up in front of the last house on Windsor Road. The property was a large mock Tudor detached, recently painted white, with an expanse of open space rolling down the hill next to it. The London sun was just rising and picking up the dark glistening green of the wet grass. Fingers crossed, it promised to be a rain-free day.

"Nice place," Inspector Grayson said, peering up at the closed curtains upstairs from the passenger seat. He was a middle-aged man with a soft pink face and thinning blond hair. His unimpressive build was hidden in a beige raincoat.

"You're in Finchley now, sir," Campbell said at the wheel, putting on an upper-class accent. "Thatcher Country."

"Are the constables in place?"

"Yes, sir. One around the back. And Higgins for backup."

"Higgins the sprinter," Inspector Grayson said. He craned his neck, peered down the hill. Ah, there she was, long and lean, in her police blues, standing by the playground. Looking smart in a woman's police bowler, with its red-and-white checked band. Stamping her feet in the cold. He could see her breath. "Very good."

"Do you want me to come with you, sir?"

"No," Grayson said. "Top brass wants to play it low key."

"Typical. He's got a 'sir' in front of his bloody name; he gets special treatment."

"I'll signal if I need help." Grayson showed two fingers. "Two fingers behind my back."

"Right you are, sir. Good luck."

"Right." Inspector Grayson got out of the Rover, adjusted his raincoat.

Up to the door of Sir Ian Ellis' house.

Rang the bell.

"Who on earth is that?" Sir Ian said, waking up.

"How should I know?" his wife said, burying her head under the covers. One pink curler stuck out.

The doorbell rang again.

"You going to get that or not?" his wife said into her pillow.

Sir Ian sighed, climbed out of bed, yanked on his dressing gown, stepped into leather slippers. Went over to the window. Pulled the curtain open no more than an inch or two.

And jumped when he saw the Rover parked out front. A figure at the wheel. He didn't know anyone with a Rover like that.

He let the curtain narrow an inch and peered down by the front door.

Another man he didn't know, in a raincoat. Looking up now. Squinting. Not smiling.

Sir Ian's heart played an unpleasant rhythm. He took a deep breath.

Friend or foe? He couldn't imagine them being friends. He didn't have many to begin with.

The police.

"Eloise," he hissed. "Get up!"

"What is it now?"

"The police. At the door. Go tell them I'm not home."

"Christ, Ian." She sat up, looking as rumpled as the bed. "What have you done now?"

"I don't know." But there was plenty to answer for. That bloody Brenda Pike girl. He never should have trusted Ev. Bloody oaf. Ev was going to be his ruin if he wasn't careful. "Go on—*please!*"

"Right." His wife climbed out of bed, fumbling for her spectacles. She pulled on a fluffy blue robe, frouffy slippers with heels. Went downstairs. Meanwhile, Sir Ian dressed quickly, got his passport, secret stash of money, American Express checks from his locked desk in his study where he kept them in case of emergency. He laced his walking shoes. Threw on a sweater and a car coat, because one never knew where one might end up. All the while he listened. At the front door, Eloise talking to the police.

"My husband's not here," Sir Ian's wife said.

Inspector Grayson put his badge away, came out with a warrant. "We have a warrant for his arrest, madam." Behind his back he showed two fingers. He immediately heard the crackle of the police radio in the car, then Campbell getting out to assist.

"But my husband's not here!" Sir Ian's wife shrieked, a little too loud. Sending a signal? "You can't come in! Do you have any idea who we are?"

Upstairs, that was all Ian needed to hear. Time to leg it. He ran to the back of the house, scrutinized the backyard from behind a curtain.

Down there by the shed at the back, a police constable. *Bloody hell.*

Ian took a deep breath as his heart hammered, then dashed into the next bedroom, the one over the garage. It was a bit of a jump from there to freedom, but he could manage it. How many times, in his mind, had he planned this? Now the time had come.

He should never had used Ev again, not after he killed that silly girl for him. Tried to pin it on Steve Cook.

While the police entered the house downstairs, he quietly cranked open the window, stepped out onto the narrow ledge over one side of the garage. Feet slipping on wet stucco. Not a good feeling. Not at all.

The constable by the shed saw him. Came quickly toward him.

"Where do you think you're going?"

"Bit of an emergency!" Sir Ian shouted. "The house is on fire."

"I don't think so," he said drily, picking up his feet into a run.

There was a bushy hedge over the tall fence, next to the park. Ian was ready as he'd ever be. He was already plotting how to get to Wales. Then the boat to Dublin. Then, who knew where? If nothing else, he'd be rid of Eloise. *Small mercies.*

It crossed his mind that he was about to do what Steve Cook did all those years ago. Flee. A chill of realization shuddered through him.

"Sorry, laddie!" One story up, Sir Ian jumped off the ledge, just missing the fence, thank God. Landed on the hedge on the other side and it heaved with his weight, dumping him unceremoniously on the grass. *Ouch.* Rougher than he liked, but his fall was broken. Leg throbbing. Nothing else, he didn't think. He was in luck.

He got up, panting.

The police constable in his garden on the other side of the fence was on his radio now. "He's done a runner! Jumped the flippin' fence! Heading for the commons."

Sir Ian actually laughed as he tore down the common space toward the playground. It would take more than PC Plod to stop him. Still a trick or two left up old Ian's sleeve.

And froze when he saw a beanpole of a police constable, female, coming at him like a whirlwind. A police radio in her hand. She raised it as she ran.

"Got 'im!" she shouted in a South London accent. Her checked hat flew off.

Good Lord!

Ian spun, frantic. He aimed for the other side of the park. Hendon Lane beyond. It would have to do.

And ran for all he was worth. Which wasn't much, compared to the thumping strides of the gazelle looming up behind him.

"Stop! Police!"

He did not heed her words.

She leapt on him from behind, grabbed him, twisting him hard, taking him down to the wet grass with a wallop that ended with a pop somewhere in his shoulder. Now that *did* hurt.

"Good morning, sunshine!" she said in his ear. She had minty breath.

His head rang with the impact. And up the hill, coming toward them, he could hear the other officers whooping with glee.

AUTHOR'S NOTE

Years ago, a homicide detective on the San Francisco Peninsula told me of a harrowing murder case he was working that involved outlaw bikers and an unfortunate individual who fell afoul of them. Among the people caught up in the investigation were a runaway teenage girl from the Midwest and her distraught parent with a dark past who came out to California looking for her. It didn't take long for me to realize that here was a character who could almost write her own story. Enter Colleen Hayes.

Thank you for reading *Tie Die*. I hope you enjoyed it as much as I did writing it. If you liked the book, please consider leaving a review on Amazon or the social platform of your choice, and tell your friends about books and authors you enjoy. It really makes a difference to those of us sitting in darkened rooms, banging out stories about people who never really existed doing things that never really happened, except in our imaginations. You are, after all, the reason we do this. I truly like to hear from readers as well and you can stay in touch with me and follow Colleen's latest exploits on my website, listed below. Another Colleen Hayes mystery is on the way.

https://maxtomlinson.wordpress.com/